THE
MADNESS
of
LORD
WESTFALL

THE ORDER OF THE M.U.S.E

MIA MARLOWE

Entangled Publishing, LLC
2614 South Timberline Road
Suite 109
Fort Collins, CO 80525
Visit our website at www.entangledpublishing.com.

Select Historical is an imprint of Entangled Publishing, LLC.

Edited by Erin Molta
Cover design by Louisa Maggio
Cover art by The Killion Group, Inc.

ISBN 978-1-943892-58-7

Manufactured in the United States of America

First Edition September 2015

To my dear husband, the love of my life and source of all my hero's best impulses.
The wicked stuff is all me.

Welcome to the Order of the M.U.S.E.

His Grace, the Duke of Camden, has recruited (some say coerced) gifted individuals from all strata of society to join his Metaphysical Union of Sensory Extraordinaires. Their purpose is to protect the Crown from arcane weapons of a psychic bent. The duke fears that one such malicious object may have slipped by them and is responsible for King George III's periodic descents into lunacy. There may be no help for His Majesty, but Camden intends to see that a similar fate doesn't overcome "Prinny," the Prince of Wales.

Meet the M.U.S.E.s

Pierce Langdon, Viscount Westfall — a telepath whose skills are the mirror image of Garret Sterling's. If Sterling is the universal dispenser of unwanted thoughts, Westfall is the universal receiver of everything rattling around in the heads of others. Unfortunately, he hasn't learned to filter anything out. Because of his propensity to "hear voices," Westfall was only recently released from Bedlam on the condition that the Duke of Camden be responsible for him should his "voices" urge him to violence.

Edward St. James, Duke of Camden — Founder of the Order of the M.U.S.E., Camden is the protector and mentor of those who display unusual sensory and metaphysical gifts. In addition to safeguarding the Crown from psychic attack, he's searching for a way to make contact with his deceased wife. He's exhausted all natural means of investigating the mysterious deaths of Mercedes and his infant son. Now he has turned to the supernatural.

Vesta LaMotte — Top-tier courtesan who is also a fire mage. She's called in to educate Cassandra in the ways of her gift... and the ways of men. She and the widowed Camden have had an on-again, off-again "arrangement" for years.

Cassandra Darkin, Lady Stanstead — Second daughter of Sir Henry Darkin who was an unwitting fire mage. Cassie risked losing her place in Society when she accidentally set Almack's on fire. But since the horrific event brought Garret Sterling into her life, she blesses the accident now. She's in full possession of both her psychic ability and Garret.

Garret Sterling, Lord Stanstead — Recently elevated to his new station after the death of his uncle. Garret is able to implant a thought in another's mind with such seductive force, his suggestions are irresistible. Garret is a libertine who carouses to avoid sleep because his nightmares have the bad habit of becoming someone else's waking reality. Usually. Cassandra Darkin seemed oblivious to his gift, which made the fact that the duke asked him to help her control her accidental fire-starting a difficult assignment.

Meg Anthony — a former ladies' maid and a psychic "Finder." Her ability to locate misplaced items and people is uncanny, but not without danger to her, a fact she tries to hide. She's in awe of the Duke of Camden and fears disappointing him if she can't learn to act the part of a proper lady instead of a domestic. She hides the truth of her parentage because she's on the run from her uncle who used her abilities for profit and to ruin others.

The defining moment of my life occurred when I was eight years old and fell from the topmost limb of an oak tree. I remember naught about the incident. They tell me my head struck several branches on the way down. I was insensible for the better part of a sennight, which was a mercy because it allowed the doctor to set my broken arm without my being aware of the agony he inflicted. For the injury to my brain, he did nothing.

Perhaps that was another type of mercy.

I only know that when I finally opened my eyes, the voices were there. They have been with me ever since.

~from the private journal of Pierce Langdon, Viscount Westfall

Chapter One

It was said that an invitation to Lord Albemarle's salon was second only to presentation at court as a means of sealing one's reputation among the *bon ton*. His soirees were glittering assemblies of all the right people wearing all the right fashions, listening to all the right sopranos, or poets, or politicians. The music was always perfect, the food sublime, and everything was stamped with Lord Albemarle's unquestioned good taste.

But this evening was not one of Albemarle's salons.

Make no mistake. The music, décor, and refreshments were as exquisite as ever, though wine and spirits flowed more freely than usual. The main difference was the guest list. On this night, Albemarle's Mayfair town house was filled to the rafters with the demimonde—disgraced lords and their mistresses, actresses and courtesans, anarchists and freethinkers.

Such company made Lord Stanstead feel very much at home. He liked nothing better than thumbing his nose at the world in general and the *ton* in particular. However, nothing about this gathering made Pierce Langdon, Viscount Westfall, comfortable.

His sense of aloneness was rarely more intense than when he was in a crowd. He could not bring himself to count Stanstead his friend. Indeed, he had no friends. Their work together for the Order of the M.U.S.E. had made them colleagues of a sort, but they were very different men possessed of widely divergent abilities.

When the pair entered Albemarle's grand parlor, the myriad minds in the room pressed up against Westfall's consciousness. It was like a disturbed hive of bees seeking entrance through a hole in a beekeeper's protective suit. He could hear them clamoring to break through, a determined buzzing trying to overpower him. Westfall drew a deep breath and fortified the mental shield his mentor, the Duke of Camden, had taught him to erect.

Steady on. Or they'll find a way to send me back to Bedlam.

"Wipe that pained expression from your face," Stanstead said. "Otherwise someone will suspect you've mastered the feat of standing on your own testicles."

"Easy for you to say. No one is battering down your defenses."

If anything, the reverse was true. Stanstead possessed the psychic gift of being able to broadcast his thoughts to others and in such a subtle way, the recipient usually couldn't tell that the thought wasn't his own. Like a cuckoo's egg in a warbler's nest, Stanstead's idea pushed aside the ones that had every right to be there. As a result, his psychic target often behaved in other than expected ways.

The *ton* was still nattering on about Lady Waldgren's impromptu soliloquy from *Macbeth* at the theater last

Season. Since the old gossip was generally disliked and universally feared, when she had mounted the stage and begun reciting "Out, damn'd spot!"—and rather badly, it must be admitted—the aberration in her deportment was met with unabashed glee. But when the poor lady's husband took an unexpected dip in a public fountain wearing naught but his birthday suit, Polite Society shook its collective heads and tut-tutted under its breath.

Living with such a wife as Lady Waldgren, his lordship was bound to break eventually. What else might one expect?

More unusual behavior, if Stanstead had his mischievous way with the couple who'd landed in his metaphysical sights.

In contrast, Westfall was Stanstead's psychic opposite. Instead of projecting his thoughts to others, he was the unhappy receiver of whatever was tumbling about in the minds of those around him. Being in the company of others left Lord Westfall drained and more than a little cynical. After all, he knew what people were really thinking behind their false smiles.

"How's your shield holding?" Stanstead asked, nodding a greeting to those he knew as they moved around the room.

"Better than expected," Westfall said. It had taken several months of mental discipline to learn how to create the shield. The first time he had managed it, his relief when the voices finally stilled was like having a weight lifted from his chest.

Then, to his surprise, if he maintained the shield too long, he began to miss the voices. The world around him seemed flat and two-dimensional. It was as if he moved through chalk drawings, peopled with pale imitations of humans, instead of living, breathing ones. Still, that was better than being bombarded by their random thoughts. He had to protect himself from the disjointed scramble of ideas that careened toward him from all sides.

"Want to try a filter?" Stanstead asked.

"Perhaps later." Westfall had experimented with lowering his shield enough to target a single mind for him to listen in on, but he hadn't perfected the process yet. He also couldn't admit to Stanstead that keeping up his shield was straining his last ounce of psychic energy.

"I'd fancy knowing what that tasty bit of muslin is thinking." Stanstead nodded toward their left.

Westfall didn't follow the direction of Stanstead's gaze to see the example of feminine beauty who had captured the earl's attention. He despised a lie of any stripe and breaking a wedding vow counted as two in his estimation—once to one's spouse and another to the third party involved. "In case you've forgotten, you are a married man."

"Make that a happily married man," Stanstead corrected. "However, that does not make me dead. I'm blessed with a wife who knows what men are. Cassandra doesn't care where I get my appetite so long as I eat at home. She knows I'd never stray. Besides the fact that I adore her too much to hurt her, she'd immolate me if I were to put so much as a toe out of line."

It was no idle threat. Lord Stanstead's wife was a fire mage, an elemental who also served alongside the gentlemen in the Order of the M.U.S.E. Westfall had no doubt the countess would singe more than her husband's eyebrows if his eyes wandered and the rest of him followed.

A full-blown thought crashed through Westfall's mental shield. The idea carried far more power than the others trying to gain entrance. It shredded his defenses and plastered itself at the forefront of his consciousness.

Here's what you're missing, you sanctimonious prig.

Stanstead had *Sent* him one of his directed thoughts, devil take the man. A mental image accompanied Stanstead's *Sending.*

It was of a young woman.

No, that didn't begin to be adequate. She was a goddess.

Languid eyes, black as the Stygian depths, invited him to plunge into her. The woman's abundant dark hair was drawn up to bare her nape and tease her delicate neck with loose curls. Westfall ached to kiss the tender skin just there, beneath her jaw. Full and plum-colored, her lips beckoned. The apples of her cheeks were dusted with just enough pink to appear virginal, but the seductive hollow beneath them suggested a smoldering sensuality that was anything but chaste.

If Westfall could assemble perfection, taking the best feature from each woman present—graceful arms here, a high, full bosom there, a willowy waist and long legs from another—the result would have been this paragon.

He prided himself on his extreme degree of self-control, but this woman had him rock hard and aching merely from the mental sight of her. He couldn't stop himself from turning toward the real woman.

"You're welcome." Stanstead chuckled. "But you'd best close your mouth, friend. You're in danger of being mistaken for a codfish."

Westfall clamped his jaw shut, chagrined at having been caught gaping but, in all honesty, this woman's beauty stopped him cold. Like the night sky in splendor, her very existence was evidence of a creative God. She was why lovesick poets wrote bad verse.

She tempted him to lower his shield.

"Well, what are you waiting for? Go talk to her."

"I can't," Westfall said, grateful not to have stammered. "We haven't been properly introduced."

"Regular rules of etiquette don't signify at these sorts of events. Start by giving her your name, if you must. Then find a way to give her a compliment. By Jove, it shouldn't be hard." Stanstead clapped a hand on his shoulder. "I'll even *Send* her a suggestion that she finds your ugly mug fine to look upon."

"No. No *Sending*." He didn't need Stanstead's help. Besides, he'd been told that he was not without a certain rugged appeal, if a woman fancied a man who had unfashionably large hands and feet to match his breadth of shoulder. Westfall's facial features were considered raw-boned rather than refined, but he didn't care. If someone didn't like his looks, they were welcome to look the other way. "If you *Sent* that she should like me, I'd never know for sure if she did. It would be cheating."

"What a bore you are sometimes."

"What a bounder you are, all the time."

"Look," Stanstead said, suddenly all business, "we can swap insults or we can do what we came here to do. The Duke of Camden has sensed the presence of a psychic relic somewhere in this town house. It may be in Lord Albemarle's possession. It may belong to one of his guests. All we know for certain is that the intention behind it is not conducive to the welfare of our future king."

That steadied him. Becoming part of the Duke of Camden's Order of the M.U.S.E. had given Westfall new purpose and new hope that his debility—he couldn't think of his psychic powers as a gift quite yet—might be put to good use. M.U.S.E. stood for Metaphysical Union of Sensory Extraordinaires. That seemed a little grandiose to Westfall, and he felt nothing like an "Extraordinaire," but the Order had proved its worth a dozen times over.

With France's military defeat, England's enemies had turned to more subtle means to harm the British royal family. Someone with resources and intelligence was intent on infiltrating the Crown's collection of art and oddities with psychically debilitating relics. The Duke of Camden was convinced that at least one object of malicious intent had slipped through his gauntlet and was responsible for the king's periodic descents into madness.

But Camden and his Order had stopped plenty of other items from reaching the royals. Often, they worked with only the sketchiest of information about the relics—a rumor, a string of unusual events or, as in this case, because the duke had experienced one of his visions about an object of power.

So now, Westfall and Stanstead were dispatched to Lord Albemarle's rout to try to ferret out the elusive item, discover who held it, and what its special properties might be. Then the Order could decide how to deal with the threat.

"So are we going to work?" Stanstead asked. "Or are you going to stand there like you've got a broom handle shoved up your arse?"

"Elegant as always, Stanstead."

"One does one's best."

"One could hardly do worse," Westfall said sourly. "Very well, I'll take the left side of the room. You circulate on the right. We'll compare notes when we reach the other side."

"Good. I'm highly gratified to learn you aren't dead. You

chose the side *she* is on." Stanstead waggled his eyebrows meaningfully. "*Bon chance*, old chap."

Westfall was tempted to clout Stanstead a good one over the head. He moved away from his colleague before he could act on the impulse. He located the beautiful woman again in a blink. She was standing behind a gentleman at the whist table. Then she leaned over and whispered something into his ear. The man laughed, caught up her hand, and kissed it.

Palm up. A lover's kiss.

Westfall's insides did a slow boil. He didn't have any right to those unsettling feelings. Didn't want them.

But there they were.

As he drew closer to the whist table, he lowered his shield by the smallest of degrees, enough to target the woman's mind only.

It was always a risk.

Very few minds were tidy, well organized, and ready for his inspection. Usually, when he opened himself to another, the mind in question flooded into his own like the Deluge, until he was swamped by their loves and hates and secret shames. To his surprise, very little trickled in from the woman.

She was a closed book.

Westfall frowned. He'd only encountered that level of resistance when he tried to peer into the minds of those who regularly trod the boards on Drury Lane. Because actors so embraced their roles, so became the characters they portrayed, nothing of their own lives, their own thoughts, broke through. It was deceit at the most elemental level, and Westfall recoiled from it in abhorrence.

Whoever she really was, this beauty was clearly trying to be someone else.

Names can be deceptive. People say they reflect the character of the person to whom they belong. I say they more accurately reveal the hopes of the person's parents. When mine named me Honora, they no doubt expected a dutiful daughter whose impeccable behavior would do them credit.

How very disappointed they must be.

~from the secret journal of Lady Nora Claremont

Chapter Two

Nora knew she turned masculine heads everywhere she went. It wasn't conceit. She was merely being honest. And she certainly wouldn't claim credit for it. Nature had simply made her this way. It had uniquely fashioned her to be an object of desire. Nora was chagrined to admit that a few duels had been fought over her, though she had done nothing to encourage that sort of barbarous behavior and had never rewarded the victor with her favors. She was simply used to men fawning over her.

She was not accustomed to having one scowl at her.

With the exception of his snowy linen shirt, the striking fellow was dressed all in black, the stark suit a perfect foil for his sandy blond hair. His ensemble was Brummellesque in its simplicity, but he'd never be considered the fashionable sort.

For one thing, he was too big, too broad of shoulder, and far too tall, towering over most of the other gentlemen in the room. The way he moved was all wrong. Men in Lord Albemarle's circles comported themselves with easy masculine grace. Walking slowly, ignoring the other guests, almost as if he were trying to escape anyone's notice, this fellow was clearly uncomfortable in his own skin. Though the fit of his jacket and trousers was beyond reproach, he seemed rather like a dockworker in fancy dress.

Even more surprising, despite his frown, the big man was coming toward her.

Probably a fire-breathing evangelist or some other crusader for public morals. Though if that were the case, what he was doing at Lord Albemarle's party was a mystery. She'd held her own against plenty of those "holier than thou" types. Never one to back down from a fight—and she certainly sensed one brewing—Nora decided to leave her place near Albemarle's whist table and meet the gentleman halfway across the room. As soon as he was close enough, she dipped in the shallowest of curtsies.

"Good evening, Reverend." Only a man of the cloth would greet her with so disapproving an expression.

His frown deepened. "You have mistaken me for someone else," he said, his voice a low rumble. "I'm no clergyman."

"Pity. They often make the best lovers—all that guilt and angst seething beneath the surface desperately seeking release," she said, her tone as sultry as she could make it and soft enough for his ears alone. If he was going to censure her with his severe expression, she was determined to give him cause. "Have you never heard the saying, 'Repressed sex is the best sex'?"

The man actually blushed to the tips of his ears. She was going to have fun with this one.

"Do not have a conniption, I pray you, sir," she said with a flip of her fan. "I'm not in the market for a lover. Not at present in any case."

"You're...I... I'm not having a conniption."

She flashed her brightest smile at him, the one known for bringing a man to his knees. "Then why are you frowning at me as if I were the town trollop?"

He blinked hard. His eyes were the pale gray of the sky just before dawn. Nora should know. She'd seen enough sunrises, albeit through bleary eyes, after her all night carouses.

"I'm not frowning at you." He was still staring at her with complete absorption. "I'm... I was thinking of something else."

"Thinking extraordinarily hard about it, then. While Lord Albemarle encourages thoughtful discourse at his salons, this is not at all that sort of party." She occasionally ran across a fellow whose attraction to her rendered him incoherent, but since this man's scowl was still in place, she began to consider that perhaps the big fellow wasn't destined to become another one of her conquests. "Have I offended you in some way, sir?"

If not, it wasn't for lack of trying. Something about him made her uncomfortable. She'd be just as happy if this man left Albemarle's party. He wasn't the jovial sort Benedick Albemarle usually cultivated at his routs.

"No, you've given me no cause for offense. Though I suspect the world has offended you more than once," he said. "I am sorry for it. You deserve a full measure of respect."

That took her aback. While she was arguably the most sought after high-flyer in London, no one had ever cared if they offended her. How on earth could this man know if she had been? Nora was scrupulous about maintaining her public reputation for gaiety.

No one wanted to be around a depressed courtesan.

First and foremost, she was an entertainer, in or out of the boudoir. If Polite Society deemed her a pariah, that was too bad. She made her living satisfying others, seeing that their needs were met and their vanity flattered.

But that didn't mean she didn't have feelings. Or that she couldn't be hurt.

She had been. Often.

In one moment, this stranger had sliced to a sensitive corner of her heart no one would ever have suspected was there. The balance of power in the conversation shifted.

"Forgive my lack of manners," he said with a stiff bow.

Now that he wasn't frowning, Nora admitted he was very easy on the eyes. One of the most attractive men she'd ever met, she decided—until he had spoken, of course. She didn't need him to uncover the parts of her she kept hidden.

"We have not been properly introduced," he said, "but as there is no one to do the honors, allow me to present myself. I'm—"

"My, my. There's no need to be so formal, not at one of Lord Albemarle's routs," she chided, determined to keep their banter light. "After all, Adam and Eve had no one to introduce them and, barring the bit about the apple, they got on swimmingly."

"God presented Eve to Adam," he said in all seriousness, "so they were arguably the most properly introduced couple in history."

"As proper as an introduction can be when both parties are bare as a baby chick," she said with a laugh.

"There was no shame in their nakedness," he said, still refusing to rise to her teasing. "Besides, it is possible to be naked in other ways besides merely shedding one's clothes."

"How?" She was considered an expert on all things sensual. As far as she knew, naked was naked and that was the end of it.

"It is possible to so possess another, to become so close, that their very thoughts become yours as well." His forceful gaze bordered on hypnotic. "When that occurs, the soul is naked, which is far more intimate than simply baring the body."

She'd never had a relationship that intense. "I don't think I'd fancy that at all. Everyone needs to be able to close the door on their own thoughts.

"Only if they are practicing deceit," he said. "If a person lives without lies, there's no need to hide what one thinks."

"Oh, I never hide what I think. I'm known for outrageous pronouncements. Ask anyone. Ask yourself. Hasn't this very conversation demonstrated that whatever pops into my head tumbles out my mouth without a second thought?"

"Outrageous I'll give you, but I doubt very much that you do it without purpose. Everything about you is controlled and calculated." The frown was back, but slighter now. "You are a woman of many secrets."

She crossed her arms under her breasts knowing full well as she did so that the man's eyes would likely glaze over when his gaze was drawn to them. "Well, then, since you're so perceptive, why don't you tell me one of my secrets?"

She expected him to use the opportunity to say something self-serving, like she secretly wanted him to take her up to one of the many sumptuous bedchambers in Lord

Albemarle's residence and let him have his wicked way with her. Ha! If they found themselves alone in proximity to a bed, she'd be more likely to have her way with him.

But instead, he cocked his head and considered her through narrowed eyes. Surprisingly, his gaze did not dip to her artfully presented bosom, but concentrated instead on her face. His brow furrowed and his jaw tensed. If Nora didn't know better, she'd swear the man was being subjected to thumbscrews.

Then he closed his eyes, and the taut muscles in his face relaxed a bit. He suddenly looked years younger. When he opened them, his gray eyes were sad.

"Emilia," he said softly.

No! she almost screamed.

The man flinched as if she had.

No one knew about Emilia. Well, only two other souls in the world knew, but they were sworn to secrecy.

He didn't know. He couldn't know.

And yet he did.

"Who *are* you?" she demanded.

"Good evening, my lady," came a welcome interruption. Garret Sterling, who'd recently been elevated as the Earl of Stanstead, suddenly appeared at her side. He was a charming fellow who always put others at ease. Her alarm over the big man's perceptiveness drained away a bit, simply from being in Stanstead's presence.

"I see you've met my friend, Lord Westfall," Stanstead went on.

"No, we haven't been properly introduced yet," the stranger said and then glared at Stanstead. "And you and I are not actually friends."

Stanstead chuckled. "Always joking, that's Westfall for you. All right, old son, we'll do it your way. Lady Nora Claremont, may I present Viscount Westfall? Westfall, the incomparable La Nora."

Westfall made an elegant leg to her, a throwback to the previous generation. "I am charmed."

"Now who's being deceitful, my lord?" She made it a point to *my lord* him. Men who were entitled expected it. Plus, it took the sting from her needling. "You don't find me a bit charming."

"If charmed means compelled, the word fits to perfection," Viscount Westfall said. "I confess I have been compelled to your side. Enchanted, one might say."

She sidled close to Lord Stanstead, slipping a hand companionably through the crook of his elbow. "After his fierce scowl, I never expected fair words from your friend."

"In truth, I never expected them either," Stanstead said with a laugh that sounded genuinely surprised, "but then that might be because, as he says, we're not really friends."

Westfall grimaced at him. "We need to leave."

"So soon?" Nora said, feeling equal parts relief and dismay. Now that the big man was speaking prettily to her, she was ready to hear more from him.

"We have what we came for," Westfall said to his companion, "and you have a wife waiting at your hearth."

What they came for? To Nora's knowledge, the pair hadn't sampled so much as a cup of the rum punch. They hadn't made it as far as the next parlor where a string quartet played and the furniture had been moved against the walls to create space for dancing. She hadn't seen Stanstead or Westfall at any of the card tables. They hadn't even approached Lord Albemarle, their host, to bid him either good evening or good-bye.

It was true that, given the guest list, the party was bound to turn boisterous as the evening wore on, but right now everyone was behaving themselves. Besides, Benedick would never allow one of his gatherings to descend into an outright orgy. Even his bacchanalias were conducted with exquisite taste. Any lewd behavior, which admittedly sometimes ensued, was kept behind carefully closed doors.

Stanstead eyed his friend for a moment. "I suppose you're right. Now that my dear Cassandra is in 'an interesting condition,' she does appreciate me keeping regular hours."

So the new Countess of Stanstead was with child. Even though the doors of Polite Society were closed to her, Nora was still interested in the doings and news of the *ton*. It was the world she'd been born to, after all.

Lady Stanstead's pregnancy explained why her husband had come to Albemarle's rout without her. Expectant mothers were coddled and tucked away and generally not allowed to have a speck of fun. But before Cassandra Darkin had become Lady Stanstead, she had cut a wide swath through the *ton* during her come-out Season and had a reputation for being a force to reckon with. That was probably why Stanstead was in the company of Westfall. Before his marriage, the earl had been something of a rake. The upright viscount could be counted upon to keep Stanstead in line and out of trouble.

But if, as Westfall asserted, the two gentlemen were not friends, and Nora was inclined to believe him because she'd rarely encountered two more direct opposites, why were they on the town together?

As the men made their obeisance over her gloved hand and took their leave, Nora's curiosity arched like a cat's back. Westfall was unlike anyone she'd ever met, and his knowledge of Emilia was more than unsettling. He would bear watching. She followed his progress until he reached the door, wondering if he would pause and look back at her.

He never did.

If a child suffers from weak eyes, he doesn't know he ought to be able to see individual bricks in buildings or separate leaves on trees. He assumes his uncorrected view of the world is the same thing everyone else sees.

So it was with me and the voices. I forgot there had ever been a time when I couldn't hear the thoughts of those around me, as if they'd spoken them aloud. I assumed others could hear my thoughts, as well, and would not object if I commented on the unspoken elements of conversation.

I could not have been more wrong.

~from the secret journal of Pierce Langdon,
Viscount Westfall

Chapter Three

"Why didn't you tell me you knew the lady?" Westfall demanded as he climbed into the Duke of Camden's elegant carriage.

"Where's the fun in that?" Stanstead followed him into the equipage. Then he rapped the ceiling with the silver head of his walking stick, signaling the driver that they were ready to go. "It was far more fun watching you meet La Nora on your own."

"You were not there for your own amusement, Stanstead. We were tasked with a mission for the Order." He folded his arms across his chest and looked steadfastly out at the row of town houses they passed. The Georgian-style homes were all identical, in number and placement of windows, in their mathematical proportions, and in the intricate dentils on the cornices. The sameness soothed him. He needed it after meeting such an unconventional woman. She made him feel jumpy, uncomfortable in his own skin. "La Nora. Why do you call her that?"

"Because, my dear chap, she is a Cyprian of the first water and all the glittering birds of paradise must have a nom de plume."

"A Cyprian," he repeated. That unwelcome boiling sensation he'd experienced when Lord Albemarle kissed Lady Nora's hand returned to his chest. "You mean she's a prostitute?"

"No, nothing so gauche. The lady is the daughter of an earl, after all." Stanstead removed his topper and set it on his lap. The chances that they'd hit a pothole hard enough to make their heads touch the ceiling and ruin their hats was small in Mayfair, but to be on the safe side, Westfall followed suit. "But Lady Nora *is* a courtesan, which is very different than your average light-skirt."

"Not in any way that matters." It made no sense that he should care that the lady was a kept woman, but the boiling sensation raged hotter all the same.

"I beg to differ. La Nora is very particular about her patrons. In fact, I doubt she's had more than a handful throughout her entire career." Stanstead chuckled. "You were clearly smitten. What was that business about being 'charmed' and 'enchanted'?"

"We were there to gain information," Westfall said, embarrassed that he'd said those things to Lady Nora and worse, that Stanstead had heard him say them. "I was taught that one attracts more flies with honey than vinegar."

"Always supposing that more flies is a thing to be devoutly wished for," Stanstead said with a grin.

"Did you *Send* me a suggestion about her?" Westfall asked. He was normally aware that the extraneous thoughts careening through his brain belonged to someone else, but

Stanstead was able to slip his suggestions in so subtly, it might not have stood out as foreign. It was the only thing that made sense. Stanstead was to blame for the odd way he was feeling.

"Lud, no. Why would I?"

Westfall turned away to peer out the coach window again. Sometimes, being a party to another's thoughts meant their sorrows became his. And in the brief time he'd allowed her mind to wash over him, he'd learned that Lady Nora had had her share of grief. Perhaps that was why he felt this strange tenderness for her, despite his abhorrence over her occupation.

"The world is very black and white to you, isn't it, Westfall? Are there no shades of gray?"

"Not about some things."

"Then I wish you joy of your rigid views and hope that someday your refusal to bend does not break you," Stanstead said. "Now, tell me what you have learned."

"Not until I can tell the duke, as well."

"Can you at least divulge whose mind yielded the information about the relic we seek?"

Westfall sighed. Truth was his one constant, the touchstone in his life. If he surrendered that, he'd have nothing left to stand on. He didn't want this truth to be so, but it was. "Lady Nora."

"Well, that's interesting. She's been Lord Albemarle's mistress for about a year now. I wonder if he's involved with the plot. Do you suppose —"

"I can't discuss it now." Westfall didn't want to hear more about Lady Nora and her patron. He rubbed his chest as if that would stop the roiling.

"Suit yourself." Stanstead yawned, slumped in the seat, and closed his eyes. "Cassandra isn't sleeping well of late, and she's been keeping me awake, too."

A vision of the fire mage who was Stanstead's wife flashed across Westfall's mind. The lady was lovely, but in the image that shimmered before him she was wearing only the thinnest of night rails. The lacy strap at one shoulder slid down.

Then a curious thing happened. In Westfall's mind, the lady suddenly looked much less like Lady Stanstead and much more like Lady Nora. Her hair was darker now, lush and unbound, falling to curl around her barely covered breasts. The night rail continued to slip off one shoulder until, like Diana the Huntress, one full orb was bared. It was topped with a taut, berry-colored nipple.

Westfall ached to suckle it.

He hastily erected his mental shield and glared at Stanstead. "Kindly keep your salacious musings to yourself."

Stanstead opened one eye. "There's nothing salacious about a man thinking about his wife."

"That thought wasn't about Lady Stanstead."

"*Hmph!* If it wasn't, then I didn't *Send* it to you. So if anyone's to blame for offending your puritanical sensibilities, it's you, my dear fellow." Stanstead grinned. "And if you're producing even one vaguely naughty thought on your own, I must say, I have renewed hope for you. In the meantime, stay out of my head."

"With pleasure," Westfall said with a snort.

Maintaining a mental shield took so much concentration, he had hoped to keep his down when he was only with Stanstead. The earl's mind was surprisingly well ordered.

Since Stanstead engaged in some of the same mental exercises prescribed by the Duke of Camden for Westfall, Stanstead's thoughts were usually disciplined, too. Because of that, he was restful to be around, which, when Westfall reconsidered, probably did make the man his friend.

But Stanstead wasn't a restful companion when he was imagining ravishing his wife, even if Westfall's mind did have a hand in enhancing the earl's musings by changing the woman in question to the courtesan, Lady Nora.

So the best Westfall could do was prop up his shield and hope that Stanstead would fall asleep between Lord Albemarle's town house and His Grace's. He'd never been able to listen in on someone else's dreams, so a napping Stanstead would be as refreshing to spend time with as a philodendron.

He closed his eyes and imagined the moist breath of the conservatory, the freshness of green growing things around him. A little sunlight, a little water, an occasional pruning. Plants were the most undemanding of companions. He could easily retreat into them and become a gardening hermit.

But that wouldn't give him a chance to make a difference in the world. Or prove that he was sane enough to take his place in it.

• • •

"Your report, Lord Stanstead," the Duke of Camden said, prowling the perimeter of the room as was his custom. Except in the mahogany-paneled dining room of Camden House, Westfall had rarely seen the man sit. His Grace was a whirlwind with feet, all bustling energy, and raw power.

"Westfall is the one with news this time," Stanstead said from his place on the settee next to his countess.

Lord and Lady Stanstead occupied the town house next to His Grace's. Previously both residents at Camden House, the newlywed couple enjoyed the privacy of their own establishment, but the proximity of their home made it convenient for them to rejoin the group whenever a meeting of the Order of the M.U.S.E. was called.

Westfall and Miss Meg Anthony were both houseguests of the duke for the foreseeable future, since they were still in intensive training. Westfall was unable to fully harness his psychic gift, so his days were filled with the duke's experimental exercises to help him grapple for control over the voices in his head.

Tiring as they were, they were miles better than the dubious "treatments" he'd endured while he had been committed to Bedlam.

Miss Anthony was already in full possession of her ability to *Find* lost objects and people by metaphysical means, so she had no mental hoops to jump through. However, she needed to gain confidence and learn the convoluted rules of etiquette required to pass as a lady, so she could move in the right circles.

Westfall couldn't say which of them had the more daunting task.

To assist Miss Anthony in her goal, the duke's sister, Lady Easton, put her through her paces like the sternest headmistress at a finishing school. Lady Easton possessed no psychic abilities, but she was adept at smoothing the way for members of the Order in social situations and kept her brother's household running as predictably and efficiently as a railway schedule.

The other member of this cell of the Order was Vesta LaMotte. Like Lord and Lady Stanstead, she kept her own residence. Or rather, she was kept in one. Vesta was a courtesan nearing the end of her career, but still much in demand. If the Order ever needed an entrée into the Prince Regent's inner circle, they could count on Vesta to supply it. Vivacious and amusing, she was always invited to Prinny's entertainments and, as far as Westfall could determine, was on intimate terms with several of His Royal Highness's chief advisors.

But she was always late.

"I do hope you haven't started without me." Vesta breezed into the parlor, wearing a diaphanous gown that would have been more appropriate on a girl half her age. However, in Westfall's estimation, she did the ensemble justice, and could easily pass for a fresh young debutante in the sheer column dress.

"You haven't missed a thing," Camden assured her. "Westfall was just about to tell us what he learned this evening."

"Oh, lovely." Vesta flashed him a bright smile. "Does this mean you were successful in opening yourself to only one mind at a time? I do hope it wasn't too hard on you, dear boy."

Westfall nodded gratefully. Vesta was the most empathetic one in the group. Only the courtesan seemed to realize how difficult his gift was to bear. "Erecting a mental shield and then lowering it slightly enabled me to detect the person's secrets fairly quickly." Even though Lady Nora's mind was unusually guarded, he'd managed to catch wind of two of her private thoughts. The one about someone named Emilia had no bearing on M.U.S.E. business, and had been couched in so much anguish, he could barely stand to hear it. That secret wasn't his to tell. But the other sounded exactly like the item they sought. "We're looking for something called *Fides Pulvis*."

"Trust Powder?" Lady Stanstead said, displaying her knowledge of Latin. Not all women were as well educated as the countess, which was a pity, in Westfall's opinion. Since he listened in on the thoughts of many ladies, he knew their minds were often as nimble as a man's, if only they had the same opportunity for learning.

"Exactly," Westfall said. "*Fides Pulvis* means Trust Powder."

"*Pulvis* may also be translated 'arena,'" the duke said.

"It would be rather difficult to tuck an arena into one's pocket, Camden," Vesta observed. "And the relics the Order usually seeks are inherently portable."

"Point taken. I've yet to hear that anyone is building an arena for the Prince Regent," His Grace conceded.

Camden's gaze lingered longer than usual on Vesta's form, and Westfall wondered about their relationship. Out of courtesy, he tried to keep his mental shield up during meetings of the Order. The last thing he wanted was for one of the members to feel violated by his gift.

Unless it was Stanstead. Westfall didn't care if he offended him.

The duke's steely gaze returned to him. "From whose mind did you glean the information, Westfall?"

"Lady Nora Claremont."

"Ah! La Nora," Vesta said as she lounged on the far end of the settee and tucked her feet up, displaying far more of her delicately curved ankles than she ought. "Lovely girl."

That was damning Nora Claremont with faint praise. She was the most exquisite creature on God's earth, but Westfall didn't dare offer his assessment. Stanstead would have a field day with him over it. He couldn't bear to be ridiculed for feelings over which he seemed to have no control.

"I fear I don't remember her," the Duke of Camden said. "Information is only as valid as its source. What can you tell us about the lady, Vesta?"

"Let me see." Vesta's blue-violet eyes shifted up and to the left, as if the knowledge might hover in the air above her. She was a repository of intelligence about the *ton* and its connections—even more thorough than *DeBrett's Guide to the Peerage* because Vesta always knew the delicious details of scandal that DeBrett's feared to print. However, she was no gossip. She only used her vault of information in the service of Camden's Order.

"Lady Nora is the third or fourth daughter of Lord Twicken. It's hard to say which. Lord and Lady Twicken had a passel of daughters before she finally gave him a son. At any rate, the earl did right by his girls. He arranged brilliant matches for them. They all married well."

"She's married?" The words blurted out of Westfall's mouth before he could stop them.

"I was about to say, with the exception of Nora. She refused the gentleman her father had chosen for her and wed without her parent's consent. Off to Gretna Green and all that, with a penniless doctor-in-training—a certain Lewis Claremont. The fellow had no family connections to speak of. I believe his people were tenant farmers in Surrey." Vesta wrinkled her pretty nose. "But young Lewis was evidently a brilliant sort and went through his medical training in half the usual time. However, that sort of thing weighs very little in the balance considering that he made off with an earl's daughter. Lord Twicken disowned Nora and cut her off completely."

"At least with him being a doctor, he'll eventually have more than two coins to rub together," Meg Anthony said.

"Only if he had cultivated the right sort of clientele," Vesta said, "but Dr. Claremont relished caring for the indigent and the downtrodden of Whitechapel. Then he went to France to serve our brave boys. Unfortunately, cannon shot reached the surgeon's tent during Waterloo, and he died. And so Lady Nora was widowed."

Westfall was ashamed of the relief that washed over him. It was a good thing he was the only thought thief in the bunch. How the others would despise him if they knew the unworthy sensations coursing through him.

"Please tell me she was reconciled with her parents after that," he said.

Vesta shook her head. "If anything, the earl was more adamant than ever that Nora should suffer for having defied him. 'She's made her bed and now she'll have to lie in it,' he reportedly said. It was terribly cruel of him because her husband had left her penniless. However, instead of languishing in threadbare gentility and imposing on distant relations as her father expected her to, she decided to become a courtesan and lie in someone else's bed." Vesta examined her bejeweled fingers, the bright gems flashing when they caught the light. "Can't say I blame her."

"You wouldn't," Stanstead said with a grin.

"And you shouldn't, either," Vesta said. "It was the only way for her to support herself in style. She wasn't a green girl, and she'd lived in poverty with her husband long enough to know it wasn't for her. It's a rare woman who knows her own mind about things. Nora made an informed choice."

"You make it sound as if being a courtesan is only a business decision." Camden finally stopped pacing long enough to lean on the mantel. The duke seemed to fight it, but his gaze was drawn inexorably back to Vesta.

She met his eyes directly. "You know it's not just business. For a lovely young thing like Lady Nora, who can pick and choose her patrons, there are pleasures aplenty to be had. And why shouldn't a woman take her pleasure like a man?"

A bit of red crept up the duke's neck. Whether it was embarrassment or anger, Westfall couldn't say without lowering his shield, and he didn't want to do that to his mentor.

"We are straying off the subject," Camden said. "Is there anything else you can tell us, Westfall?"

That he'd fallen hopelessly under La Nora's spell. That the idea of the lady taking her pleasure with anyone else had him tangled up in hopeless knots. That he was as smitten as a spotty-faced boy in the throes of his first calf-love.

He couldn't report that.

Besides, it made no sense, even to him. He'd never been one for forming quick attachments, but there was something about Nora Claremont, something that plucked at him deep down. He didn't understand what he was feeling, would have torn it from his breast if he could have, but he couldn't deny it, either.

Westfall cleared his throat. "I had the distinct impression that the *Fides Pulvis*, whatever it is, is in Lord Albemarle's possession." As was Lady Nora herself. His chest began to heat again, but he tamped it down. He had no business being jealous over the lady. Especially since she wasn't terribly ladylike.

He'd been raised to value chaste and demur women. Nora qualified as neither. Stanstead had told him once that the heart has a mind of its own. Such an irrational thing made no sense and had certainly never happened to Westfall.

Until now.

"Very well, that narrows the field of search to Albemarle's town house." Camden turned to Miss Meg Anthony, the Order's only *Finder*. "Do you think you can locate the item now that you know its name and general vicinity?"

"I'll try, Your Grace," Meg said, ducking her head in a deferential nod. "I can find a person easily that way, but for an object, a description of the item is better than what it's called."

"Will you make the attempt?"

"Of course. I never meant for anyone to think I wouldn't." Meg laced her fingers in her lap and closed her eyes before they had the chance to roll back in her head. Her body went rigid, and then limp. To other members of the group, she seemed to be deep in a self-imposed trance.

Westfall knew different. He opened himself to her mind as her spirit left her body and began sending back detailed images to her brain. Meg seemed to flit over the rooftops of London, quick as thought. She dived through the slate roof and whipped through each room of Albemarle's town house like a disembodied wraith, always seeking, always surging forward. She hovered over the powdery flour sacks in the scullery. She stopped for a blink to watch a serving girl empty a coal hod filled with ash and dust into a bin in the alley behind the residence. Lord Albemarle toyed with a snuffbox in his firelit study. Lady Nora draped herself over the back of his chair, reaching around to massage his neck and shoulders. The two seemed deep in conversation, and Westfall was grateful when Meg's consciousness darted away from them.

He didn't want to see Nora and her protector in such a cozy, domestic scene.

Meg fluttered from one room to the next, like a garden faerie leaping from blossom to blossom, pausing to inspect a dust-like substance on a vanity here, a horn of black powder draped over a musket there. Finally, her search complete, she shot back to Lord Camden's parlor faster than a pistol ball.

Meg's body jerked as her spirit reconnected with her flesh. Her eyes popped open, and she blinked in rapid succession. Then, blushing furiously, she looked around as if surprised to find everyone's attention fastened on her.

"What did you *Find*?" the duke demanded.

"Give her a moment," Westfall said. He alone knew what it cost Meg Anthony to exercise her psychic gift. She risked not making it back to her body every time she went on one of His Grace's quests. Of course, she never complained. Never even explained the danger to herself, if indeed she understood her peril. It was not in her nature to grumble. Besides, she would say she owed His Grace more than she could repay. If there were a more grateful soul on God's earth than Meg Anthony, Westfall had yet to encounter it.

Meg cast him a shy smile and dabbed a handkerchief at the corner of her mouth where a small bit of foam had formed. Then she relayed all the types of powdery substance she had found in Albemarle's home.

"But I can't say which of them might be the *Fides Pulvis* we need to find. I'm not sensitive to psychic energy like His Grace is," Meg explained.

"There was nothing in a wall safe? Nothing under lock and key?" Camden asked.

She shook her head. "His lordship keeps a goodly stack of banknotes and a cache of jewelry in the safe behind the painting over the head of his bed," Meg said. "Nothing that we need concern ourselves with, but I collect there's a number of folk in Whitechapel what would love to relieve him of it."

"My money's on the snuffbox," Stanstead said.

"Don't discount the others. It might be that sack of flour in the scullery. Something called Trust Powder could be baked into anything." Lady Stanstead seemed to delight in contradicting her husband. "Is Lord Albemarle hosting the Prince Regent for a dinner any time soon?"

"We need to find out." Camden motioned to Mr. Bernard, the steward who kept scrupulous notes of the Order's meetings. The faithful servant nodded and scratched away on his parchment. He'd no doubt make use of the servants' grapevine to contact his counterpart in Lord Albemarle's household. Those who lived belowstairs in the great houses of London always seemed to know more of what was really going on than the families they served.

"The powder on the vanity can't be eliminated either," Vesta said. "Prinny isn't above using a little paint if he's less in his looks than usual."

Since the Prince Regent would never be considered a handsome man in any case, when was he not in less than good looks?

Westfall let that disloyal thought slide without voicing it.

"His Royal Highness will be headed to the country for the shooting season," Camden said. "The black powder might be what we seek. Clearly, we need more information."

"Well, since Westfall had success using his filter on Lady Nora, I propose he make it a point to put himself in the lady's path as often as possible," Stanstead said with a barely suppressed grin. "Let's see what he turns up when he has more leisure to explore her brain. And whatever else the lady may allow."

Westfall glared at him. No, Stanstead was definitely *not* his friend.

"An excellent idea," Vesta said. "We simply need to know where she'll be and arrange for dear Pierce to be there as well."

Vesta was the only person on earth who called him by his given name. He heard it so rarely, it almost didn't seem to belong to him anymore. He had vague recollections of his mother using it. At Bedlam, his keepers had called him Mr. Langdon when they weren't calling him all manner of filthy things, but since his release from that house of horrors, he'd insisted on using his title. He was Lord Westfall. A viscount. A peer.

It was his shield against the world.

"I'll pay a call on Nora tomorrow afternoon," Vesta said, "and see if I can wheedle a bit of her schedule from her. Then dear Pierce can take matters in hand."

Outstanding. The last thing I need to know is when and how often Lady Nora's lover comes to visit.

When I was young, a benevolent God smiled kindly on my life. I let my heart rule my head. I lived for adventure and gaiety and could scarcely put a foot wrong in the world's eyes.

Since my Lewis was taken, my heart still appears to lead, but it is only an illusion. My heart is dead. My days are filled with frenetic activity, poor substitutes for adventure and true joy. Polite Society, while intensely interested in my doings, hasn't a single pleasant thing to say about me.

And God has not so much as twitched His lip in my direction for years.

~from the secret journal of Lady Nora Claremont

Chapter Four

"Wonderful party, Benedick. Another triumph under your belt," Nora said as she closed the door to Lord Albemarle's bedchamber behind her. His lordship was seated in one of the leather wing chairs before his banked fireplace. A letter dangled from his fingertips, and his chin rested in his other hand. Usually a man of carefully composed features, he was frowning as intently as Lord Westfall had been earlier that evening.

The only difference was that Benedick's scowl was directed toward the fire instead of her. In fact, Lord Albemarle seemed not to be aware of her presence.

"Lord Farraday and his new light-o-love seemed to enjoy themselves in the card room," Nora said. "Of course, it helped that you arranged for him to win."

"*Hmm*? Oh, yes. And next time I'll arrange for him to lose an amount he can't afford. After that, he'll be in my pocket. Useful in the future when I want something done in the House of Lords, I shouldn't wonder." His voice was usually a deep rumbling purr that sounded more ominous the softer he spoke. It had a ragged edge now.

"What's troubling you?"

Without a word, he raised the letter to her. Nora recognized the seal.

"Another one?" She took it from him and wandered closer to the wall sconce for better light as she read:

> *My dear Lord Albemarle,*
>
> *Your reticence in this pressing matter puzzles us. You have everything to gain by assisting us in swaying His Royal Highness to support our position at the Concert of Europe in Aix-la-Chapelle in the fall. Our operative tells us he has not changed his views.*
>
> *Use the* Fides Pulvis *and get it done.*
>
> *Otherwise you have everything to lose.*

The missive was unsigned, but it was stamped with an enigmatic seal in red wax. The design was a convoluted one, a pair of snakes twisted together in such a way that they devoured their own tails. It was a Gordian knot for deviousness. Nora feared that, unlike Alexander the Great who was first presented with the conundrum, her patron would not be able to unravel it in one stroke.

This was not the first letter Benedick had received from this entity, but it was the first one he'd let her read. She folded it back up and put it on the top of his bureau. Then she went behind his chair and reached around to massage his shoulders. His muscles clenched so hard it was like trying to soften iron.

Benedick had no compunction about ordering the lives of others. He regularly compelled them to his will, but he deeply resisted someone trying to do the same to him.

"Are you going to do as they ask?"

He pinched the bridge of his nose. "I don't see that I have a choice."

"What are they threatening you with?"

"The usual." Every few years or so, the same rumor about Lord Albemarle resurfaced, but he always managed to laugh it off.

Benedick was not laughing now.

"No one will believe them," she leaned down to whisper in his ear. "You have me, after all."

"Yes, my dear, I have you," he said wearily. "But they have some letters I was unwise enough to write to someone of whom I was enamored back when I was younger and very much more foolish. We met in Italy and, though the affair burned itself out in a few months, we continued a rather lusty correspondence for years."

"Still, letters would be difficult to use as proof."

"Not if they are in my hand. I do tend to write with a recognizable flair. And I made the mistake of sealing the letters with my signet." He glared accusingly at the cabochon topaz on his forefinger that was carved intaglio-style with the Albemarle crest. "I wrote a number of things to my dear Italian that were…quite unwise."

"Then you and I were made for each other. Being unwise is one thing at which I excel." She settled a hip on one of the arms of his chair, and he put a companionable arm around her waist. "No doubt you were in love, and that makes a fool of the wisest soul."

He laughed mirthlessly. "Love. If ever I tell you I've been reduced to that sorry state again, you have permission to use the derringer in my cupboard and put a bullet between my eyes. I would consider it a mercy."

She leaned down and planted a kiss on his forehead. "None of that. I won't have it. Not only would the world be a less cheerful place without you, it would be terribly unfair to me!"

"To you. How so?" he asked, an amused smile tugging at his lips.

"My reputation would suffer irreparably if it were known I'd killed my protector. Imagine how hard it would be for me to find another patron after that."

He laughed again, this time with something approaching real amusement. "Sometimes, my dear, I wish I…but no matter. Perhaps a strawberry may yet be gleaned from this situation." He reached into his waistcoat pocket and drew out an intricate silver snuffbox.

"That's it? The substance your blackmailers meant?"

"*Mmm-hmm. Fides Pulvis.*" He opened the top gingerly, taking care not to jostle the contents. "Trust Powder. One pinch and whoever takes it from me will believe whatever I tell them is gospel. Damned handy thing in the right hands."

"If it works, you could do some mischief with it right enough."

"Oh, it works," he said with a wry grin. "I tried it out on Smedley. Of course, it may just have been that my footman was delirious over taking snuff with his lord."

"What did you convince him was true?"

"I'm afraid I cast a bit of a love spell on the lad. Our

upstairs maid, Jane, has been mooning around after the boy for months. She's a good girl and a willing worker, but she has a smile like a muddy picket fence." He closed the snuffbox with a snap and returned it to his waistcoat pocket. "However, after a snootful of *Fides Pulvis* and a few choice words from me, our Smedley is convinced she's a goddess."

Nora covered her mouth with her hand to stifle a giggle. "Perhaps she is a goddess on the inside and you've only helped Smedley see the real Jane more clearly."

"Perhaps."

"If they find happiness with each other, you did a good deed with the Trust Powder." She shifted from the arm of the chair to his lap and crossed her legs. "Perhaps you could influence His Royal Highness for good as well."

"What are you suggesting?"

"Well, you might convince the Prince Regent to restore his wife to court." Everyone was in sympathy with Prinny's estranged princess. Even Nora's favorite author, Jane Austen, wrote that she would support Princess Caroline's cause as long as she could, "because she is a Woman and because I hate her Husband."

"Ha! Why stop there?" Benedick said. "I should persuade him to take her back to his bed."

Nora gave up and giggled uncontrollably. "Lud, what a lark. That would set the *ton* on its ear. They'd think he'd gone as daft as the king. Do you remember what he said to Lord Malmsbury the first time he saw her?"

Benedick raised the pitch of his voice half an octave to ape the Prince Regent's higher tones. "Harris, I am not well. Pray, get me a glass of brandy."

"Now he'd ask for a double portion!" Nora chuckled

and was pleased that Benedick joined her, laughing so hard he was forced to swipe at his eyes. He'd been so depressed when she'd first entered his chamber. If she could lift the man's spirits when he faced such a daunting problem, she'd done her job.

"But you know, while I suspect Princess Caroline would very much appreciate being restored to court, I highly doubt she pines to be reconciled to her husband," she said. "Not after the way he treated her after Princess Charlotte died."

"You're right, my dear. No one should read in the press that their only child has died in childbed."

"And His Royal Highness kept her from their daughter for years before that." Nora's face burned. She didn't have to imagine the Princess of Wales's pain at being separated from her daughter.

"True, then perhaps I should do something constructive instead of devious. Just a reinstatement, so she can be crowned queen when the time comes. You know, that's not a bad idea at all," he said, massaging his forehead in thought. "A grateful queen would be a wonderful asset."

Benedick had innumerable "assets"—people who were beholden to him for one reason or another—scattered across the British Isles.

"Oh! And while you're influencing our future king, you might want to convince him to recall Beau Brummell and settle his debts," Nora suggested. "No one has had the courage to dress His Royal Highness properly since that charming man fled the country."

"That would be a good deed, wouldn't it? We might actually have a prince who looks the part." He chuckled again. Now that Brummell was gone from London, Benedick was the ruling epitome of sartorial splendor. His dark good looks turned heads wherever he went, and his signature sense of style was copied, without much success, by would-be dandies all over town. Then his levity faded, and he sank back into the worried frown he'd sported when she first entered the room.

"We're being a bit silly about it, but *Fides Pulvis* is obviously dangerous as well," Nora said. "How did they ever discover you possessed such a thing?"

"How do you think? They sent it to me. I never should have opened the package." Benedick shook his head. "Why did I not remember the Trojan Horse?"

"You haven't told me. What is it they want you to convince the Prince Regent to support exactly?"

"They want him to reject the withdrawal of the Allies' troops from France. If that happens, it will stir up French sentiment against a settlement of any kind. In short, my blackmailers want a return to war."

Nora squeezed her eyes shut. Not more war. Hadn't enough young men been sacrificed on that altar?

Men like her husband.

When she had first been widowed, Lewis's image would come to her fresh-faced and clear, but lately, he'd been harder to picture in her mind. His features wouldn't come into focus, no matter how hard she tried. She no longer thought she heard him say her name in the dark watches of the night. She'd lost him entirely on that one horrific day. Every day since then, she lost a bit more of him as the memory grew more shadowy.

She shoved away her husband's shade. Benedick wouldn't like it if he knew she was pining.

"What do you mean to do?" she asked.

"What can I do? If I'm exposed, it means the gallows."

Bringing a lord before the bar on capital charges, let alone hanging one if convicted, was as rare as hens' teeth. "Surely they haven't enough proof for that."

"I've made it my business to cultivate well-placed friends, but every man also has well-placed enemies. If those letters make it into court, I'll swing." As if his cravat was suddenly too tight, Benedick tugged at one end of his waterfall and the starched cloth unraveled to drape on either side of his neck. "There's nothing the *bon ton* loves so much as a good example being made so long as it happens to someone else. And hanging a baron for this offense is one they'd take right to their hearts."

"But if you're caught trying to use the *Fides Pulvis* on the Prince Regent, might you not also be accused of treason?"

Benedick nodded. "Yes, but amazingly enough, treason wouldn't taint my nephew as much as the other." His sad smile pricked at her heart. Benedick's heir apparent was nearly of age and hadn't much use for his doting uncle other than as a source of unlimited banknotes. Nora thought the next Lord Albemarle was a pimply-faced wretch who didn't deserve the current lord's favor. "If I'm destined to hang, I'd rather pick my own offense."

The ormolu clock on his mantel chimed. Nora stifled a yawn.

"Do you think it's been long enough?" she asked as she rose from his lap.

"Considering how late it is, an hour with the incomparable La Nora speaks well of my manhood."

Servants watched everything that happened in the great

house, including how often and how long a time their master spent with his mistress. Of course, Benedick paid them well enough to instill loyalty, but one could never be too careful.

Those rumors came from somewhere.

Benedick kissed the air at the sides of each of her cheeks. "You looked lovely this evening, Nora. I could not have wished for a more gracious hostess for such generally unworthy company. However, into each life a little riffraff must fall."

"Many of them are highly useful riffraff."

"Quite so."

But how many of those who hung on Lord Albemarle's arm now would turn on him like a pack of wolves if the rumors swirling about him were proven true?

She let him walk her to the door. "Shall I send Mr. Rivers to you?"

Benedick shook his head. "No need. He'll come. Good night, my dear. Remember we've an opera to attend later this week."

Being seen at all the right places with his glamorous mistress on his arm was part of maintaining Benedick's reputation as a man about town. While Nora might be shunned by the ladies at these entertainments, their titled husbands would send surreptitious glances toward Lord Albemarle's box all evening, ill-concealed envy in their eyes. And Benedick's stature would rise on account of his beautiful paramour.

Nora stepped into the darkened corridor as the door closed behind her and started toward the stairs. Before she reached the corner she almost stumbled into Desmond Rivers. The handsome young valet had been watching his master's door like a tabby before a mousehole, waiting for her to emerge.

"Oh, there you are," she said. "He's ready for you."

"Very good, my lady." Then as she swept past she could have sworn she heard Rivers mutter, "About bloody time."

She left the baron's residence and rode in the Albemarle coach back to her gem of a town house. Benedick had chosen it for her, but she'd have picked it for herself if she'd had the coin. Elegantly appointed with slender columns on either side of the bottle-green door, it was located on a quiet street in fashionable St. James Park. As her devoted footman, Glover, met her coach and saw her safely inside, her mind was awash in thoughts of secrets and rumors and servants.

And she wondered if Benedick was right to put so much trust in his Mr. Rivers.

One good thing about German opera—it's so deucedly loud, it drowns out the voices of the minds around me. However, when the soprano is bellowing like a cow that wants milking and the tenor squalls as if he's being gelded on the spot, I'm not sure the exchange is worth it.

~from the secret journal of Pierce Langdon,
Viscount Westfall

Chapter Five

Westfall was the sole occupant of the Duke of Camden's box. Stanstead was supposed to accompany him to this production of *Fidelio*, but at the last moment, the earl had begged off.

"Cassandra is wanting a bit of a diversion, and she can't go out during her confinement, you know. So she's adamant that we host a small card party. Her relatives are coming," Stanstead had explained. "Truth to tell, I'd rather brave a German soprano than face a bunch of third cousins who want to play loo, but a woman in a delicate condition must be humored."

Westfall had declared he understood. After the first act of the opera, he had perfect understanding. Any number of cousins and cards would be preferable to suffering through the throes of such heavy-handed angst set to music.

The one bright spot of the evening was that the Duke of Camden's box was perfectly situated in relation to Lord

Albemarle's. The baron's box jutted above the proscenium onstage right where the gas footlights illuminated Albemarle's party as well as the players on the boards. Obviously, that was the point of the box's location. Albemarle and his glittering mistress were a better show than anything that might happen on stage.

Westfall took one of the rear chairs in His Grace's box where he could sit in darkness and watch Lady Nora the entire time with no one the wiser. As lively as quicksilver, her expressions mirrored the frequently changing mood of the music.

He'd hoped that his memory of her was exaggerated, that he'd somehow inflated the lady's charms. Now that he saw her again, he realized the image he carried in his head of Nora Claremont was woefully inadequate.

He was captivated afresh.

Each time she leaned to whisper to her patron, Westfall's chest heated. He crossed his arms over it to keep his heart from boiling out.

While he writhed in hopeless longing for Lady Nora, he also wallowed in self-loathing. He'd never thought himself the shallow sort who'd be so undone by a woman's face and figure. If he kept this up, he'd be no earthly good to anyone.

But when he'd invaded her mind briefly and heard her heart's cry, he had been touched by her raw pain. He'd known his own share of that emotion after his family had abandoned him to Bedlam. It made him tender toward others who hurt in silence. Nora clasped her grief so firmly that no one could slip so much as a piece of parchment between her and her sorrow. So powerful it was, he was amazed that she was a good enough actress not to let a bit of it out where the world could see it.

But equally surprising, the name he'd heard in her mind wasn't her husband's. And it wasn't the father who'd turned her out. It was this mysterious Emilia.

There was more to La Nora than anyone suspected. When Westfall had glimpsed into her mind, a connection between them had been formed, the likes of which he'd never experienced before. He was broadsided by the force of these unexpected feelings. He could either retreat from them in disgrace or forge ahead and try to make sense of them.

At least, that's what his daft lovesick side tried to tell himself.

His stern side, the part of him that struggled to present a sane face to the world, reminded him that she was little better than a trollop who sold herself to the highest bidder. A man who had doings with such had best look to his wallet, never mind the havoc she'd wreak in his heart.

But when she rose toward the end of the first act and left Lord Albemarle's box, Westfall followed suit. He told himself he was just on the Order's business, but that was a lie.

He ached to speak with her again.

He waited at the head of the stairs on his side of the auditorium until he saw her on the landing below. Then he hurried down the steps, tracking her movement as she glided through the grand foyer and into one of the chambers along the side of the room.

Without slowing his pace, he followed her in.

He found her standing before a looking glass, dabbing her eyes with a handkerchief. Her nose was slightly red, as if she'd been crying or at least fighting tears. Part of him wanted to comfort her and the other part remembered he was there on the Order's business. He ought to lower his shield now while she was vulnerable, but he couldn't make himself do it.

It smacked too much of a violation to invade her mind when she wasn't aware he was even there. Then she saw him behind her in the mirror's reflection.

"Oh! Lord Westfall," she exclaimed. "You startled me. You must be lost. This is the ladies' retiring room."

"I'm not lost." He knew exactly where he was. He was with her and for reasons he couldn't fathom, very little else mattered.

"It won't do for you to be found in here. You should leave quickly, before the end of the act. The stampede of ladies will begin then and if you're caught alone with me, Lord Albemarle won't like it one bit."

Westfall could not have cared less what Albemarle liked, but he wondered if she was afraid of her patron's wrath. He was not by nature a violent man, but if the baron threatened her in any way, he'd be pleased to do the man some serious damage.

"I checked the program. There are two more musical numbers before the end of the act," he said. "The way Herr Beethoven can stretch a few phrases into thirty minutes, we aren't in danger of being interrupted soon."

"Well, I'd better get back in any case. Lord Albemarle will be wondering where I am."

"Why did you leave in the first place?"

"I don't know." Her eyes swam as she dabbed at them with her handkerchief. "I suppose it's because the story of

Fidelio is so sad. I mean, the heroine isn't even sure her husband is still alive, but she won't give up. Not until she exhausts every possibility. And a woman would have to be more than a little desperate to pose as a man so she could search that horrible prison for her lost husband."

"But you would do the same if it would return your husband to you," he said quietly. He sensed love for the dead man, still simmering inside her. She might be a courtesan, but she knew what real love was. That much was certain. "Wouldn't you?"

She blinked at him in surprise and frowned. "That is none of your business." Then she composed her features, offering him a mask-like smile. It was as if she were a marionette whose job was to please, and her puppet master had just jerked her strings. He hated that she felt she had to smile at him when he knew she was still sad inside.

"Forgive me, Lord Westfall. Sometimes music…strikes me in a place where I have no protection, and I have to go away and weep for a bit."

"And I interrupted your weeping. I am the one who should ask forgiveness." He took a step back and folded his hands before him. "Pray, do not mind me. I will be happy to wait until you are finished crying."

She made a noise that sounded suspiciously like a cross between a snort and laugh. "I fear the moment for weeping is past. I cannot call back my tears simply to oblige you. They wouldn't be real."

"Why not weep in any case, if it will help? After all, you fawn on Albemarle and pretend to be amused by him when it's not real."

Her frown was back with a vengeance. "What I do with

his lordship is no concern of yours."

"Yes, it is. I don't want it to be, but it is very much my concern. In fact, I'm quite concerned about it." Without realizing he did so, Westfall moved toward her. She matched him step for step, only going backward, until she was stopped by the mirror at her spine. He surprised himself by lifting a hand and stroking her cheek.

He feared her skin wouldn't be as soft as he'd imagined, but he was wrong. She was like silk, the most supple kind. He had no words to describe how her skin felt or how he felt while he stroked her, only that it was a moment bathed in magic. Nora was beyond anything in his experience. She trembled under his touch, but she didn't seem afraid.

Westfall lowered his shield a bit to make sure. If he were scaring her, he'd back away immediately. But as soon as her mind invaded his, he realized she was trembling because she wanted him to touch her.

Her disjointed thoughts and feelings washed over him. She was curious, and about him, no less. Needy and, at the same time, puzzled by her need. Trying to hide, always trying to hide her deeper self, but he caught glimpses of it between the other random ideas zipping through her brain. Her lively intellect spawned them so quickly, he was hard pressed to get a net around one.

Then finally one coherent thought smacked him between the eyes.

Why doesn't he kiss me?

"To be honest, I'm not sure how," he blurted out before he remembered that other people didn't enjoy having him continue a conversation that they had started in their thoughts. He raised his mental shield and hunkered behind it.

"Not sure how to do what? What are you talking about?"

"I've never kissed a woman. Never let myself get close enough to be tempted." Before he'd learned to shield his mind, the things rolling about in a woman's head had been enough to warn him away. He always knew exactly what they thought of the men in their lives. His Aunt Beatrice, for example, had nothing kind to think about his Uncle Horace and yet she had turned a pleasant face to him every day.

Smiling on the outside, despising on the inside. Westfall couldn't bear for a woman to do that to him.

Nora tipped her head to one side. "How did we get on the subject of kissing?"

"You brought it up."

"I most certainly did not," she said indignantly.

Oh. Right. She'd only thought it. His lack of experience with women, coupled with his inconvenient psychic gift, left him hopelessly adrift. "Well, I suppose you're correct. Talking about kissing is not what you had in mind in any case."

"I beg your pardon."

"Why? You've done nothing that requires apology."

"No, I mean... I'm not...oh, botheration," she said with a shake of her head that made the gems tucked into her coiffure catch the candlelight and send tiny prisms dancing around her. "You are a very confusing man, Lord Westfall."

"Pierce. My name is Pierce."

He didn't know why he said that. It always made him feel odd when Vesta LaMotte called him Pierce. He didn't think he was close enough to anyone for them to use his given name.

But to his surprise, he wished Nora would call him Pierce instead of his title. If she did, it might mean that she knew who he really was—his faults, his struggles, his weakness—and in spite of everything, could still bear his company.

"No, I'm not confusing," he corrected. "I'm confused. A very confused man most of the time, but not at this moment. I know exactly what I want."

He wanted to kiss her. More than he wanted to serve the Order. More than he wished the voices in his head could be permanently silenced. More than he wanted to keep breathing. More than—

To hell with wishing or wanting, he *needed* to kiss this woman.

So he leaned in, meaning to brush his lips on hers, but something stopped him halfway to his goal. His gaze swept over her exquisite face.

She was beyond beautiful. She was perfect. He was an unworthy pilgrim about to touch his lips to a shrine.

So instead of kissing her lips, he pressed his mouth to her cheek. Well, he missed a little. It was more the corner of her mouth actually, in that sweet place where her soft skin gave way to the moist intimacy of her lips.

She tasted of mint and lavender with a hint of apple-ish tartness. It was as if those flavors and scents had become ingrained on her skin and were a part of her uniqueness.

He pulled back to look down at her. She did not run from the retiring room screaming. In fact, her eyelids fluttered closed, her dark lashes resting on those lovely cheekbones. She raised herself a little on tiptoe.

My God, she wants me to kiss her. Really kiss her.

Even more surprisingly, he'd been able to divine that

amazing piece of intelligence without lowering his shield and letting her thoughts swamp him again. He bent to cover her mouth with his.

The kiss began as a gentle exploration. An acknowledgment.

I am I and you are you and we are moving tentatively toward us.

Then it turned into a quest. His mental shield melted away.

Yes, you are Other and yet I allow you in.

Know me. I need you to.

Discover me. No one else has.

Find yourself in me. I will never let you be lost again.

Were those his thoughts or hers? He always told himself so long as he could distinguish between his own ideas and the ones rattling around in the heads of others, he was sane. Now he wasn't quite sure.

Surprisingly enough, with his lips on hers, it didn't matter so much if he couldn't tell whose thoughts he was thinking. And it didn't matter that Nora belonged to another man. For this glorious slice of a moment, she was his.

What was life but a string of moments, in any case, some shining more than others? For these glittering heartbeats, he held the incomparable La Nora and—wonder of wonders!— she held him.

The whole world went wet and pliant and liquid while he heated and hardened and gathered her closer than his next breath.

Kissing was really quite something once one got the hang of it.

In some ways, a kiss is far more intimate than the ultimate act of love. It is a shared breath. We inhabit each other's bodies. Taking another's essence in with each breath, letting your own go with each exhale. It means trusting someone enough to allow them to carry a bit of you inside them. It is a joining of souls.

Why does it not break our hearts to take such chances?

~from the secret journal of Lady Nora Claremont

Chapter Six

He missed.

Lord Westfall hadn't kissed her full on the mouth. Then, when she looked up into his steely gray eyes, she realized he'd done exactly as he'd intended.

He wanted to *give* her a kiss, not take one from her. It was a fine distinction, but it meant something to Nora.

She hadn't met a man like that in years.

Not since Lewis...

She tried to shove the memory of her dead husband away but, wavering and indistinct, he appeared at the edge of her vision. If she looked in that direction, she knew from sad experience that he'd only vanish. She closed her eyes so she wouldn't be tempted.

Westfall seemed to take it as an invitation and covered her mouth with his warm lips.

That was fine with her. She hadn't been well and truly kissed in ages. Of course, if this was really Lord Westfall's first kiss, she wasn't likely to be well kissed. Besides, no man ever kissed a courtesan truly. There were always layers of deception on both sides.

Let Lewis's ghost watch if he liked. It would serve him right for leaving her.

She knew it wasn't logical to blame her husband for being killed in the king's service. Most widows honored the memory of their fallen heroes. If anyone mentioned Lewis to her, and that happened very rarely nowadays, she would claim she was proud of his sacrifice.

The more often a lie was repeated, the more easily it dropped from one's lips.

It had been more than five years, and she was still furious with him for dying and leaving her desolate. She'd given up everything for him—her home, her family, her place in the world. She'd lavished all she was on him. How could he die and make her go on breathing without him?

She knew it was petty and irrational of her to feel that way. Lewis hadn't intended to leave her in order to be of service to the Crown and he certainly hadn't meant to die. But her feelings on the subject resisted all efforts to mold them into something society would accept.

Not that they accepted anything about her.

To top it off, she also felt guilty about being angry with Lewis. So she shoved those emotions down into a tight little part of her heart where no one ever ventured. Then she poked and prodded at her shadowy husband until he disappeared from the edge of her mind.

Lord Westfall was quickly filling up the rest of the available space. He made her breath hitch and her chest tighten.

Nora was a connoisseur of the kiss. An expert, even though it had been a long while since she'd done it. Yet this man's halting attempts at kissing plucked at a deep place inside her. His mouth on hers was gentle. Sweet.

He gave her a long kiss of unhurried adoration.

That's ridiculous. He doesn't adore me. It's the aura of La Nora that draws men in. The mystique of the courtesan. I know what they are and what they want. I'm safe in a way the respectable women in their lives aren't.

Then Westfall's kiss suddenly turned decidedly unsafe. His tongue swept in with full assurance that she wanted him to, and surprisingly enough, she did. It was as if he sensed what she needed before she had the chance to know herself.

Bruise me. I don't care. I don't deserve easy.

He brutalized her mouth for a moment with just enough raw aggression to make a drumbeat begin between her thighs. She ached over her emptiness.

Then his kiss turned suddenly soft. Unbearably gentle. Tears pressed the backs of her eyes, but she kept them squeezed shut.

Oh, God, his kiss is like grace dripping from heaven.

Everything she needed and shouldn't have. Didn't merit. Unqualified favor. She was coated with it. His mouth caressed her, beguiled her. Little by little, the wall she'd erected around herself began to crumble.

He was seeking the deep Nora, the one she kept hidden. Looking for a way inside her secret self, a place she never allowed anyone to roam.

If this is truly the man's first kiss, I'm lost.

Nora wedged her arms between them and flattened both palms on his chest. He broke off their kiss before she could give him a push. Again, he'd anticipated her need.

Lord Westfall touched her cheek. It was wet.

"If you're ready to weep now, I can wait until you're finished to kiss you again."

Nora pulled away from him and swiped her eyes. She was probably smearing the paint she'd used to enhance them, but she didn't care. Westfall's kiss had made her cry. No one had ever done that to her. Not even Lewis.

Who was this man?

"You will not be kissing me again," Nora said firmly. The last thing she needed was someone who made her cry. She went to great pains not to feel that much. She pushed past him to leave just as Lady Waldgren was entering, followed by her circle of cronies and sycophants. The despicable old gossip gave Nora the fisheye, then her mouth fell open when she discovered Westfall, standing bold as brass in the midst of the feminine retreat.

"Lord Westfall! What on earth are you doing here?" she screeched. "If you insist on invading the ladies' retiring room that may be all it takes to convince your poor family to have you committed again."

Committed?

The word rolled around Nora's brain as she threaded her way through the milling crowd in the theater's grand foyer. Albemarle was holding court in one corner of the great room, surrounded by an assemblage of gentlemen who were listening to him with avid attention. When he set himself to charm, no one was better than Benedick. Whatever he wanted from this group, she was sure he would get.

She caught his eye for a moment, but he didn't signal for her to join him. Sometimes having her draped on his arm was a help and sometimes a hindrance, depending upon whom he was trying to impress. She'd given up feeling hurt or happy about it, no matter which he needed from her at the moment. She made her way back to his private box to wait amid the crushed velvet seats and gilt cherubs that cavorted around the box and above the stage's curtain. The other opera-goers greeted their friends and acquaintances as they returned to their seats.

A few of them glanced her way, but none sent her any hint of acknowledgment. This was the respectable crowd. The one that followed her exploits in the tabloids with glee while shunning her in person with equal delight.

She lifted her chin to show them she didn't care.

When she had begun her career as a courtesan, her mentor had advised her that beauty was her stock in trade. She must be diligent in the application of lotions to protect her skin and keep it supple and youthful-appearing for as long as possible.

No one had warned her that she also needed to make it as tough as a rhinoceros hide.

The second act began. Benedick didn't return until the opera's unhappy prisoner Florestan was well into a wistful aria about freedom in his dank Seville dungeon.

"Sorry, my dear," Lord Albemarle whispered. "The business of the House of Lords waits for no man."

Some aristocrats served in that august body only to speechify about social injustice and rail against the oppression of the downtrodden. They made themselves feel important while accomplishing nothing. By contrast, Benedick was pushing through a number of reforms that would benefit his friends and confound his enemies. He made full use of the system of laws and statutes and bent it to his will.

It wasn't altruistic, but it was what he did best.

She smiled at him. When she started to turn her attention back to the action on the stage, something caught her eye in the audience instead.

Lord Westfall was taking his seat in the box across the theater from her. Why had she not noticed him there before?

He met her gaze steadily and then looked down at the action on the stage. Her chest constricted as she continued to study him. When she'd first met him at Benedick's party, she'd thought him awkward, a bit clumsy. Rather like an overgrown puppy.

That was before he'd kissed her. He had seemed singularly accomplished for someone who claimed he'd never kissed a woman.

Westfall was beyond odd. The things he said didn't fit society's rules for acceptable conversation. He made her feel exposed, as if he'd somehow seen her naked. She waited for a prickly opinion of him to sprout in her chest. Instead, she felt only confusion and the sort of soppiness she despised in other women.

All because he kissed like a god.

What a befuddling man.

"Penny for your thoughts." Benedick's whisper interrupted her musings. She jerked her gaze from Lord Westfall and fastened it on her protector's face.

"Only a penny?" she said with false gaiety. "Everything about me is far more expensive than that."

He chuckled. "And worth every sovereign, my dear. I don't fault you for ogling Viscount Westfall. The man is striking."

Albemarle was on top of everything. Trust him not to miss her interest in Westfall.

"However, I'd rather you not do it when Lady Waldgren is likely to catch you."

The Waldgren box was located next to Lord Albemarle's, close enough that if Benedick wished, he could reach across and hand the beleaguered Lord Waldgren a handkerchief if he needed one to stop up his ears when his wife began nattering on. Now however, the waspish woman was gawking, not gabbing. Her lorgnette was trained not on the stage, but on Benedick and Nora.

Nora cast Lady Waldgren a poisonous smile to let her know she'd been caught snooping. The lorgnette shifted guiltily to the singers below.

"I understand Lord Westfall put in an appearance at my last party, but I didn't get the chance to meet the man," Benedick said softly. "Did you?"

She was tempted to lie. It might be better to say that she knew nothing of Westfall, that she'd been staring off into space instead of mooning over him and reliving the feel of his lips on hers. Instead, she leaned toward Benedick. She had myriad acquaintances, but he was her ally in most matters, the closest thing she had to a friend. She owed him truth.

"Yes, I met him, but he didn't stay long. He's not... Well, he didn't seem comfortable in a crowd," she whispered behind her fan. "Why did you invite him in the first place?"

"Because he and Lord Stanstead are both known associates of the Duke of Camden. Since I can never lure His Grace to one of my fetes, I thought I'd start with his friends and work my way into the duke's good opinion through that backdoor," Benedick explained. "He may be a recluse, but Camden swings a good deal of weight in some very important circles. Circles I may find myself in need of someday."

"And you hope to make him an asset," Nora concluded. Almost every relationship in Benedick's life was balanced by how it might benefit him. Even his relationship with her. Yes, he found her company amusing, and they'd formed something approximating a partnership, but if she ceased being useful to him, she doubted he'd trouble himself over her long. Not that he'd be cruel. Benedick wouldn't send her away without a generous pension, but then he'd move on to someone who would benefit him more.

"The Duke of Camden an asset? Lud, no. Someone of Camden's stature is no one's 'asset.' Unless I discover that His Grace hides some hideous secret, I'd never be able to bend him to my will." Benedick sighed. "No, in the Duke of Camden's case, I have to be content with politics as usual. *Quid pro quo* and all that. But we still might be able to help each other in areas of mutual interest. Unfortunately, I can't seem to get close enough to the man to find out what those might be."

"So in the meantime, we should cultivate the duke's friends." She stressed the "we" a bit to remind him that she did bring something to the table besides her pretty face.

He patted her forearm. "Yes, my dear. You may pursue Lord Westfall, if you like. But be discreet."

"When am I not?"

He arched a brow at her. "You mean other than a few minutes ago when you were practically disrobing the man with your eyes?" Benedick tossed an appraising glance across the theater toward Westfall. "Not that I blame you."

"I was not disrobing him." Now that Benedick had mentioned it, all she could think about was what Westfall might have hidden beneath his superfine jacket and starched cravat. The male form held no surprises for her, but every man had his own unique strengths and, sadly, weaknesses as well. Westfall was a large man, broad through the shoulders, and tall. She wondered if he was proportional in other places as well.

"Frankly, I'm more puzzled by him than attracted," she lied. "What's this I hear about him being...committed?"

"Now we come to it. I wasn't going to burst your bubble, since you're clearly besotted with the fellow. Don't fret. The gossip wasn't about him being engaged or otherwise committed to some young lady." Benedick smirked. "It's actually much worse."

Since Lady Waldgren was glaring in their direction again, Benedick took Nora's hand and brought her knuckles to his lips. When he released her hand, she let it settle on his leg. Then she ran her palm up and down from his knee to mid-thigh.

Might as well give the old biddy something to gossip about. Of course, by the time Lady Waldgren was done with her account of the exchange, the tale would be that Lady Nora Claremont and Lord Albemarle had all but rutted each other blind in the dim light of the opera house.

For the gossip's sake, Benedick leaned over and bussed his lips on Nora's neck before continuing to whisper, "According to all reports, your Lord Westfall is mad as a hatter."

"Mad?" Her hand stopped its light massage. He wasn't

her Lord Westfall, particularly if he was mad, but this was not the place to argue the point.

To further scandalize Lady Waldgren, Benedick removed his pristine white gloves, then tugged off one of hers. He took his time about it, stroking her palm before lacing her bare fingers with his. With this sort of attention to detail, Nora suspected Benedick was a gentle and thorough lover, though she'd never know from actual experience.

"Westfall's family tried to hush up his condition, of course. Evidently, the problem showed itself when he was quite young. He was tutored at home instead of being sent to Eton or Harrow. They kept him in the country as much as they could, but when his father died and he came into the title, it was impossible to keep his madness a secret any longer." Benedick shrugged eloquently. "His uncle had him committed to Bedlam a few years ago."

Bedlam. Something inside Nora stiffened at the sound of the name. Its proponents argued that Bethlem Royal Hospital for the Insane was a necessary evil to protect society from lunatics. But rumors about the cruelty of the dubious "treatments" practiced on Bedlam's inmates leaked from its walls like filth from a cracked chamber pot.

"Once someone enters Bedlam, they rarely emerge," she said. *Unless they are wrapped in a shroud.*

"It is a wonder that Westfall is out and about in society." Benedick nodded. "Blame it on the Duke of Camden. A few months ago, His Grace inexplicably interested himself in the fellow. He crossed enough palms with coin that he was able to have Westfall released to his care. Heaven only knows what that cost him." Benedick's gaze flicked to the viscount and then back to her. "I must say, the poor man cleans up well, but still, one wonders why Camden bothered."

Obviously, Benedick suspected this was the tip of some secret that might serve his interests. Nora had never met the Duke of Camden, but she blessed him for his compassion.

Bedlam, of all God-forsaken places, and sent there by his family, to boot. Good Lord, what Westfall must have endured. "What does Lord Westfall's family think of him being out?"

"His uncle is less than pleased, I'm sure. After all, his nephew is the only thing that keeps him from inheriting his dead brother's title and lands."

"So Westfall's commitment may have been motivated solely by greed. Perhaps he isn't truly mad at all," Nora said softly as Benedick stroked her forearm. If he meant anything by the caress, she might have found it pleasurable.

"Aren't you the clever girl? I believe I'm rubbing off on you." As if to suit his actions to his words, he nuzzled her neck. "But unfortunately, no. Westfall is quite dotty. The fact that his parents recognized it in childhood proves his troubles predate his uncle's actions."

Then Benedick turned suddenly to Lady Waldgren, who was still leering at them from the neighboring box. "Perhaps you might wish to hire a painter, Madam. If you capture Lady Nora and me on canvas as we take ease of each other, you may gawk at us at your leisure."

Lady Waldgren sputtered. "Well, I never —"

"Probably not," Benedick interrupted. "Therein lies your problem. Good evening, my lady." He nodded to Lord Waldgren who was half asleep in the chair behind his wife. "My lord, you have my deepest condolences."

"Why?" Lord Waldgren asked, blinking stupidly as he jerked to full wakefulness. "Who died?"

"We are at the opera. Everybody dies," Benedick quipped. "But I refer to your patience, sir. It must be totally expired by now. Good evening."

Benedick raised Nora to her feet and started to shepherd her out without asking if she wished to stay until the entertainment's end. He'd accomplished what he wanted with that group during intermission. It didn't matter a jot to him that Nora was engaged in the opera and wanted to know how the story ended. She cast a glance at the stage where the heroine was still searching for her imprisoned husband amid the forbidding cells. Then she looked once more across the theater toward the Duke of Camden's box.

Lord Westfall's gaze was fixed on her, a look of concentration on his handsome features. It wasn't the glazed-eyed stare of lust she was expecting. It was more as if she were a museum piece whose meaning he was trying to unravel.

She wasn't sure what to make of it.

Or of him.

Everyone always talks about the advance of scientific knowledge as if it's an unqualified good thing. The vivisectionist, for example, has added considerably to our knowledge of the body and how it all works. He is hailed as forward thinking and courageous, because he is willing to brave certain taboos as he hacks up his living subjects in search of further understanding.

However, no one asks his subjects what they think of the process.

~from the secret journal of Pierce Langdon,
Viscount Westfall

Chapter Seven

Water spewed from his mouth and nose. This was it. He was dying for certain this time. He'd never get enough out. He gagged and sputtered, fighting to clear his airway. Then he gasped and, God be praised, the dank air of the subterranean chamber invaded his oxygen-starved lungs.

I'm going to live, shrieked through his brain.

No one was more surprised than he.

His head lolled forward. He fought the gathering blackness at the edge of his vision. If he sank into it, his tormentors would only use the cattle prod to revive him again. He forced himself to look up at his doctor's face.

"Very good, Mr. Langdon," the quack said. Pierce couldn't remember the man's name. Couldn't remember ever hearing it. Or if he had, subsequent water "treatments" must have rinsed it right out of his brain. "You came through that surprisingly well."

Pierce was strapped naked to a wooden chair whose

surfaces had been scoured smooth by countless thousands of gallons of water. The only rough spot was under Pierce's bare backside, but that discomfort was minor compared with the other indignities he suffered. He shivered so hard his teeth knocked against one another. If his tongue got in the way, he'd bite it in two. He had no sensation below his ankles. Cold leached up his shins from the wet stone floor.

"As you can see, my device is a significant improvement over Van Helmont's full immersion therapy," the doctor jabbered on to his colleague who was taking copious notes. "It completely pacifies the belligerent patient and puts him in a suggestible state."

"Not to mention that the patient, he is less likely to drown than with Van Helmont's method." The new doctor had an Italian accent. His nasal tone danced up and down Pierce's spine, pausing at intervals to grind in its sharp heel.

"Quite. I'm happy to report we've only lost four this month."

The Italian made a noise of approval. The men's thoughts, small-minded and self-aggrandizing at the same time, vied with each other for supremacy in the air over their heads. Pierce tried not to listen to them. The words coming out of their mouths were confusing enough.

Instead, he stared at the drain in the floor. It was between his feet. He thought they were his feet, but he couldn't be sure because he couldn't feel them any longer. The last of the deluge pooled around his blue toes and glumped down the drain in belching hitches, ready to be forced through a system of pumps back into the massive tank above his head.

"A quantifiable improvement, indeed. What is Signor Langdon's diagnosis?"

He might as well have been a dumb beast, the way they spoke about him as if he weren't even present. Perhaps he wasn't. Not in any way that counted.

"Pitiable case, sir. Pitiable. You'd never know he was a lord to look at him, would you?"

No one looks lordly if you strip them naked and strap them to a chair, *Pierce thought defiantly, but he was careful to keep his eyes downcast lest the doctors see bloodlust swirling behind his irises. If he wasn't so weakened by the "treatments," he'd tear off his bonds, cheerfully strangle the pair of them, and sleep like the just, once the deed was done.*

"But his title is no proof against what's going on in his poor brainpan," the doctor went on. "He first presented with mania, claiming he heard voices. Even more incredible, Langdon believed he was hearing the thoughts of those around him. He was quite adamant that I believe him on that point and, I must admit, he did come up with some rather amazing guesses that might have fooled those who are disposed to believe such rot. However, after a few weeks of treatment he stopped trying to coerce me into joining in his manic fantasy and became sullen and uncooperative."

The Italian doctor made a tsking noise. "Melancholia, you think?"

The first doctor nodded. "Now I fear he may be slipping into dementia. He often cannot remember his own name."

"Neither would you if someone half drowned you every day," *Pierce mumbled, but the words were so garbled as to be unintelligible.*

"He speaks. Oh, good. It's very important to implant the desired change when the mind is at its most pliable. Now, Mr. Langdon, I want you to repeat after me. I CANNOT

HEAR THE THOUGHTS OF THOSE AROUND ME. Say it. Say it just once and the orderly will come and dress you and you can return to your cell. I CANNOT HEAR THE THOUGHTS OF THOSE AROUND ME."

Pierce forced himself to focus on the doctor's gaunt face. The man was so pale and his cheekbones protruded so sharply as he leered down at him that Pierce couldn't shake the thought that he was looking at a skull.

"I can see your bones," he muttered.

"Dear me, now he's delusional," the doctor said, making a mark on the paper in his folder. "Fill the tank again, if you please, Dr. Falco."

Pierce screamed.

"For the love of God, no!"

His own shouting woke him. All his muscles were clenched. Even though he recognized his surroundings, and he knew he was safe, it was some minutes before he could slow his racing heart.

Only a dream. It was only a dream.

Westfall wasn't still held captive in the lower reaches of Bedlam. No quack was about to administer yet another treatment. He was warm and dry and comfortable on a thick feather tick in one of the Duke of Camden's sumptuous guest quarters.

But he couldn't seem to stop shivering.

Fortunately, the servants at Camden House were accustomed to all manner of strange noises coming from his room and no longer came running when a nightmare chased him from sleep.

However, someone had probably heard him cry out. He cringed with embarrassment over the fact that his weakness had been exposed once again.

Westfall forced himself out of bed and got dressed. His wardrobe needs were simple. Besides, he didn't want to bother with a valet's attentions. It would only mean one more mind from whom he'd have to shield himself. As usual, a servant had slipped into his chamber while he slept and left a breakfast tray for him. He suffered through suppers in the dining room with the entire household, but this small concession saved him from having to sit with the other minds around a table for his morning meal as well.

So far, Westfall was allowed to live in monk-like seclusion whenever he wished. Eventually, however, the duke would expect him to be more sociable with the other residents and guests of Camden House.

Since he'd been venturing out into society on behalf of the Order and he had to erect and maintain his mental shield most of the time, he appreciated the leisure of being able to relax his vigilance in the mornings. After taking his tea and wolfing down three rolls with clotted cream and jam, he wandered down to the solarium.

The fresh green breath of plants met him at the door. The duke's gardener cultivated a number of exotic species, but the man was careful to make himself scarce when Westfall entered. The duke must have left orders in that regard. Since Pierce had demonstrated a knack for it, the gardener even allowed Pierce to do some of the watering and a bit of minor pruning.

Plants were so much easier than people.

A number of African violets needed repotting, so Pierce

removed his jacket, rolled up his shirtsleeves, and went to work. It felt good to get his hands dirty, to feel the tender roots loosen and then settle into their new home.

If he could hear the thoughts of plants, he suspected they'd be breathing a sigh of relief and saying, "Thank you." He smiled at the imagined chorus of greenery expressing their gratitude. They'd have sweet, bloodless voices.

Like angels.

He'd always enjoyed his own company and rarely felt solitude was a burden. For the first time, though, he began to wish he could tolerate someone else's presence well enough to share his passions and pleasures. Would anyone else be amused by the thought of his angelic violet chorus? What would Lady Nora think about it?

"Where are you hiding? Oh, there you are, Pierce."

He'd wished for company, and now he had it. "Be careful what you wish for," he grumbled to himself as he quickly refastened his cuffs and donned his jacket.

Vesta LaMotte stepped gingerly down the narrow path between the new beds.

"I was hoping I'd catch you alone," she said gaily.

"Of course, I'm alone." As if he ever sought out the company of others. Still, Vesta was always unfailingly kind to him, and he had the sense that she carefully guarded her thoughts when she was near so as not to shock him unduly. Her mind never battered away at his shield like Stanstead's did.

"How are you?" he asked because it was the "done" thing to inquire.

"Getting old," she said because it was not the "done" response. Vesta often advised him that if one couldn't be witty one should at least strive to be surprising. "But I suppose I ought not to complain, considering the alternative. Now what's this I hear about you turning into a recluse again? Camden tells me you have gone to ground since the opera last week. You'd been making such great strides prior to that. Why are you refusing to venture out?"

He shook his head. "I didn't do the Order any good at the opera. I'm not likely to do any better at a piano recital or a gallery opening or a bear baiting, for that matter."

Those were all places where Lady Nora was expected to be, probably on the arm of her patron Lord Albemarle. Westfall could have made an appearance at any of them since they were public events and no invitation was required. But he didn't want to have to grit his teeth and watch as the baron made love to Nora in the open again the way he had in his box at the opera.

"I'll have you know that it was not easy for me to tease the lady's schedule from her," Vesta said. "Quite tedious, actually."

"I would have thought you and she would enjoy each other's company. You have a great deal in common."

"A sisterhood of tarts, as it were? Oh, I am sorry. I can see that word shocks you, but believe me when I say I was censoring myself. Polite Society calls us much worse." She gave a dismissive wave of her bejeweled hand. Vesta never wore gloves if she could help it. She liked showing off her rings far too much. Some fingers boasted more than one. "Well, since Lady Nora and I have chosen similar paths, I suppose one might expect that to lead to a sense of camaraderie, if not for the fact that our line of work is extremely competitive. And since the care and pleasing of the male of the species is our bread and butter, we tend not to be disposed toward female friendships. However, she surprised me yesterday afternoon. Lady Nora paid me a call."

His ears pricked. "Oh?"

"Yes." Vesta slipped her hand into the crook of Pierce's elbow and gracefully forced him to escort her through the greenery, stooping occasionally to smell a beckoning blossom. "She disguised her purpose well. At first, she asked my advice about how to set up the annuity her current protector wishes to settle on her. But then as soon as I finished giving her the barest of guidance about her financial matter, she turned the conversation to you almost immediately. You have definitely piqued the lady's interest."

Something snapped to attention inside him. "What did you tell her?"

"That you're a hopeless neurotic who hears the thoughts of others but won't use his formidable power to control them."

"What?" The cardinal rule of the Order of the M.U.S.E. was that one never discussed the psychic gifts (or burdens, in his case) of its members.

"I'm only teasing, dear boy. I'd never betray you." She patted his forearm. "But you could, you know. Control others, I mean. The ability you bear is ripe with ever so many powerful possibilities. It's fortunate for the world that you're the one to whom it was given. Just imagine if Bonaparte had possessed your gift—or even our own Prinny!" She shuddered delicately.

Privately, Pierce thought it might be good for those in power to know exactly what the others around them thought. As it stood, they were more likely to be advised by people who said only what their ruler wanted to hear. No one should be guided solely by thoughts that mirrored their own. No one was smart enough or principled enough for that.

"In any case, I told Lady Nora that you're one of the duke's trusted associates which, Lord knows, is true. Honestly, I don't know which of you is the most misanthropic, you or Camden, but he does seem to like you well enough. He seeks out the company of so few. At least you have good reason to avoid others, while Edward…but that's neither here nor there." She made small circles with one hand, another of her expressive gestures. Tiny sparks seemed to shoot from under her lacquered nails, a small indication of the power of a fire mage which she kept under firm control most of the time. "At any rate, you seem to have captured the lady's attention."

He shook his head. He'd made a cake of himself at their last meeting. Given his limited experience with the fair sex, why on earth had he dared to kiss a courtesan? "You're just saying that."

"No, this letter is just saying that." She drew a slender sealed parchment from her reticule and waggled it in the air. The violets he was working with had very little smell, but the scents of mint, lavender, and apple wafted from the missive.

The heady mix was Nora's fragrance.

He reached for it, but Vesta snatched it away beyond his grasp.

"Not so fast," Vesta said. "First, the courier must have her pay, and I've decided mine will be to know what's in this message."

"Agreed." He'd have licked the sole of her foot if she'd demanded it. "Now give it to me."

"As you wish. But pace yourself, dear boy. It's only a letter."

Only a letter. Only something she'd touched. Only words she'd thought and committed to foolscap. And addressed to him. Maybe she didn't think him mad. Maybe...

He tore open the seal, pausing for a moment to close his eyes and drink in more of her scent as it emanated from the missive. Then he unfolded the foolscap and read:

> *My dear Lord Westfall,*
>
> *I understand from my good friend, Miss LaMotte, that you are a horticultural enthusiast. My gardener has done some miraculous things with orchids of late. If you would like to see them, I will be at home on Thursday between the hours of two and four.*
>
> *Yours truly,*
> *N. Claremont*

"She invites me to visit her on Thursday. That's today," he realized. Vesta was looking at him expectantly, as if she couldn't hear his heart thundering in his chest. He read the letter over a few more times to make certain he hadn't misunderstood.

"You'll go, of course." Vesta's smile was so brilliant, it hurt to look at it.

"But won't Lord Albemarle be upset if I visit his mistress?"

"If he isn't, you're not doing it right," Vesta said dryly. "And if he is, worse things could happen. You are more likely to learn something of worth from an upset man than one who is in perfect charity with the world."

He'd forgotten completely that his association with Nora was supposed to be about discovering the nature and whereabouts of the *Fides Pulvis*. That reminder steadied him a bit.

Then too, he ought to be repulsed by the notion of pursuing a courtesan in the first place. If a woman's favor could be bought and sold, how could he put any value on it?

But when he thought of Nora, things like right or wrong, respectable or beyond the pale, took wing and flew out the window.

"What's wrong with me, Vesta?"

The fire mage leaned her head on his shoulder, and he noticed for the first time that a few strands of silver were interspersed with her golden locks. "Not a thing, Pierce. Not anything you can help, at any rate, so there's no point in fretting over it."

"What do you mean? What can't I help?"

"Falling in love, my dear boy. Falling in love."

"That's ludicrous. I barely know the lady."

"I would beg to differ. Because you can hear Lady Nora's thoughts, you are able to know her deeply and well, in short order," Vesta said. "Besides, you're exhibiting the classic signs."

But what was Lady Nora exhibiting? She was interested in him, Vesta said. Was he a curiosity, like her orchids? Was he an amusement for when her patron wasn't looking? No, someone tenderhearted enough to weep over the plight of opera characters wasn't likely to use real people for sport.

But he wasn't like real people. Westfall was different and always would be. Would she run from him in horror once she knew what he was?

Thanks to the generosity of my protector, I am a woman in possession of my own fortune. My supposed lover showers me with jewels and gifts and demands very little in return, beyond my loyalty and discretion. If they were honest, most women, even the married ones, would envy my place in the world.

So why am I willing to risk everything because I can't stop thinking about a madman's kiss?

~from the secret journal of Lady Nora Claremont

Chapter Eight

That afternoon, Nora paced in her first floor parlor, waiting for Lord Westfall to make an appearance. It was inconceivable that he wouldn't come. After all, what man would decline an opportunity to spend time alone with La Nora?

"This one, most like," she fretted to herself ruefully.

She had the feeling that he disapproved of her but that he was still weirdly fascinated by her. He reminded her of a field mouse who is charmed immobile by a snake's glassy stare, terrified but unable to look away.

"Oh, Lud, that makes me the serpent," she muttered.

"My lady? Is something amiss? Do you require anything?"

She'd forgotten that her butler, Mr. Whittles, was in the room. He was of medium height and build, pale-haired and of sallow complexion. The butler's general appearance was that of a man crabbing sideways into his middle years and had been for as long as he'd been in Lord Albemarle's employ. Benedick liked to joke that if Whittles stood naked before a beige wall and closed his eyes, he'd disappear entirely.

"No, Whittles," Nora said. "After you bring up some tea, you may take the rest of the day."

"Begging your pardon, my lady, but it's not my half day off till Saturday."

"Nevertheless, you will take the day." She'd dismissed her lady's maid and Cook at noon. Before that, the rest of the servants had been given orders not to return until tomorrow evening. She would have dispensed with Whittles sooner, too, but it was unheard of that she should answer her own door. "And don't hurry back tomorrow. You know I never rise before noon, in any case."

"Yes, my lady. Very good."

"Oh, and Whittles, bring tea for two."

"Ah!" Whittles laid a finger alongside his nose in the time-honored gesture of collusion. "His lordship is coming. Say no more."

"I'm not expecting his lordship, though Lord Albemarle knows of my...friendship with the gentleman who's coming to visit. However, I'd rather there was no confusion on the matter among the other servants, so let's keep this between ourselves. I hope I can count on your discretion."

"Of course, my lady." His head bobbed a few times like a water bird feeding in the shallows before he glided toward the door. "I am yours to command."

But Benedick's to pay, she finished silently. Nothing would happen in her home that Lord Albemarle didn't know about. She'd considered replacing Whittles, but he'd come with the house and had served Benedick for years. It didn't seem fair to penalize the man for loyalty.

She just wished she could inspire some for herself.

Someone rapped the knocker on her front door.

"That will be Lord Westfall. He's come to see the orchids," she added, wishing she hadn't. She owed Whittles no explanation. "But first show him up here, and we'll have refreshments."

"Right away, my lady." The butler hurried to answer the door and then do her bidding over the matter of tea.

She didn't know why she insisted on the formality of tea. Westfall was such an unconventional fellow, she might as well have worn a gardener's smock and met him in the hothouse behind her town house. Instead, she'd taken great pains with her appearance. She wanted to show him that, though she was a courtesan, she could receive a caller like a lady.

Whatever had befallen her, whatever choices she'd made, she was still the daughter of an earl and knew how to behave like one when she wished.

She draped herself gracefully on the settee, carefully arranging the flowing panels of her morning gown. Then she opened the book of poetry that had been left on the side table, though she didn't really attend to the words.

Nora felt his presence before she caught a glimpse of him from the corner of her eye. A ripple of feral pleasure coursed through her. He seemed to fill the parlor doorway, his broad shoulders nearly touching on both sides.

She changed her mind. There was nothing of a field mouse about this man.

He made a stiff bow, but he didn't speak.

Nora looked up, aware that most men loved to catch a woman in this state. She was wearing half-dress, her hair unbound, her expression appropriately dewy-eyed and hopeful after supposedly letting Byron's lush verses surge over her.

"Hullo, Westfall," she said.

"Your book is upside down."

"Oh!" She laid it aside as quickly as if it were a viper.

"But you looked lovely pretending to read it. I assume that was the point, so, well done."

"Well, I have read it, you know." In fact, it was one of her favorites. *Fugitive Pieces* was Lord Byron's first privately published collection of poems, some of which were vehemently disapproved of by his lordship's boyhood preacher. Byron had been quietly trying to buy back all the copies that had been sold, but Nora would never part with hers.

Westfall stared at the cover for a moment and began reciting:

"'Ye rhymers, whose bosoms with phantasy glow,

Whose pastoral passions are made for the grove;

From what blest inspiration your sonnets would flow,

Could you ever have tasted the first kiss of love!'"

That very stanza had just flitted through her mind. It was uncanny and reminded her of their kiss at the opera enough to set her insides a-jitter. "Oh, you know your Byron."

"Not really," he said, "but it appears you do."

She rose hastily. "Where are my manners? Please have a seat."

Nora had chosen to meet him in the parlor located on the first floor toward the back of the house instead of in the more formal one in front. Here the chairs were overstuffed and comfortable instead of ostentatious and gilded. She'd surrounded herself with things she loved, not things meant to impress others. Rather than housing gewgaws and gizzwickies, the shelves along one wall held books whose spines showed wear. Instead of a fashionable Turkish rug, the hardwoods were bare and gleaming so the parquet's design was shown to best advantage. While she wouldn't throw rocks at a Gainsborough landscape, the walls in this room were graced with a simple framed set of pressed flowers.

Westfall ignored her invitation to sit. The flowers caught his eye, and he wandered over to inspect them.

"You collected these yourself," he said. It was a statement, not a question.

"Yes, when I was a girl in Surrey." What a very intuitive man he was. "They grow wild there."

"*Solanum dulcamara*," he said before the specimen with a five petal blossom whose purplish blue color had faded slightly over time.

"It's also known as bittersweet. The crofters on my father's land consider it a weed, but I think it's lovely all the same."

"It is."

"I have another name for them." She didn't know why she told him that. She'd never confided the notion to anyone. It was a silly little thing from her childhood, certainly not full of the wit and charm for which she was known, but "in for a penny, in for a pound." "I call them God's flowers."

"Because they're the ones no one else wants," he said as if he was finishing her thought.

"Exactly." She'd pitied the poor unloved plants when she was a child. Now that she was grown, she knew what it was to be the one no one wanted. Even after Lewis had died, her father had refused to see her. She'd defied him, and he'd never forgiven her for it. She was the weed in his garden. The earl had plucked her out with ruthlessness, root and all.

Whittles bustled back in with the tea tray and made a great show of setting things up on the low table before her. Lord Westfall sat, quite properly, in the Sheridan chair opposite her. Nora was relieved when he did. It was a mistake to meet him in this room. If he continued to prowl around the space, poking into her special things, what else might he learn about her that she wasn't quite willing to share?

"I'll pour out myself," she said to her butler. "That will be all, Mr. Whittles."

Her butler eyed Lord Westfall for a moment, and then scraped a bow to her. "Very good, my lady." He was too well trained to sneak another glance at her guest as he made his exit.

"How do you take your tea, Westfall?"

"I'd like it if you would call me Pierce."

She blinked in surprise. He seemed such a buttoned-up, formal sort of fellow. "Of course," she said. Even though he'd told her his Christian name at the opera, he hadn't invited her to use it. "I'm honored you would count me among your intimate friends."

"I have no friends, intimate or otherwise," he said matter-of-factly. "No one but Vesta LaMotte calls me Pierce."

She bristled a bit. "And since she and I are similarly employed you thought—"

"No, it's not that." He lifted a hand to forestall her indignation. "I never asked Vesta to use my name. She simply does it. I have no idea why. But I'd like to hear you say it. If you would."

"Very well...Pierce," she said, slightly mollified. She

was, it must be admitted, a fancy whore, but she was quick to guard her dignity. No one else would. "You may call me Nora."

"But that's not your given name, is it?" He leaned forward. "You were christened Honora."

"How do you know that?

"I am an associate of the Duke of Camden. He has means of acquiring information throughout England that I can't even begin to fathom."

So he'd used his association with the duke to learn more about her. It made her uneasy. No one's past would bear much scrutiny. Certainly, not hers, but Benedick would be pleased. It meant Westfall was on very good terms with His Grace and that made him much more valuable as an asset.

"No one has called me Honora in years," she said.

"Then Honora will not mind if I take the name out of mothballs and give it a bit of practice. Will she?"

He said the strangest things, but she rather liked them. She smiled her assent.

"How do you take your tea?" she repeated.

"I didn't come here for tea, Honora."

"Oh." She stopped in mid-pour. "Yes, of course, the orchids. Come."

She was a little disappointed that she wouldn't be allowed to show off her skills with a teapot. There was something genteel, yet sensual, about preparing a perfect cup. Benedick loved to watch her stir in the lumps and add just the right amount of milk.

"Ambrosia," he'd say. "Just the way I like it."

But she reasoned that a good hostess falls in with the wishes of her guest so she abandoned plans to coax more information from Westfall over her brew. She might call him Pierce, but she'd continue to think of him as Westfall. It was safer.

Allowing him close would give him the power to hurt her.

She rose and guided him back down the elegant stairs to the ground level of her home. Then they swept through the beautifully appointed salon that, like her front parlor, was designed to over-awe visitors with the taste and wealth of her patron. There was nothing of her in either of those rooms. They were all Benedick.

Without the quiet bustle of servants, the empty house seemed to breathe with them. The swish of her kid-soles on the floor was the sound of its soft inhalations, Westfall's noisier footfalls its loud exhale. He held the back door for her, and they stepped into her small garden.

The kitchen squatted to one side, detached from the house so as not to be a fire hazard, and the hothouse sat opposite it, across the small garden. Beyond a tall wall at the rear of the property, a stable housed her horse and provided a place for Benedick to park his equipage when he visited. A grassy patch ornamented by a pattering fountain and a granite bench was located between these three structures. It was a place where the lady of the house could take her leisure while servants worked around her on all sides.

But now all her servants were gone. She didn't know why it was important to her not to be under their watchful eyes. It was not that they weren't paid well enough to be discreet. Benedick wouldn't care that she had invited this man here. He'd told her she was free to pursue Lord Westfall. He'd even encouraged it since he believed it might lead to a closer association with His Grace, the Duke of Camden.

But part of her didn't want this visit to be about Benedick's schemes. There was something about Lord Westfall—Pierce, she corrected, reasoning that perhaps she *could* think of him as that so long as she didn't become maudlin about what it might mean that he wanted her to use his given name.

She didn't know what it was that drew her to him. His madness placed him on the furthest edge of her experience and so few things were. Perhaps that was why she'd arranged for this meeting to take place away from prying eyes. She sensed he'd be more comfortable with fewer people around, though why this should be, she couldn't say.

Her insides fluttered as she entered the hothouse with him dogging her steps. A tart, fresh smell tickled her nostrils.

"Oranges," Pierce said.

"Yes. I have the cleverest gardener. He manages to trick a couple of small trees into growing and bearing year-round. The smell is heavenly, isn't it?"

"I prefer a mix of mint, lavender, and apple myself but yes, the scent of oranges is very nice."

She allowed herself a small smile. He'd almost given her a compliment. While most of the *ton* was dousing itself in heavy floral or musky scents, that unusual trio—mint, lavender, and apple—were the high notes in a fragrance her perfumer compounded specifically for her use. The process had cost Benedick the earth, but he always claimed it money well spent.

"You'll never be able to sneak up on me, my dear," he had joked. "I shall always catch a whiff of you first."

Pierce looked around the hothouse at the plethora of exotic plants. "Lord Albemarle is very generous."

It was as if he knew Benedick had crossed her mind.

"He gets value for his coin."

"Of that, I have no doubt."

Why had she said that? It wasn't as if Benedick had ever taken her to his bed. Her value to him was measured in other ways, but she couldn't betray him by telling Westfall what those were. Let him think what he would.

A smile played about his lips, as if something had struck him funny.

"Do you mind letting me in on the joke?" she said, wishing now that she hadn't invited him. This was a mistake. She wasn't ready to be with someone like this. It had been too long since she'd been with a man, let alone someone as decidedly odd as Lord Westfall.

"There is no joke. I was just thinking about orchids. People think they are parasites, you know, but they really aren't." He stooped and, from beside a begonia, he plucked a cankerwort up by its long root. "Most orchids actually don't take anything from their hosts except a place to live and grow."

"I didn't know that." By those lights, she supposed she was Benedick's orchid—a frilly spot of color on his arm, a mark of manhood for him and a source of envy among the bucks and dandies of the *ton*. She asked only her keeping in return—a place to live and grow.

Lord Westfall didn't meet her gaze often, but when he did, she looked away, feeling the heat of his eyes on her. There was something feral behind his cool gray irises. Was that madness flickering there?

Despite his tightly controlled demeanor, even though the Duke of Camden had vouched for him, Pierce Langdon seemed a dangerous, unpredictable man. She didn't want to admit it, even to herself, but that raw edge excited her.

"Of course, there is a possibility that the orchid will eventually harm its host," he warned.

She remembered that she considered herself the orchid in her relationship with Benedick. Perhaps she and Pierce were both dangerous. "How?"

"By virtue of its placement. The orchid can weaken the host if its roots become too invasive."

No danger of that with Benedick. She wasn't the clingy sort. She'd never harm him. He was too important to her. How would she support Emilia without him?

"Who is Emilia?" he asked suddenly.

"How do you—oh, of course, the Duke of Camden. He must have dozens of Bow Street Runners at his beck and call." So His Grace had discovered her secret. Lord knew, her father had never cared enough to try. The weight of the burden grew the longer she carried it by herself. She still wasn't sure having Westfall here wasn't a mistake, but when she looked into his eyes, no madness leaped in them. She decided to trust him.

"Emilia is my daughter."

He nodded with no hint of shock. "I thought so."

"My husband died in France before I could tell him I was going to bear his child. And since I had defied my father to marry, I decided not to return home."

"You mean you couldn't return home," he said simply and without pity. His words smacked more of understanding than sympathy. "I, too, know what it is to be pushed away by family."

So he did. At least her father hadn't had her committed to Bedlam. "Not to put too fine a point on it, but no, I was not welcome at home."

"And your family still doesn't know about the child." Again his remarks that should have been questions sounded more as if he were simply rehearsing facts he already knew.

"Why should I tell them? Once Emilia is old enough, they would probably only blame her for my shortcomings. After all, she is the walking, breathing evidence of my disobedience. I would never put her in that position." Nora wandered along the narrow path between the raised benches covered with potted specimens. "At any rate, she is safe and well-tended where she is."

"And kept as far away from you as you can bear."

Tears pressed the backs of her eyes. What was it about this man? Every time she was with him, he either caught her crying or moved her to weep.

"Emilia doesn't need to be tainted by having a mother who…" she began.

"Who loves her more than anything?"

She was going to say, "Having a mother who is a whore," but Pierce had reached inside her chest and pulled out the real reason Nora kept her daughter at a distance. She was a pariah. She couldn't bear to taint her child with her sordid reputation. "How do you know so much?"

"I know very little really," he said, his voice husky. "But I want to know more."

"Well, the orchids are over there on the north wall and—"

"Honora, I didn't come for tea. I didn't come for orchids."

"You didn't?"

He shook his head. "I came for you."

When I began confiding my thoughts to this journal I wrote that the defining moment of my life occurred when I was eight years old and I fell from a tree. I was wrong. It happened when I was thirty-two and I fell in love.

Both events have had equally devastating effects upon my mind.

~from the secret journal of Pierce Langdon, Viscount Westfall

Chapter Nine

Pierce ached to take her right there on the cool stone floor of the hothouse, but he held himself back. It was bad enough to be labeled mad. If he was also discovered to be a rutting beast, they'd lock him up and never let him run free again, no matter how much the duke vouched for him. He had to go about this the right way.

But what was the right way?

"You said you'd never kissed a woman before that night at the opera," Honora said.

He nodded as he moved closer to her.

"Then am I correct in assuming you have also never… been with a woman?"

"I haven't." Not for lack of interest. Pierce might be put off by what was swirling around in women's heads, but he was very much curious about their delectable forms. From the time he'd been about fourteen and his body first had begun to rouse and spill into his bedclothes by night in hopeless erotic dreams, he'd surreptitiously watched the women in his sphere. From the buxom chambermaid Lily, who had been known to have extremely light heels, to the vicar's daughter whom he only dared look upon while everyone else's head was bowed and eyes closed, he became a voyeur of the mysterious female. Both extremes of women found their ways into his wet dreams.

But in the waking world, he didn't dare approach either of them because of the disturbing racket of their thoughts. Until the Duke of Camden had shown him how to erect a barrier against another's mind, he thought he'd forever have to rely solely on his own right hand for his body's release.

Now that he had a measure of control over how fast and how much information vaulted toward him from another's head, he found he actually wanted to know what was going on in Honora's mind. He lowered his shield a bit more.

Amazingly enough, his inexperience seemed to excite her.

"Would you like me to show you what to do?" she asked.

"I think I can figure that out for myself," he said as he continued to close the distance between them at an unhurried pace. She'd never know what that deliberation cost him. "If you don't mind going slow."

Her breathing hitched. "Slow is good."

He opened himself more to her thoughts.

Oh, God! He's beautiful.

That was so surprising it almost stopped him in his tracks.

What is he waiting for?

He didn't want to rush. He wanted to savor. Each moment would be etched on his psyche forever. This was the first time he was going to bed a woman, and he wanted everything to be perfect for him and for her. Lovemaking was a journey. The last thing he wanted to do was miss something wonderful along the way because he was in too much of a hurry to reach the final destination.

"We ought to go to my chamber," she said abruptly and started toward the door. He caught her wrist, stopping her.

"We will," he assured her. Then he lifted her palm to his lips and kissed it. He drew little circles around the spot with his fingertip and traced each of her fingers. "You have lovely hands."

I have lovely other things, too. Don't you want to see them?

"I ache to see all of you," he said as if she'd spoken aloud. It was a hard habit to break, responding to half a conversation he wasn't supposed to have heard. He needed to be careful. She already believed him a bit mad. The last thing he wanted was for her to think him a freak, as well. He raised her hand to his mouth and suckled the tender skin of her inner wrist. "I want to taste all of you. I don't want to miss anything."

Her lips fell slack at that.

Touch me. Handle me. Know me.

So he did. While he kissed her, his hands went roaming. They slid down her back to cup her bum and snug her next to him. Oh, the feel of her soft abdomen against his hardened cock. He feared he might spend on the spot, so he distracted himself by listening to her thoughts.

I ache so. Please God, let him know what to do.

Her breasts were a revelation. He palmed them, kneading her soft flesh through the layers of her clothing. It helped that she wished he would. He even found her nipples, hard little buttons, under all that muslin and linen and thrummed them with his thumbs. Then he gave them a pinch, just the way she hoped.

She groaned into his mouth. He didn't think he could get any harder, but even his balls tightened at that sound.

Oh, God, it's been so long.

That surprised him. He already knew from exploring her mind a bit that she and Benedick weren't lovers in the traditional sense. She had no sexual thoughts about him at all. No memories, either good or bad, of his lovemaking.

But for a woman with an unabashedly sensual reputation like Nora to be celibate was unthinkable.

He searched her memories again and found a few fleeting recollections of past patrons. But the recollections were indistinct, shrouded in mist, as if she didn't want to retain them and hoped they too would dissolve, like a mist, in the morning sun. Her memories of her husband were a little more vibrant, but Pierce didn't want to violate those.

It would be like spitting on an altar.

She tipped her head back.

Kiss my neck. Nibble along the tops of my breasts.

He did so with great enthusiasm. She made such helpless little noises of need, he was inspired to undo the first few horn buttons that drew a line between her breasts. Then he peeled back the fabric so that more of her lustrous skin was exposed.

How does he do that? Know what I need before I need it? The man is like magic.

For the first time in his life, he was grateful for his gift.

But his mind was so filled with her body, he had no room to spy out her thoughts. He decided to play fair and he pulled up his shield. Instead, he concentrated on the way she breathed, the way she smelled, the way she moved when he touched and sucked and kissed.

They slow-walked down the hothouse aisle like a pair of drunkards clinging to each other so they'd stay upright. Pierce was unwilling to break off their embrace. He lifted her so he could more easily suckle her nipples through the thin fabric of her chemise. Once her underthings were wet, he could see them through the linen, all berry-colored and taut, winking up at him, begging him for more.

As he continued to move toward the door, he knocked several containers of seedlings off the benches and upset one of the orange trees in its pot. The oranges rolling on the pavers sent fresh bursts of their glorious fragrance into the space.

"Wait, please wait." She wiggled out of his arms with her spine pressed against the door. "I have a very nosy neighbor on the eastern side. We have to walk through the garden as if nothing is amiss."

"Nothing is amiss," he said as he continued to torment her nipples. "I just want to swive you like no one has ever swived anyone before."

Her smile was bright enough to illuminate all of Vauxhall's Dark Walks. Even on a moonless night.

But her fingers trembled as she did up her buttons again.

He peeked once more into her mind.

She wasn't cold. She wasn't afraid. She was trembling with need. She wanted him quite desperately.

He was doing surprisingly well for his first time. Barring the destruction in her hothouse, of course.

She smoothed down her hair and then straightened his

jacket on his shoulders.

"Race you to the door?" he said with hope.

"No. We must walk. Sedately. As if we have no pressing need to—"

"Swive each other senseless," he interrupted.

There was that smile again. He could live for weeks on just one of them, and he'd been given two in one glorious afternoon.

"May I at least offer you my arm?" He suited his actions to his words.

"Oh, my dear viscount," she said as she slipped a hand through the crook of his elbow, "I'm depending on you to offer me far more than that."

"I shall do my best not to disappoint." They strolled into the sunshine as if their insides weren't pounding.

"If you continue as you've begun, I'll never believe this is your first time."

"This is your first time as well."

She cocked her head.

"Your first time with a madman."

She attempted to lighten the moment with a little laugh. "I do not think you mad."

"Yes, you do," he said without rancor, "and what's more, you like the idea."

She started to protest, but they'd reached her back door and he held it open for her most properly. Then, once it closed behind them, he pressed her up against the wall and reached under her hem, sliding it up her thighs.

"You think because I'm mad, I'm dangerous. And I am," he admitted. "But I will not harm you. Not for worlds."

Her skin was silky smooth and hot, almost feverish.

Where her pantalets ended, an apparently open crotch began in the garment. Pierce silently blessed the modiste who had come up with that idea.

Touch me.

So he did.

She was wet and welcoming, and holding her was like holding a piece of her soul, all trembling and naked. When his fingers moved, she grasped the lapels of his jacket as if she were drowning, and he was all that would keep her afloat.

There were no more words, no more thoughts forming in her mind for him. Nothing he could make sense of, in any case. Instead, a burst of sensations shivered through him.

Harder. Ah, just there. That's it.

The sensations gathered themselves into a fist and punched his heart. His knees nearly buckled.

Whether they were her sensations or his, he wasn't sure.

Maybe it didn't matter.

The pleasure between them built to an almost unbearable tension.

They started a dipping, turning waltz to music only they could hear. When they kissed, it was her hands that began roaming now. First, his cravat unraveled and fluttered to the floor. Somewhere between the salon and the foot of the stairs, his jacket came off. Then his waistcoat. By the first landing, she was tugging his shirt over his head and raking her nails across his bared chest.

Pierce undid her buttons, not stopping with only a few this time. He popped off a couple in his haste. He'd promised himself he'd go slow, but those urgent little sounds she made as he kissed her went straight to his groin. No one would call them words. Even when he opened his mind to her, nothing he recognized as a fully formed thought materialized. It was far more primal, more basic than thought. But he didn't need to understand those noises to know what she wanted.

Somehow, he found himself laying her down on the stairs and, wonder of wonders, she went willingly. He kissed her in unexpected places—the crease of her elbow, the juncture of her shoulder and neck, the hollow of her temple—to distract her from the oddness of unevenness beneath them.

He began to peel away her layers. The gown was easy. Once he undid enough buttons, it slid off her shoulders and down her body as they inched up the stairs. His clumsy fingers snarled the laces in her stays so badly, he had to resort to his boot knife to cut them.

Her eyes widened at the sight of the blade.

"I meant what I said. I'll never harm you, Honora," he promised. "However, your laces are in imminent danger."

She laughed. Lord, the woman had a laugh that would tempt angels. It was low and liquid and full of pleasure. It was a hot bath a man could sink into and, even if he drowned, he wouldn't care a whit.

After he sliced the laces, she joyfully shed her stays and they were left on the stairs alongside his boots, which she had to help him out of. A trail of discarded clothing traced their progress from the rear of the house and up the flights of stairs.

His trousers came off next and then she practically tore off his smalls.

"Pierce, you're huge," Honora said when she came up for air after one of their kisses. She gasped, like a pearl diver who'd been submerged too long. She grasped him and ran her fingers over his full length. Pleasure lanced through him, sharp as a blade.

"I take it that's a good thing," he said, knowing full well she was delighted with him from the joyful little thoughts that came tripping into his mind from hers.

Then she did the most surprising thing in the world. She didn't even think before she did it. If she had, he'd have had warning and could have braced himself for the shock. She moved down his body, rolled him over on the second floor landing, and took his cock between her sweet lips.

He'd heard of such things, of course. Stanstead had been a wealth of sensual information before he'd married Miss Cassandra Darkin. After that, the earl kept his sexual knowledge to himself, which was all right with Pierce, who had never expected to be able to use any of it, in any case. But the idea of a woman taking that part of him into her mouth, into that soft, warm place where her tongue could lash him, that notion had stuck with him. Pierce had never thought such unasked-for bliss would ever happen to him.

He'd nearly died many times in Bedlam. He had never felt closer to death than he did right now.

And welcomed the manner of his demise with much gratitude.

They always say misery loves company, but the reverse is true as well. Bliss is not bliss unless it is shared.

~from the secret journal of Lady Nora Claremont

Chapter Ten

Honora reveled in the feminine power of reducing a man to helpless need. Never had one shattered before her like this one.

Pierce groaned. He gasped. He clutched her head and murmured an odd mix of blessings and profanities while she tongued him. He seemed about to burst out of his own skin.

Finally, I'm convinced he's a virgin.

In addition to the joy of instructing an unbedded man, it added immeasurably to her pleasure that Pierce was an incredibly quick learner. He might have been the proverbial bull in a china shop in her hothouse, but he'd demonstrated no clumsiness with her. He seemed to anticipate her every need. She wouldn't have believed it his first time except for the shock on his face when she'd whorled her tongue over him.

She ached to do this for him. To give to him without expecting anything in return. His bliss was enough.

Of course, if she were honest with herself, she'd have to admit that sucking him made her insides pound as well.

She sensed the tension building in him and didn't want their interlude to end too soon, so she sat up and straddled him where he lay on the rectangle of Aubusson carpet on the landing. Then she pulled her chemise over her head. Her pantalets were no impediment to their joining, so she moved quickly to guide him into her.

He cried out as he slid in. So did she. It was an incredibly tight fit, but she did her best to engulf him. Once he was fully seated, she slumped down to lie on his chest, to give them both a moment to settle, to prepare for what was to come. His heart hammered under her ear. She willed it to slow, for his breathing to return to some semblance of normal. She didn't want him to spend too soon.

As if she'd spoken her wishes, he began to take measured breaths. Then he sat up, bringing her upright with him, still joined, still throbbing inside her, still burning up with heated passion, but struggling to control it.

"If we stay here, one or both of us is going to get a rug burn," he said with maddening practicality.

Then, with seeming effortlessness, he rose to his feet, careful to support her bum so his cock remained firmly inside her. She wrapped her legs around his waist and hooked her ankles at the small of his back. He was every bit as strong as he looked.

"Which one is your bedchamber?" he asked as if he were asking for directions to the nearest market.

"One more flight up. End of the hall. I'd rather face the garden than the street."

"You'll only be facing me for a while," he said with a

grin.

It was so unusual for him to smile, the whiteness of his teeth caught her by surprise. "You should do that more often."

"If one smiles without something to smile about, one is generally considered a bit nipped in the noggin." He shrugged as he climbed the remaining stairs with her still clinging to him. "Of course, in my case, it would only confirm the general consensus."

"I don't think you're really mad."

He smiled again, this time wryly.

"Well, I don't." She swatted his shoulder as he homed in on her chamber door. He jiggled the latch a few times. It was sticky sometimes, but he managed to open it and push through. "I just think you've had some unfortunate experiences."

He barked a laugh. "That's putting it mildly."

She palmed his face. She wanted him to see she meant it. "You have a beautiful soul."

"Given the brevity of our association, that's not something you can know."

"You're right," she said. "It's not something I *know*. It's something I *feel*."

He walked her over to the canopy bed that occupied the central portion of the room and sat on the edge. She pushed against his shoulders so that he plopped back onto the soft feather mattress and counterpane. She smiled down at him and whispered, "And now, here's something I want *you* to feel."

Amazingly enough, once they settled into the bed and stopped talking, they started communicating in earnest. It was as if her flesh spoke to his, and he answered immediately.

The merest wish would slip into her mind, and he was quick to fulfill it.

She rode him with abandon, sliding up and down the length of his thick cock, luxuriating in her own arousal. If she angled her pelvis just so, she got the loveliest bit of friction right where she needed it. A bit more of this and she'd come with him inside her, fisting around him. She hadn't done that since Lewis—no, she wouldn't think on her dead husband. She would think on the live man beneath her.

Then he rolled her over and began pounding away and she couldn't think at all.

Oh, he was just what she needed. Rough, then tender. He slipped out of her, and she cried out, bereft, until he substituted his talented fingers for his thick cock and played a virtuoso performance on her most sensitive spot.

She unraveled under him, her release pounding her insides. When she stopped convulsing, she pulled him to her, took him in, and led him to his own shattering climax. He arched his back and emptied himself into her in hot spurts. Then he collapsed onto her, taking care to support himself with his elbows lest his full weight bear down on her.

She'd never had a more considerate lover. Not even Lewis.

Nora stroked his back, running her fingertips over his spine. Too late, she remembered the French letter in her vanity. It had been so long since she'd needed to concern herself with avoiding conception, she'd forgotten all about it. Pierce probably would have objected to wearing the lamb-gut condom in any case.

"I'll wear anything you want, if only you'll let me stay close to you," he murmured into his neck.

She hadn't said anything about the condom. She was sure of it. And this wasn't the first time he seemed to know exactly what she was thinking.

"If I ask you a question, will you promise to answer it?" she said.

He raised himself to look down at her, his eyes still glassy with the I-don't-give-a-damn-about-anything haze that follows a good hard swive. "If you ask me to flap my arms and fly to France right now, I'll climb up to your roof and make an attempt."

She laughed, but then stopped abruptly when she saw the seriousness on his face. "I believe you would."

He started to rise from the bed.

"No, come back here, you." She caught his arm and pulled. "Just answer my question, and I'll be satisfied."

He settled back down, his lower body resting between her splayed legs.

"Why did your family believe you mad?"

He sighed, rolled off her, and lay beside her, staring up at the fleur-de-lis stitched into her canopy. At first, she thought he wasn't going to answer, but then he began speaking about a boy who climbed an oak tree and a catastrophic fall and finally waking to hear voices all around him whether anyone's lips moved or not.

"You mean to say that you can hear my thoughts?" she said incredulously.

His face was a mask of misery. "I can hear everyone's thoughts."

She sat up and tucked the linens under her armpits. She was naked save for her pantalets and stockings, but she hadn't felt really exposed until that very moment. It couldn't be true.

"That's the most absurd thing I've ever heard."

"Now you see why my uncle had me condemned and committed. It *is* absurd," he admitted. "It's also unfortunately true."

"Really? What am I thinking now?" She cast about for something she was certain he couldn't simply guess. *Ah!* Fides Pulvis. *He'll never come up with—*

"*Fides Pulvis,*" he said wearily. "It means 'Trust Powder.'"

She scrambled from the bed and pulled on her wrapper which was draped over her vanity chair. "You can't know about that. No one knows about—"

"No one but you and Lord Albemarle. And now officially—me."

But this was terrible. What else might he glean from her mind? Benedick's confidences—all of them—were no longer safe. A large part of her value to her protector was her discretion. His secrets were legion and against her will, several of them flitted across her consciousness.

"If you're worried that I'll tell someone that Lord Albemarle likes men, you needn't be. I'm glad he's of that disposition," Pierce said. "It means you're not really his mistress, and that makes me happier than I've ever been about anything."

But he didn't look happy. He was frowning in her direction with intense concentration. Even so, she'd never seen anything quite as compelling as the naked viscount in her bed. His arms were massive, his chest well-muscled, and beneath those sheets—she jerked her gaze away from him. She didn't need him to be a party to those sorts of thoughts.

Not now.

"But this isn't right," Nora said as she paced with nervousness. "You can't simply invade people's minds like this."

"That's not how it works. I don't try to do it. It's more as if your mind invades mine. If I want to keep the thoughts of others out, I have to slog away with a will to hold up a mental shield. They shoot about like darts, thoughts do, ricocheting here and there." He dragged a hand over his crown as if his fingers might gather up the stray thoughts and yank them out. "As you can imagine, I'm not very good in a crowd."

"I don't want you to hear my thoughts," she said with vehemence. "Why did you even tell me you could?"

He shrugged. "You asked why my family thought me mad. I told you."

"You might have lied. People do, you know." Hadn't he ever heard that ignorance was bliss? She'd never be able to relax around the man again. "Uncomfortable truths are best left unspoken."

"The truth is all I have."

"But you can turn it off, can't you?"

"Yes, with effort." He grimaced. "There. My mental shield is up. Now I have no certain knowledge of what's swirling about in that pretty head of yours, but I can guess." He climbed out of bed and crossed the room to her. "You think I'm a monster."

"No, I don't." Then because she could be truthful, too, she added, "Maybe a little."

To her surprise, that made him chuckle. "That makes two of us."

Then he reached for her and drew her into his arms. She went willingly, though she knew she shouldn't. He felt so good, so warm and big and comforting.

But he really wasn't a comfortable sort of man. She'd never know if he was plucking thoughts from her willy-nilly. It wasn't right.

It wasn't safe.

"Wait a moment. You said something a moment ago." She pulled back and searched his face. "Something about you knowing *officially* about the *Fides Pulvis*. What did you mean by that?"

"This is not the first time you've thought about it in my presence. I saw it in your mind briefly that first night at Lord Albemarle's party. The same night I saw an image of your Emilia." He stroked her cheek and tucked a stray curl behind her ear. "She's a beautiful child. But then she would be with you as her—"

"Hold now." She wiggled out of his arms. "You let me believe the Duke of Camden's sources of information led to you knowing about my daughter."

"No, I merely implied it. You came to that conclusion on your own."

She narrowed her eyes at him. "What about your devotion to truth?"

"What I said about His Grace's resources was true. It just wasn't relevant to the subject at the time," he said with such an earnest expression she was tempted to believe him, but she held herself back. The man had just admitted to deception, after all. "I'm sorry if you feel deceived. That was not my intention."

It was exactly his intention. "Why did you come here today? Really?"

"You invited me to see your orchids."

He seemed genuinely surprised by her growing outrage.

An innocent unjustly accused. Well, Satan could masquerade as an angel of light, too.

"No, you said you came for me, Pierce," she corrected. "But that's not right either, is it? What did you really hope to accomplish?"

"But I did come for you, Honora."

"Stop calling me that." He was trying to change her back into someone she no longer was. Her cheeks heated and not with embarrassment. She was angrier than she'd been since her father had slammed the door on her for the final time. "My name is Nora."

"Not to me," he murmured, then raised his voice. "All right, if you must know, the Duke of Camden is concerned about the psychic properties inherent in that Trust Powder. He wants to know Lord Albemarle's intentions for it. How does he plan to use it?"

She forced herself to think of anything other than Benedick's plans to influence the Prince Regent to a policy that would lead to a return to war with France. "So you came here with the express purpose of spying on my mind."

"No, I—"

"The truth, Pierce. It's all you have," she parroted. "Remember?"

"Yes," he admitted. "I came to spy."

He came to invade her. To violate her. She felt like retching, but she swallowed back the rising bile. She wouldn't give him the satisfaction of seeing how his betrayal affected her. "Leave now."

"But that's not all I came to do."

"I know. You also came to lose your virginity. Very well. Mission accomplished all around." She trembled with rage.

The man had used her on several levels. If he didn't leave soon, she'd fly at him, nails bared. "Now get out."

He bowed correctly to her, as correctly as a naked man could bow, and strode to the door. He closed it behind him softly. She waited with an ear to the oak for his retreating footfalls, for some indication that he was retrieving his discarded wardrobe from the stairs and landings and by the back door, but she heard nothing.

He was still standing on the other side of the door.

"Go away, Westfall," she said.

"Not until I tell you."

Silence stretched between them for the space of ten heartbeats.

"What?" she asked in exasperation, trying to keep her mind blank, determined not to think anything she didn't want him to know.

"I never expected this to happen."

"Then let's just say you experienced extreme good luck and leave it at that," she said crossly.

"You're right about one thing. I did hope to learn how Lord Albemarle will use the *Pulvis Fides*, because if he intends to harm the royal family, I'll try to stop him somehow."

"You are mad, Westfall, if you believe I won't tell him that."

"I won't blame you if you do," he said. "But there's something else at work here. Something I don't understand. The truth is, I think I love you, Honora."

He walked away then, but she didn't move until she heard the heavy front door close with a thud. Then she slid to the floor with her knees tucked to her chin and her back to the oak.

Westfall didn't love her. The man was half mad and she

just happened to have been the first woman he'd ever lain with. If he'd lost his virginity to a doxy in Whitechapel, he'd have told her the same thing.

He thinks he loves me. How ridiculous.

Her chest constricted. She needed someone to love her. Wanted it with a fierceness that threatened to suck all the air from her lungs.

But she didn't deserve it.

Love is a right puzzle box of an emotion. What engineer can unravel its mysteries? It is a surging tempest of wants and needs and desires. No captain can pilot its waves with surety of reaching safe harbor. Yet I'm told that saints pray to love more completely rather than to be loved in return.

Alas, I am no saint.

~from the secret journal of Pierce Langdon,
Viscount Westfall

Chapter Eleven

When the Duke of Camden signaled to Mr. Bernard, the steward rapped a small gavel on the escritoire at which he sat. "This meeting of the Order of the M.U.S.E. will please come to order."

Westfall had been slumped in his seat, elbow on the settee's arm, chin in his hand, concentrating on keeping his mental shield erected. Now he sat upright as the others took their places. They'd been chatting with the newcomer, a fellow by the name of Gaston LeGrand.

His surname was a misnomer. There was nothing the least grand about him. The Frenchman was small and wiry, built close to the ground. But that, too, was misleading, because he wasn't an earth mage. The newest member of the Order had an affinity for water and could bend it to his will in the same way Vesta and Lady Stanstead controlled fire.

Westfall wasn't as concerned about the fellow's psychic gift as he was his nationality. His Grace had explained that

LeGrand's mother had been an Englishwoman, but the man's surname was definitely French.

And didn't His Grace claim most of England's troubles came from that part of the world?

Still, it wasn't his place to decide who was welcomed into the Order. If the duke trusted LeGrand, Westfall should, too. However, he promised himself a peek into the fellow's mind later, just to make sure.

"Vesta isn't here yet," Stanstead said. "We can't start without her."

"When is she ever on time?" the duke said with an ignoble snort. "Perhaps if Miss LaMotte misses a few important things, she'll make room in her oh-so-busy schedule for—"

"Oh, good!" her familiar voice called out. "You're all here."

The courtesan breezed into the duke's study, a cloud of flowery scent wafting in her wake. She was dressed in pale green silk with layers of petal-like epaulets on her white shoulders. Westfall decided the gown was designed to make a man wish to pluck them off one by one—sort of a haute couture version of "She loves me, She loves me not." He wished it was Honora in that gown. And when he got to the last petal he hoped the answer would be the right one.

The thought surprised him. Before lying with Honora, he'd never been one for such flights of fancy. He shot an accusing glare at Stanstead, in case the idea had come from that quarter, but the earl wasn't even looking at Vesta.

I'm becoming a hopeless nit, he thought sullenly. *Outstanding.*

"I, for one, cannot wait to hear Lord Westfall's report." Vesta perched in the chair usually reserved for His Grace and leaned toward Westfall expectantly.

He scanned the circle of eager faces. Since his mental

shield was drawn up as tight as he could make it, he got no sense of what they were really thinking. Without that input, they were like caricatures of themselves, two dimensional renderings of the real people. Still, it was easier to concentrate in a group if he kept himself boxed in.

"When Miss Anthony searched Lord Albemarle's home for the *Fides Pulvis*, she found several powdery substances," he began with a nod in Meg's direction. "I learned from Lady Nora that the one we seek is in the silver snuffbox."

It was like a betrayal to share what he'd heard in her mind, but he had little choice. The Order demanded the information and didn't care how it was acquired. At least he wasn't giving away any of Honora's secrets. They didn't need to know about her daughter or how much she suffered to keep her safe.

"I suspected as much," Camden said, "but it is good to have confirmation."

"Good? How is this good?" Vesta said, glancing over her shoulder at the duke with unexpected waspishness. "The man is likely to have it on his person at all times except when he retires for the night. When will we be able to relieve him of it without resorting to burglary?"

"You're getting ahead of yourself, Vesta," Camden said with a deceptively calm tone. Westfall suspected the duke meant to infuriate rather than placate her but without lowering his shield he couldn't be sure. "Rushing headlong is always your strong suit."

"As yours is dithering for the sake of it."

The group gave a collective gasp. Even for Vesta, who could always be counted upon to say something outrageous, the remark was beyond the pale. No one addressed a peer of the realm in such a disrespectful way. Something dangerous flashed in the duke's eyes. If Vesta had been a man, His Grace would have called her out for it, even if he had contributed to the verbal sparring.

Vesta refused to be cowed by his dark scowl.

"His Grace is right," Stanstead said in an attempt to smooth things over. "We shouldn't rush matters. First we need to consider how Albemarle intends to use the Trust Powder."

Fortunately, before Honora had thrown Westfall out, her mind had provided the answer. She'd tried mightily not to think of it, but such powder-keg thoughts weren't easy to keep at bay. "He intends to influence the Prince Regent over a question to be decided at the next Concert of Europe in Aix-la-Chappell," Pierce said. "Albemarle wants His Royal Highness to refuse to support the withdrawal of the Allies' troops from France."

"But the withdrawal, it has always been part of the peace agreement. The French countryside, she is just settling now," LeGrand said, gesturing wildly with his hands. If he'd been handcuffed, Westfall suspected he'd be struck dumb. "If the troops, they do not withdraw, it will be like the poking of a hornet's nest. There will be war again."

Westfall nodded. "I know. And so does Lord Albemarle."

"Why on earth would he want war?" Lady Stanstead asked.

"Albemarle is working on our enemies' behalf. No doubt the French hope for a different outcome if hostilities resume," the duke said. "Treasonous. Absolutely treasonous."

"The baron may not be motivated by politics, Camden." This time, Vesta didn't sound as if she were disagreeing solely to be disagreeable. "Wars are expensive propositions. Fortunes are made in such ways if one is situated to take advantage of the event. What do we know about Albemarle's finances?"

The duke shot a searching look at his steward. Bernard opened the dossier on Albemarle and glanced through the pages.

"He seems as sound as a pound on paper," Mr. Bernard said. "Lord Albemarle has no excessive debt. If anything, he's been a lender more often than a borrower. I see nothing here that indicates he's invested in armaments or essential commodities or anything which would be necessary to the nation should war with France recommence."

"And there's nothing in Albemarle's life that indicates a predilection for aggression for its own sake. He's a sybarite, a *bon vivant*," Vesta said. "He'd sooner launch a new poet on Society than interrupt the peaceful conclusion to old hostilities. War is a messy business. It might interfere with Albemarle's calendar of salons and dinner parties."

Silence settled on the group as they considered Vesta's well-taken point.

"What if using the *Fides Pulvis* to influence His Royal Highness wasn't Albemarle's idea?" Westfall said, almost to himself.

"Wait. Didn't you just say using the *Fides Pulvis* to undermine the peace treaty was his intention?" Lady Stanstead asked.

"I did, but what if he were being coerced somehow?"

"Is he?" Vesta lifted one brow in a shrewd expression.

"I got the sense that was the case," Westfall said, "but I didn't learn any of the particulars."

It would have meant lowering his shield and letting

Honora's mind wash over him while he quizzed her on the subject. She wouldn't have liked that one bit. It still made little sense, but what Honora liked mattered to him more than anything else.

"No matter his motivation, the fact remains that this Lord Albemarle, he means to do mischief with his Powder of the Trust," LeGrand said. "It is not our place to understand why. That is of no import. It is our duty only to stop him, no?"

The water mage had a valid point, but it irked Westfall that the newcomer should have been the one to make it. Pierce had been a silent party to Order meetings for months before he'd felt emboldened to speak out at one.

"Well put, LeGrand," the duke said. "Miss Anthony, would you please locate Lord Albemarle for us?"

"Certainly, Your Grace."

The Finder closed her eyes and slipped into the trance that would enable her to search for Lord Albemarle. Westfall held his breath as her spirit slipped from her body and went winging over the chimneys of London. While her mind roamed free, the shell that usually housed it sat still as death in the Duke of Camden's palatial home.

The others around him murmured softly to one another about inconsequential things. They had no idea Miss Anthony risked staying away from her body too long each time she embarked on one of her quests for His Grace.

But Pierce knew.

He watched her intently, hoping for the twitch beneath her closed eyelids that showed she had returned. Her cheeks paled. Her lips turned blue.

Still, the others chattered on as if a life didn't hang in

the balance. More than once, Westfall had been on the verge of warning His Grace what was involved in the Finder's psychic searches, but it wasn't his secret to tell. When he'd confronted Meg Anthony about it, she'd begged him to keep his knowledge to himself.

"Please don't peach on me, my lord. *Finding* is all I can do for His Grace," she'd told him. "Leastwise, all that's respectable."

She was right about that. Once, Meg Anthony had tutored Lady Stanstead on the fine art of pickpocketing when the Order's business had called for it. No doubt, she had a number of other nefarious skills in her bag of tricks. But Meg had yet to master the task His Grace had set for her to accomplish—being able to pass for a wellborn lady.

As seconds stretched into minutes and she still hadn't returned, Westfall wished he'd ignored Meg's pleading and told His Grace about the danger she was in each time she was ordered to "fetch" something.

"She's been out a long time," Stanstead finally said.

"Longer than usual," His Grace allowed, and stopped his habitual circuiting of the room. He crossed over and reached out a hand, intending to give Miss Anthony's shoulder a shake.

"No!" Westfall was on his feet and batting Camden's hand away before he considered the impropriety of swatting a duke as if he were a toddler reaching for a candle flame. "Don't touch her. If she's on her way back, you may interfere with her return."

"On her way back?"

"Her spirit leaves her body when she does this for you," Westfall said testily. Concern for her safety made keeping her secret fade into insignificance.

"I had no idea," the duke said with a frown. "I thought her ability was akin to mine when I sense the presence of another Extraordinaire."

Camden suffered vivid visions when he encountered a new psychic to be brought into the M.U.S.E. fold. He had even been physically injured by events that occurred in his visions when he made use of his psychic sensitivity. But the hurts had been minor, and his spirit remained firmly attached to his body at all times.

"Why would she risk such a thing?" Camden asked, aghast.

"She'd do anything for a scrap of praise from your lips," Westfall said. He didn't need the duke's approval, but he'd dare quite a bit for Camden's sake as well. After all, without His Grace's intervention, he'd still be at the mercy of that quack in Bedlam.

One way or another, everyone in the Order was beholden to the duke. It was not an obligation His Grace ever trumpeted or used as a means of coercion, but the sense of indebtedness was there nonetheless.

Meg Anthony suddenly gasped for breath, and everyone began talking at once.

"Oh, you wicked, wicked girl." Vesta nearly hugged the stuffing out of her. "You scared the life out of us."

Westfall stifled the urge to correct Vesta. Meg was the only one whose life had been in danger.

The duke planted his feet before her. "Now that I am aware of the risks you run when you embark on a *Finding* mission for us, Miss Anthony, you will do no more of them until we can discover a way to mitigate the danger to you. Is that understood?"

"But Your Grace—"

"No arguments." He stopped her with a raised hand. "You are far too valuable to the Order to expose yourself to such danger." Westfall had never heard the duke raise his voice, but he was shouting now. "I forbid it, do you hear?"

"Yes, Your Grace." The world trembled when a peer of the realm thundered like that. Meg Anthony greeted the words with a shaky smile. Then she shot a reproving look in Westfall's direction. He couldn't find it in him to feel sorry he'd betrayed her. She shouldn't take such chances. "I won't *Find* again until you give me leave."

Camden nodded curtly and tugged down his waistcoat, a sure sign he was still miffed. "Yes, well, see that you don't. Now tell us what you learned while your soul went kiting about all over London."

"That was just the trouble." Color slowly returned to her lips. "I wasn't in London, you see. I was in Wiltshire. Lord Albemarle is headed for his country estate, Albion Abbey."

"Is Lady Nora with him?" The words tumbled from Westfall's mouth before he could get a net around them to keep them in.

Meg Anthony nodded.

"Well, that settles it," Camden said. "Someone has to go to Wiltshire and retrieve the snuffbox filled with *Fides Pulvis*."

"I'll go if I must, but you know how I loathe the countryside," Vesta said. "All that fresh air and early rising— it's enough to drive one quite dotty. Oh! Westfall, I do beg your pardon."

He waved away her apology. He was so used to being

thought mad, it no longer raised his hackles when someone assumed he was one brick short of a load.

"I'll go," Stanstead offered. His wife skewered him in the ribs with her elbow. "Oh, perhaps not. Since my countess cannot accompany me, she being great with child and— Ow!" There was the elbow again. "What? A biblical reference to your condition isn't good enough?"

"It would be if only the one you chose didn't make me sound as big as an elephant," Lady Stanstead said with meekness in her tone that belied the flame flashing behind her eyes. "You don't truly think I've reached pachyderm proportions, do you, dear?"

"Never, my darling." Stanstead raised his lady's hand to his lips and kissed it. "Your Grace, I must respectfully decline to participate at this time."

"If you please," Meg Anthony began, "I will— "

"Miss Anthony, I determine when my operatives are ready for the field. Since I have only just discovered this disturbing new information about your psychic gift, and I must say, it troubles me that you were not forthcoming about the risks you take, I cannot allow you to take part in this enterprise until we've discovered a way to lessen the hazard to you."

For the first time, Westfall saw a glint of mutiny in the Finder's mild eyes, but she folded her hands in her lap and studied her knuckles before anyone else could see it.

"So Westfall," His Grace said, "that leaves you."

There were a number of things wrong with that plan, not the least of which was that he was certain Honora didn't want to see him again—either in London or Wiltshire. "I've not been invited to Lord Albemarle's countryseat. I cannot simply present myself at Albion Abbey's doorstep."

"Of course not." The duke waved his hand as if he could swipe away all difficulties as easily as swatting a gnat. "That's why you'll be heading for my hunting lodge. It abuts the Albemarle property on the eastern side. I'm sure you can arrange a chance meeting once you're that close. Country society is somewhat sparse by comparison to London. You'll be invited to the Abbey soon enough."

"But how am I to retrieve"—he wouldn't let himself even think "steal"—"the baron's snuffbox? I'm not an accomplished pickpocket."

Given Miss Anthony's skills in that regard, he thought the duke wrong to dismiss her out of hand.

"You shouldn't attempt it. You have too honest a face and a good pull requires a bit of acting. Besides, you'd never get close enough to Albemarle," Vesta said. Meg nodded her agreement. "But you know someone who can."

"Lady Nora?" Pierce guessed.

Vesta smiled and tapped the tip of her pretty nose.

Pierce shook his head. "She won't betray her protector."

"Perhaps you can persuade her that she'd be *protecting* him. After all, he is contemplating treason," Vesta said. "If she were to substitute the *Fides Pulvis* for some ordinary snuff, Lord Albemarle wouldn't be any the wiser. Without the power of the Trust Powder behind him, he'd just be another courtier trying to turn the opinion of the Prince Regent and frankly, Prinny's too lazy to change his own cravat, much less his mind."

"Thank you for that nearly treasonous assessment of our future sovereign, Vesta. But we ought to have a backup plan in place, in case Lady Nora proves...stubborn." Camden shot a glare at the courtesan. "Women generally are."

Then the duke eyed LeGrand.

"Monsieur LeGrand will go with you, Westfall," His Grace said. "He'll pose as your valet. Then once he's belowstairs at Albion Abbey, he can befriend Albemarle's valet. Servants can sometimes be tempted to petty thievery if they are assured of not being caught."

"It wouldn't hurt for Miss Anthony to come, too. As another option for retrieving the *Fides Pulvis*." The words were out of Pierce's mouth before he could stop them. Meg Anthony had looked so crestfallen at being passed over in favor of the newcomer that he had to come to her defense. Her quick smile told him he'd won forgiveness for telling her secret with that suggestion. "Country society is different than in the city. You said so yourself. It should be easier for Miss Anthony to slip into that setting so she can practice passing as a lady."

"He's right, Camden," Vesta said with a sigh.

"A journey to Wiltshire." Lady Easton, the duke's sister, had been quietly embroidering in the corner. When she spoke up, there was wistfulness in her tone. "It's been ages since I've seen the Chalk Horse country. I'd be happy to accompany Miss Anthony as her chaperone."

"Oh, why don't we all go?" Vesta said sharply. "If I can bear a little fresh air, you can too, Camden. You could do with a bit of rusticating. Far too much of your time is wasted on chasing mediums and riddling with the past and not enough on the problems at hand."

The duke tugged at his waistcoat, though it hung on his frame with an impeccable fit. "How I spend my time is none of your concern."

"It is when it affects the operation of the Order," Vesta said. "You know full well that things will progress more quickly if you're in Wiltshire too. Albemarle won't be able to resist inviting you and your party to dine once he knows you're in the vicinity."

"But it isn't hunting season," the duke protested.

"Which didn't matter a flibbet to you when you decided to send dear Pierce off to your precious hunting lodge." Then Vesta's voice dropped into seductress range, and she sent a sizzling look across the room to the duke. "Besides, you know full well that for some of us, it's always hunting season."

His Grace expects me to use Honora in the furtherance of the Order's goals. I can think of nothing more repugnant. If by some miracle I have not already destroyed whatever we might become to each other, I cannot risk losing her. Not even for King and country.

I'd rather return to Bedlam and the water chair.

~from the secret journal of Pierce Langdon,
Viscount Westfall

Chapter Twelve

Camden dismissed the others with instructions to pack for an extended trip to the country. Only Lord and Lady Stanstead would stay behind in London. In Camden's absence, Bernard had instructions to relay any incoming intelligence from other cells of the Order to them. Garret and Cassandra could be trusted to act independently, if the occasion warranted.

Vesta, on the other hand, couldn't be trusted at all.

As the last of his Extraordinaires filed out the door, only she remained. The woman lounged in his leather wing chair as if she were doing the piece of furniture a favor by allowing it to support her tight little bum. She cast a feline smile at Camden.

"I hope you have an explanation for the way you tried to undermine my authority in the meeting," he said testily.

"Your authority? Why should you lord it over the rest of us in the Order? Aren't you the one who's always expounding on how extraordinary we all are? Why should it surprise you when we act like it?"

She rose in a single, graceful motion and swanned across the room to stand before him. The way the daring bodice on her gown was cut, if he looked down, he knew he'd be able to see the sweet hollow between her breasts, perhaps even a rouged nipple peeping from the froth of lace. He fought to keep his gaze locked on hers.

"If we're that bloody exceptional, we don't need a keeper, Edward."

The sound of his name on her tongue zinged straight to his groin. "There's no need for profanity," he growled, irritated that she could rouse him so thoroughly when he was so thoroughly angry with her. "And I am not your keeper."

"Obviously." She slid a cool hand around the back of his neck, pulling his head down so the warmth of her breath feathered over his lips. "If you were my keeper, I'd be bound to acquiesce to your every demand. Satisfy your every wish…"

Vesta LaMotte might be one of the most powerful fire mages ever born, but her real gift was bringing a man to his knees.

He was still annoyed with her, but he ached to kiss her. He wanted to flip up the woman's skirt and take her right there on his Aubusson carpet. He needed to pound her into such a shattering climax, she'd never try to subvert him again.

"I could be yours, you know." Vesta nearly purred as she smoothed her cheek against his. Then she ran her open mouth along his jaw.

He couldn't hold back. He clasped her roughly to him and claimed her lips. She didn't seem to expect gentleness, and he gave her none. They devoured each other, tongues thrusting, lips bruising.

Her hands were everywhere, her clever fingers stoking him to white-hot fury. She reached around him and drew a thumbnail along the seam in his trousers that divided his bum cheeks. He nearly spent into his smallclothes.

It had been so long since the last time she'd tempted him beyond what he was able to resist.

Vesta was a sickness. A recurring fever that left him weaker and more prone to succumb to her wiles with each indulgence. When she knelt before him and worked the buttons over his hips, he abandoned all hope of restraint.

As his trousers slid down his thighs he collapsed into the wing chair. She settled between his knees and went to work.

The heaven of her tongue on him. The warmth of her mouth as she took him in. The scrape of her teeth over his most sensitive spot. He dug his fingernails into the arms of the chair hard enough to leave marks in the leather.

"Succubus," he murmured as the pressure built in his shaft.

"No, I'm definitely flesh and blood," she corrected between long licks of his entire length. "But I suppose I do fall on the dark side of the scale. Your Mercedes was the angel of light."

It was the only thing Vesta could have said that would deflate him completely. His gaze jerked up to the portrait of his dead wife above the mantel. Mercedes was smiling down at him with that enigmatic glow of hers, her lips softly parted as if she was about to share the most delicious of secrets.

And there he was with his trousers around his ankles and his cock in another woman's mouth.

Camden pushed Vesta away so forcibly that she rocked back off her knees and landed with a thump on her bum.

He wished he'd been less brutish, but if he hadn't thrust her away that very second, he wouldn't have had the will to do it. He rose, yanking up his trousers and stuffing his shirttail back into them.

"Damnation," he muttered.

"My thoughts exactly," Vesta said without bothering to get up. Instead, she splayed her legs before her and leaned back on her palms. "We were having a delicious time. Do you mind telling me why you felt compelled to kill the joy?"

"What do you think? I can't do this. Not with you. Not…" He waved a hand toward the portrait. "Not here."

Vesta's gaze flicked upward and her wicked mouth formed a perfect "Oh." "It seems my words were poorly timed—"

"You think so?"

"But Camden, when will you realize that Mercedes loved you? Wherever she is, if she is able to see you, she would want you to be happy."

He leaned on the mantel and pressed his forehead against the cool stone of the fireplace. It steadied him, made it easier to think clearly. He wished he could put out the fire that still raged in the rest of him as easily. "If she wanted me to be happy, she'd still be here."

"It's not as if she chose to leave you."

"Isn't it? She should have stayed home."

It had only been a few days after she had given birth to their little boy. The child hadn't even been christened yet. Mercedes hadn't been churched—usually the first outing for a new mother, but instead, she'd ignored Camden's wishes and set off for an unsafe part of the city on an unknown errand.

Days later, after the funerals were over and all the mourners had left, Camden had realized that Mercedes had tried to talk to him about something, but he'd put her off. He had been too busy with plans for his Order of the M.U.S.E., too puffed up over producing an heir for the estate, and too engrossed in the running of said estate to believe his beautiful wife had anything of consequence bothering her.

Certainly, nothing so pressing that she'd bundle up herself and their newborn and go to Whitechapel in the dead of winter.

Camden wandered over to the window and stared out at London. His home was on a small rise so that, from his study, he could see over the rooftops across the street. The city was settling into evening, myriad chimneys belching smoke into the sky. Lit by flames extended on long poles, gas lamps winked on in the better neighborhoods. So many lives intersecting, so many souls living cheek by jowl, and none of them the one he most wanted to speak to.

"Why?" he whispered.

It was a measure of how finely attuned Vesta was to him that she seemed to sense the direction of his thoughts. "I know you spent a small fortune on Bow Street Runners trying to answer that question."

He heard a rustle of silk. Vesta came up behind him and slipped her arms around his waist. She laid her head against his spine between his shoulder blades.

His feelings for the courtesan were a tangled mess. She was blindingly attractive and she knew it. She could make him her slave, if he didn't take care. He alternated between lusting after her and being repulsed by his need for her. Either way, she was the most exasperating woman he'd ever known.

Now, however, he covered her hands with one of his, grateful beyond words.

Sometimes, she was too good to him. Mercedes had been, too.

He didn't deserve any of the women who'd come into his life.

"There are some questions that have no answers," Vesta said.

"That's not true of this one. Mercedes went to Whitechapel for a purpose and I need to know what it was." The Runners had discovered no reason for her visit to the sketchy district or even who she had been meeting there, so Camden had turned to seeking a way to contact his wife directly. If he could locate a medium worthy of the name, he'd be able to speak with Mercedes. But so far, all the mediums he'd discovered were charlatans preying on the bereaved. None of them could really communicate with the dead.

At least, not *his* dead.

Vesta tugged her hand free. "Good night, Edward."

"Wait a moment." He turned and caught her wrist. Her lovely eyes were hooded, but he could still read hurt in them. "My behavior toward you has been abominable of late."

She merely looked up at him. After a long pause she said, "Oh!" Then she gave herself a slight shake and batted her long lashes at him, her professional courtesan's smile firmly in place. "Were you expecting me to disagree?"

"Always, but perhaps not on this point," he said with a chuckle. "Vesta, for what it's worth, I am sorry."

"So am I." Her smile drooped. "I'd hoped to give you ease. And take a bit for myself as well."

She was between patrons, he knew, and the fire mage's gift was always accompanied by a voracious sexual appetite. The least he could have done was sate that hunger for her a little.

"I should have—"

"Yes, you should have," she said with a genuine smile this time. "But that ship has sailed, for this evening, at least. And now I must be off."

He cocked his head at her.

"Someone we know and have little reason to love at the moment has commanded me to take a journey to the country." She dipped in a low curtsy. "So that means I must pack."

She turned and sashayed toward the door, her luscious hips swaying. He damned himself for a fool. She was right. Mercedes was gone. He'd mourned her for far more years than most husbands. He would always love her, and the mystery of why she was taken from him would always haunt him, but his wife wouldn't begrudge him the comfort of a mistress now.

Vesta stopped at the threshold. "Even though you don't deserve it, sleep well, Edward. Heaven knows, I shan't."

Then she slipped out the door before he could call her back. Even if he had, she was contrary enough not to have come.

"Neither will I, Vesta," he said with regret. When it came to women, even being a duke was no guarantee of unquestioned obedience. Or a restful night's sleep. "Neither will I."

. . .

Nora didn't know why she'd ridden this way. It wasn't her usual route through the woods surrounding Albion Abbey. But when she'd learned that the Duke of Camden had a hunting lodge nearby, she was drawn to see it, as surely as a lodestone to true north. There was no logic to it. She was compelled to view the lodge for no other reason than her strange sense that seeing it would ease the disquiet in her breast.

Which was how she'd come to be leading her mare along the rutted road instead of riding. The beast had thrown a shoe, and Nora couldn't bear to see her lamed. She was closer to the Camden property than Albion Abbey, so she trudged on in hope of finding a hostler on site who could help her.

When she crested a small rise, the hunting lodge and its accompanying outbuildings spread out before her. It was ringed by an ancient grove of beeches. Clematis and wisteria clung to the limestone walls, bright spots of color against weathered gray. It seemed far too grand to be a hunting lodge. While undeniably rustic, Camden End was more of a manor house than most estates could boast. The three-story stone structure was shaped like a stone butterfly, wings extended on either side of a central tower.

The symmetry pleased her, but she wasn't there to study the architecture. Even her lame horse wasn't the real reason she kept walking toward the tower, though she'd have disputed it with her dying breath.

Since Viscount Westfall was an intimate friend of the duke, Camden End was a link to him. It was a slender connection, but it was all she had.

Pierce was the most unusual man she'd ever met. She couldn't stop thinking about him. More specifically, she couldn't stop thinking about his final words to her.

I think I love you, Honora.

She could still hear his voice. It shivered through her in deep tones. It touched places she'd forgotten she had. Her insides quaked each time the remembered phrase washed over her.

The words weren't true, of course. Of course, he didn't love her. By his own admission, he wasn't even sure of it himself. Men desired her. Men were obsessed with her. Men wanted to possess her.

None of them loved her.

She kicked a rock down the lane ahead of her. Benedick would be upset if she ruined her new riding boots. Since the pointy-toed things pinched abominably, she didn't think it would be a great loss, but they were designed in the first stare of fashion. The way she was turned out reflected on her protector, Benedick always said. In his own way, he was good to her. Benedick cared for her as much as he was capable of caring for any woman, but it wasn't the same thing as love.

"Of course, Westfall's declaration wasn't the same thing as love, either," she muttered to herself. It was more like the aftermath of lust. A man would say anything to the first woman he bedded.

She reminded herself that he claimed to be able to hear her thoughts. Considering how many secrets she guarded for Benedick, Westfall was a decidedly dangerous man for her to know.

But she couldn't help wishing to see him again. As she drew near, she even thought she saw a resemblance to Pierce Langdon in the brawny shoulders of the gardener who was trimming the shrubs beneath the ground floor windows.

I am losing my mind.

The gardener turned then and removed his disreputable hat, revealing a head of honey-blond hair, darkened with sweat.

"No, you're not, Honora." His familiar voice rolled over her. "You're the sanest person I know."

Never trust the opinion of a madman. Especially on the subject of sanity.

~from the secret journal of Lady Nora Claremont

Chapter Thirteen

"Lord Westfall, what are you doing here?" And how could she keep her heart from leaping out of her chest?

"Pruning the rhododendrons," he said. "I can't imagine what the duke was thinking to allow them to be planted in this spot. They aren't native to Wiltshire. The wicked things will take over if they aren't kept in check. You see—"

"No," she interrupted. "I mean, how did you come to be here?"

He grinned indulgently at her, as if she were a not-quite-bright child. "By carriage, of course. Well, I rode some of the way. His Grace likes to keep his favorite gelding with him so we traded off on either horseback or rear-facing squab—"

Was the man being purposely obtuse? "But *why* are you in Wiltshire?"

One of those rare, full smiles of his spread across his face. "To see you, of course."

It was suddenly hard to breathe. She had to consciously

push the air in and out. *Down, Nora. You need him like you need a second head.*

"It's a bit of a step to travel to deliver an apology," he said, "but I do hope you've forgiven me for the last time we were together."

Was he asking forgiveness for the best time of her life? No, it was that other thing, she reminded herself. The fact that he'd used her to spy on her patron. She had to keep that in mind, but when she met his gaze, she couldn't keep the corners of her mouth from turning up.

"Am I forgiven?" he asked.

Despite her best intentions, her smile exonerated him.

"Good." He smiled back at her, his face the picture of someone at perfect peace. Her own breathing relaxed. Pierce accepted her without condition. She hadn't felt this comfortable in anyone's company since she'd lost Lewis.

"While I was trying to think of a way to accidentally make our paths cross, I thought I'd take care of these shrubs." He applied the shears with vigor and more purple-sheathed limbs fell to the ground. "You saved me from having to come up with some sort of ruse. I'm glad you came to see me instead."

"I haven't come to see you." Where had he gotten that idea?

"You're here, aren't you?"

She had to give him that. "Other than the apology, is there any other reason you want to see me?"

Pierce stopped his pruning and met her gaze steadily. "Of course, but you already know what it is."

He didn't say the words this time, but something that looked an awfully lot like love showed in his eyes. Whether the emotion was real or not, Westfall seemed to have convinced himself it was. If she didn't look away quickly, he'd have her convinced, too.

"Yes, well, I had no idea you were here and I was simply out riding and...and..." The reason she was there finally slammed back into her mind. "And my mare has gone lame."

This time he flashed her a damnably smug smile.

The man knows. He's invading my mind. He'll see that I can't stop thinking about him.

"Stop that," she ordered.

"Stop what?"

"That thing you do." She pointed at him accusingly. "You're doing it right now, and I won't have it."

His brows nearly met over his fine straight nose. "What thing?"

"You're listening to my thoughts."

"No, I'm not. After that first thought of yours I intercepted, I knew you'd want me to shield my mind," he said. "Don't worry that it's a burden on me to do it. When I work with plants, I find it so restful, it's easier to keep up my mental shield."

He bent to yank out a cankerwort. The sight of the man's beautifully muscled bum encased in his tight buckskins nearly took her breath away. She longed to see him in the altogether again. He tossed a grin over his shoulder at her.

Her cheeks heated. "If you can't hear what I'm thinking, why are you smiling?"

"Because I'm happy to see you. Or won't you have that, either?"

"No, I...now you're making me seem unreasonable."

"Madmen have that effect, I'm told." He stepped forward

and took the lead reins from her. "Come. Let's see what can be done for your horse."

He led the mare toward the stables without waiting to see if she'd follow.

Of course, he wouldn't need to look over his shoulder at her. He'd be able to hear the way her mind was churning as she bobbed in his wake. She schooled herself to concentrate only on the fresh green smell of newly cut hay in the meadow and the warmth of the sun on her face. When Nora tipped her nose to admire the robin's egg blue of the sky, sunshine slipped in under the bill of her bonnet. She'd sprout a crop of freckles if she wasn't careful.

But she needed a distraction. She refused to entertain the notion that he really loved her. How could he? And Nora certainly didn't want to fixate on the fine view of Westfall's bum as he walked ahead of her. The man's stride was long and loping and made his muscular backside undulate in a beguiling manner.

He tossed a look over his shoulder at her and smiled again.

Drat the man! She could feel her cheeks flooding with color. His claim that he wasn't listening to her thoughts notwithstanding, Pierce seemed to know she was ogling his bum. And more to the point, he'd made her blush about it.

Who knew that a courtesan could even remember how to blush? She had so much more sensual experience than he, but somehow, everything felt fresh and new with him. It was as if she'd never been with those others.

Not even her dead husband Lewis.

She didn't want to contemplate what that meant.

She waited in the cool shade of the stable door while

Lord Westfall—she tried not to think of him as Pierce— discussed her mare's situation with the master of horse for the Camden estate. After much wrangling, the fellow advised that the remaining shoes should be removed and the horse be allowed to rest there for a day or so.

"I'm sure His Grace would welcome you at Camden End, too," Westfall said.

"No, I can't stay. Albemarle is expecting me back in time for tea."

The sun was at its zenith. Westfall swiped a bronzed forearm across his forehead. "It's a long while till teatime."

"Still, I must be going." She turned to begin walking, cursing her tight riding boots with every step.

"Wait, my lady. I'll take you in the gig."

She stopped, shifting her weight from one foot to the other.

"You won't get far in those boots."

She rounded on him. "There, you see. You are doing it. You're in my head, listening to my thoughts."

"No, I'm not. I'm using the eyes God gave me. If those boots aren't hurting you, why are you mincing around in them?" He crossed over to her and took both her hands. "I know how you feel about my...ability and I promise you, I will not let my shield down while we're together. You deserve the privacy of your own mind and frankly, I deserve the peace."

She blinked hard at that. She hadn't considered until that moment that being able to hear other people's thoughts might be a burden.

"So will you let me take you home?"

She nodded. "Get the gig."

. . .

The Duke of Camden kept a sporty little gig at his countryseat that could fly over the dirt roads. Pierce had a similar equipage on his own estate, but since his committal to Bedlam he hadn't been home to drive it. His uncle might well have sold the gig along with the matched pair of grays that pulled it. If Pierce had been in his own conveyance, he'd have driven hell-for-leather over the country lane for the pure joy of speed.

Instead, he held the horses in check, driving at a sedate pace.

May as well not give Honora one more reason to think me mad.

He nearly burst with the need to tell her he loved her, that he was more certain of it now, but he knew she wouldn't appreciate it. She'd certainly not responded to his declaration the first time. After all, given his lack of experience with women, he would have been astounded if he hadn't botched it somehow. He tried not to feel despondent about it. After all, she was there with him, wasn't she?

That was more than a madman had a right to hope.

The sun beat down upon them warmly. The scents of earth and ripening grain filled the air. Birdsong greeted his ears. Those things alone were cause for him to be in charity with the world.

To be wedged onto the narrow seat with Honora as they drove through the green English countryside was almost enough to tip him over into euphoria. After they'd driven for a while, she broke the silence.

"You seem different," she said.

"I'm not," he assured her. "I'm the same fellow who put you on edge in London." *And I do still think I love you.* "The difference is you're seeing me where I belong. I'm a country man at heart."

London was such a train wreck of clamoring voices at all hours of the day and night. There were fewer souls in the country, fewer minds trying to tramp through his.

"You do seem…less intense here," she said.

"Is that good?"

She smiled thinly at him, and he wasn't sure what it meant. He wished he hadn't promised to keep up his mental shield. He was sorely tempted to let her thoughts trip through his mind, even if it meant she'd be upset with him. Still, a promise was a promise.

She leaned forward and slipped a finger inside the high rise of her boot. The footwear was an odd cross between blue and green. Pierce wasn't sure what color to call them. He'd seen Vesta wearing something similar so they were undoubtedly all the crack. But when Nora fiddled with the buckle that held one fastened around her ankle, he realized however stylish they might be, the boot was hurting her.

When the gig passed over a small bridge above a meandering stream, he pulled the horses up short. "Give me your feet."

"What?"

"You're in as much pain over how you're shod as your mare was. Let's see what may be done." He patted his knee. "Now."

To his surprise, she obeyed, lifting her leg to set her ankle on his thigh. He made short work of the buckle and eased the boot off.

"Ow!" She wiggled her stockinged toes gingerly.

He reached under her hem in search of the lacy garter holding up her stockings.

She grasped his forearm to stop him. "What do you think you're doing?"

Granted, there was no one near them for miles around, but he supposed his actions did cross some sort of line. "The stocking needs to come off, too. What did you think I was doing?" His fingertips found the garter, and he gave it a tug. The silky stocking sagged.

"When a gentleman's hand slips under a lady's hem, he's not generally after her garter." Nora's dark eyes rolled expressively. "At least, not *only* her garter."

For a moment, he allowed himself to remember what it was like to hold her most vulnerable parts, all wet and soft and trembling. He'd be less than a man if he didn't want to do it again. "I may not be very experienced, but surely you didn't think I'd force my attentions on you that clumsily."

"No, I suppose not." Her eyes softened and he suspected she, too, was thinking about how he'd held her. But he couldn't be sure. Not without lowering his shield, and his promise not to do that held him back.

"Inexperienced or no, you're not a bit clumsy," she said.

She tugged off her stocking and turned her ankle this way and that. Her toes were red and the boots had chafed an angry, raised blister on her heel. "I'll have to wear backless mules for a week."

"Maybe not." He climbed down from the gig and lifted his arms in invitation. "If we cool your feet in that stream, the blister may go down."

She bit her lower lip, considering. He ached to take that little lip and suckle it, but he made himself stand still. The last time they were together, she'd been as eager for their joining as he. Now he sensed a wall between them.

The wall of his oddity, no doubt. If he were an ordinary man, they'd be regular lovers already. Nora was a sensual enough being not to withhold her body from him, but she was definitely skittish about sharing her thoughts and feelings.

How could he convince her that he cared for her and would never betray her?

By keeping his promise to erect his mental shield when he was around her, no matter what the effort cost him. They'd parted so badly, he had no idea how much repair work was ahead, but he suspected it would be far harder than clearing out those rhododendrons. He was relieved beyond words when she slipped off her other boot and stocking and let him help her down from the gig.

"Give me a moment to tend to the horses, and I'll carry you to the stream," he offered.

"No need. I like the feel of grass under my feet." She started toward a flat outcropping of granite that overhung the rippling water.

"Wait. Take my jacket to sit upon." He peeled off his jacket and handed it to her. "You'll ruin that gown otherwise."

She rewarded him with one of her sparkling smiles.

Pierce led the team and gig off the road and tied them in a shady spot. He was careful to leave enough slack in the tether so that the beasts could grab a few mouthfuls of grass if they wished.

He knew what it was to be bound and helpless. He didn't

want anyone, not even a horse, to feel that way. By the time he joined Nora beside the stream, she'd removed her bonnet since a trio of birches cast a dappled shadow over her. The trees leaned toward the water, looking for all the world like three skinny spinsters trying to screw their courage to dabble their toes in the current with Nora.

Her luxurious dark hair had tumbled down a bit. Leaning back on her elbows, she looked like a fallen angel, disheveled, slightly dirty, and missing her wings. Pierce fancied that a bit of heaven's grace still gilded her around the edges.

My angel. That's how I'll think of her always.

When he approached, she leaned forward and splashed in his direction. "The stream is so deliciously cool. What an excellent idea this is."

He removed his scuffed boots and stockings and settled beside her. The water was bracing, and he sighed in contentment. "Even a madman can have a good idea from time to time."

"I don't think of you like that, Pierce."

She'd called him by his name, not his title. Surely that was a good sign. "But you don't think of me as...normal."

"Perhaps that's not such a bad thing. Have you any idea how horrid most normal men really are?"

Well, she doesn't think I'm horrid. That is a start.

Then, because he wasn't sure what to say, he said nothing. If they'd been in London, the silence would have stretched between them, taut and hungry, begging to be crammed with anything, even the banality of discussing the weather or one of the other *ton*-approved topics of conversation. Here, the quiet seemed satisfied with the twitter of birdsong, the burbling voice of the stream, and the drowsy hum of bees at work on the bittersweet blooming amid the grass.

Nora sighed and lifted her wet foot to examine the damage on her heel. A few drips slipped up around her ankle to disappear under her soggy hem. "Still a bit angry looking, but it feels ever so much better. We should probably go on."

But she made no move to rise.

Neither did he. Instead, he simply sat there, content to feel her soft shoulder against his. She let her feet sink back into the stream, her small toes undulating like water grass beneath the surface. Pierce drank in her scent. A gorse bush, laden with yellow blooms, effectively blocked them from view should anyone pass by on the road. He could wallow in the happy conceit that he and Nora were the only two people in the world.

"You really aren't listening to my thoughts, are you?" she finally said.

He shook his head. "I promised I wouldn't. How can you tell?"

"Because if you were, you'd know I'm dying for you to kiss me."

The advantage to being thought mad is that nothing one does ever really surprises others. Whether I behave outrageously or do an imitation of a rock, my supposed condition explains all.

The truth is, when confronted with a beautiful woman, I am neither more nor less bewildered about what to do than any other man. Which is to say, rather more than a little mad.

~from the secret journal of Pierce Langdon,
Viscount Westfall

Chapter Fourteen

If Nora had issued such a blatant invitation to kiss her to any other fellow, he wouldn't have hesitated for a second. Most men would have swept her into a hurried embrace. But Pierce Langdon was not most men.

"Why are you dying for me to kiss you?" he asked.

She cocked her head at him in surprise. "Because... because for a man who claims to have had little sensual experience, you kiss rather well."

That wasn't strictly true. Pierce wasn't a technically adept kisser. He'd even missed her mouth on one occasion, but since Lewis's death, no other man's lips on hers had made her feel so tinglingly alive. Nora had no idea why, but she was sure she could figure it out if he kissed her again.

"So you like the way I kiss," he said, as if confused by the idea instead of flattered. "Is that all?"

"Isn't that enough?"

"No." His gray-eyed gaze seemed to reach into her soul.

"I believe I love you, Honora. Don't you feel anything about me?"

So he *believed* he loved her now. That was more positive than merely *thinking* it, but she still couldn't reciprocate. She didn't dare. If there was one constant in the universe, it was that men were inconstant. Love was a risky business. It was hurt. It was loss. And even if a lover was the exception that proved the rule and was faithful all his days, like her Lewis had been, love still ended in the ultimate betrayal—the abandonment of death.

"I scarcely know you," she admitted. "How can you expect me to have feelings for you?"

"You know me better than most. After all, I confided my deepest secret to you." A corner of his mouth twitched up. "I'd say you know enough to know whether you care for me a bit."

He *had* entrusted her with his claim that he could hear the thoughts of others. A secret equaled power. Benedick had taught her that. If she repeated Pierce's assertion in the right person's ear, she could have him sent back to Bedlam in short order. Not that she'd do that to a dog, much less to Pierce. But he had no right to demand that she care about him.

"I don't see how my feelings for you one way or another have any bearing on whether or not I allow you to kiss me."

"*Ask* me to kiss you, you mean."

Indignation rose in her. She'd never had to beg for a man's attention before. "Forget I mentioned it."

This time both sides of his mouth turned up. "I can't. You want me to kiss you. That makes me happier than a madman has any right to be."

"And I would have thought being mad was a perpetual giggling feast," she said with a laugh.

His smile faded. "You'd be wrong. Not being able to trust one's own mind is...well, I wouldn't wish it on anyone. Not even my uncle."

The man who'd sent him to Bedlam in the first place. Pierce Langdon was either a saint or he truly was mad not to wish a bit of retribution on his relative for that act of treachery.

Something tightened in her chest. And glowed a bit. She didn't want it to. Feelings were always messy. A courtesan had no business allowing them.

But she had no way of controlling this feeling. Even as she tried to tamp that strange warmth down, it spread through her. Nora reached over and rested her hand on his forearm.

"My heart is not a whole one, Pierce. Bits of it are missing, probably some rather important bits, and what's left is bruised and battered." She leaned over and kissed his cheek, missing the mark and catching the corner of his mouth, much as he'd done to her in the ladies' retiring room at the opera. "But as much as I'm able, it seems my poor heart does care for you. More than a bit, for what it's worth."

"It's worth everything." He cupped her cheeks and his mouth was suddenly hot on hers.

His kiss is a whole world.

Her body thrummed to life. But even in this idyllic bower, overhung with green and lulled by the voice of the stream, Nora wasn't about to let matters progress further than a kiss. Surely not. She wasn't some milkmaid to settle for a tumble in a haystack, but Pierce's kiss tempted her to it.

Just a kiss, she chanted to herself.

Everything spiraled down to his mouth, his tongue, the way he suckled her bottom lip for a moment. He pressed a string of baby kisses along her jaw, up to her temple, and then on each of her closed eyes.

The nattering gossips would never believe it. The tabloids would call her a liar.

Pierce Langdon's kisses were more stirring than a whole night with any of her previous lovers.

It wasn't that he was smooth about it. He wasn't. But the fervor with which Pierce kissed her stole her breath away. And when his kisses turned tender and his big hands caressed her breasts through her riding habit, her chest constricted so, she feared her heart might stop beating altogether.

Then he pulled her feet out of the stream, laid her back, and settled between her spread-eagle legs. He moved down her body and hitched up her riding habit to expose the open crotch of her pantalets.

"What do you think you are doing?"

"Kissing you. All over," he said with a wicked grin. "You rendered me a similar lover's service. Would you deny me the opportunity to return that pleasure?"

Words failed her. She settled down onto Pierce's jacket spread beneath her, lifted her arms above her head in surrender, and bent her knees over his massive shoulders to give him better access.

His mouth was heaven. His tongue, oh mercy, his tongue. What with the warmth of the rock beneath her, the heat of the man over her, and the fire he kindled inside her, she was burning up.

Helpless noises of need escaped from her throat as

Pierce redoubled his efforts. His big hands cradled her bum, lifting her to meet his mouth. She fisted the cloth of his jacket, every muscle contracting. It wasn't that he tongued her with the sure knowledge of how to play a woman's body. He often slipped away from that all-important spot of ultra-sensitivity or changed rhythm just as she was building toward release. She ought to feel frustrated.

Instead she'd never been wound so tight. Or enjoyed the journey more.

The fact that he believed he *loved* her made all the difference.

Then, with little warning, she peaked and unraveled under him in a frenzy of bucking limbs and heaving gasps. There was nothing the least refined in her release. Every bit of her was flooded with bone-jarring joy.

I love you, Honora.

That was no memory. There was no qualifier, no "I think" or "I believe." But somehow, she did seem to hear his voice in her head, repeating the phrase. It echoed in the ripples of the stream. It breathed out in the fresh green exhalation of the birches. Even the bees seemed to be humming it.

"I do, you know," Pierce said as he came up for air.

"Do what?"

"Love you." He moved up her body, holding his weight on his elbows while his hips settled between hers. He was still fully dressed, but she could feel the hard bulge of him pressed against her entrance. "I know you're thinking about it, trying to decide if I mean it. I do, with all that's in me."

Joy burst inside her, flooding her entire being. But she wasn't quite ready to trust it. Joy was such a dangerous thing. So fleeting. So fragile. And in her case, so undeserved.

"I know I promised to keep my mental shield up, but it's

hard to concentrate with so many things going on at once," he said.

"I forgive you." Nora wrapped her arms around him and pulled him down for another kiss. She tasted a bit of herself, all musk and salt, on his lips. "Just don't let it become a habit."

It was all right for him to listen in on her thoughts now. They were all about him.

She was so lost in the man that she didn't hear the approaching hoof beats on the road until the rider stopped and shouted to them from the small bridge.

"Halloo!" The voice belonged to Albemarle. "Is anyone there? Your horses and gig are about to make a break for it."

"Botheration!" Fortunately, the gorse bush effectively blocked them from his view. Nora scrambled out from under Pierce and yanked down her hem to cover her legs. She jammed her discarded bonnet back on her head. Then she leaped to her feet and peered at her patron over the bush. Benedick had left the bridge and neck-reined his buckskin gelding down the road, stopping near the Duke of Camden's gig. He raised himself in the stirrups when he caught sight of her.

He waved his hat and grinned.

Then Pierce stood as well, and Albemarle's grin faded a bit. It was one thing for Benedick to give her permission to pursue a liaison with Lord Westfall. It was quite another for him to catch her at it.

"Albemarle, how very fortuitous. We were just on our way to Albion Abbey." She hurried across the grass to the gig to retrieve her boots and stockings. The equipage did seem to be inching ever closer to the road as the matched pair of horses continued to munch the sweet long grass. Pierce must have been in a hurry when he tied up the beasts because the tether had come undone.

As had she.

"I had a spot of trouble while I was riding and Lord Westfall has been so very helpful," she explained.

"So I see," Albemarle said dryly.

"My poor horse went lame and—"

"And Lady Nora nearly went lame as well, so she was soaking her feet," Pierce filled in. Nora shot him a sharp look. His tone was even. He wasn't breathing irregularly. Nothing betrayed the fact that his face had recently been buried between her thighs. "Her boots are charming, but not conducive to long walks."

"We shall have to rectify that, my dear," Albemarle said. "You shall ride pillion with me, and I'll see that your lovely feet are tended posthaste."

Benedick leaned down to offer her a hand up with a stern expression that brooked no refusal. She stepped on his stirrup and mounted behind his saddle, tugging her billowy riding skirt around her to cover her exposed ankles.

"I don't believe we've been properly introduced. Lord Westfall, isn't it?" Albemarle said.

Pierce gave him a curt bow from the neck. His eyes narrowed. He obviously didn't like Benedick much and wasn't trying to disguise it. She'd have to speak to him sternly about keeping up appearances if they were going to make this liaison work.

"It seems I am in your debt, but perhaps you might indulge me further by doing me another favor," Benedick said, ignoring Pierce's scowl. "I was on my way to Camden

End to invite His Grace to dine this evening. I wonder if you would relay that invitation so I can take Lady Nora home as quickly as possible."

"Certainly," Pierce said, "though I do not know if His Grace will be able to break free. He is hosting a large party of guests at the moment."

"Then by all means, he should bring them along. How many shall I tell my chef to expect?"

Pierce ticked off the members of the duke's party on his fingers. "There's Lady Easton, Miss Anthony, Miss LaMotte—"

"Ah! Vesta. What an enchanting woman. I remember the time when she—"

"And myself, of course," Pierce interrupted.

"And yourself, of course," Benedick said with a smile that did not reach his eyes. "I'm depending upon you, Westfall. I shan't take no for an answer. Shall we say eight o'clock? Tell His Grace my chef does miracles with squab. And please invite the duke and his guests to plan on spending the night at the Abbey as well. There's a fair in Patterlane Green on the morrow that I believe His Grace will enjoy. The village is much closer to the Abbey than Camden End, so an overnight stay will be easier all around. Until this evening…"

Benedick dug his heels into his horse's flanks, and the gelding leaped into a gallop down the road in the direction of Albion Abbey. Nora was forced to link her hands around Benedick's waist and hang on tight lest she fly off and land on her bum. Once they were out of Pierce's earshot, he slowed his mount to a walk.

"When I gave you leave to seek out Westfall, I didn't think you'd turn into such a randy little tart about it," he said, his tone surly.

"My horse went lame. Lord Westfall was being helpful. I have no idea what you mean."

"Don't you? You fairly reek of the man."

Benedick couldn't possibly be jealous. "You're being ridiculous. I don't chide you about the time you spend with Rivers."

"Of course, you don't," he said snippily. "The man is my valet."

"And your lover."

"And you're my mistress. At least as far as the world knows, you are mine, and I intend that you should keep it that way." He covered her clasped hands at his waist possessively. "Now that I've met him, I don't like the look of that Lord Westfall, not by half."

What he meant was he didn't like Lord Westfall shagging his mistress. And she had to admit that Pierce had not presented a deferential face to Benedick.

"You needn't worry," she told him. "We can trust Westfall to be discreet. He won't breathe a word about our assignations to anyone. He's convinced himself that he loves me."

"Love, bah! Never was there a more mercurial emotion. A lover may promise the moon and the stars in the first flush of lust but, as the heavens change with the seasons, such promises are later forgotten entirely."

She felt certain there was more to Benedick's surliness than simply catching her with Westfall. "What's wrong? Is Rivers giving you trouble?"

"Heavens, no." He sighed. "He's biddable as a hound. If you must know, it's that ghost from my past. My Italian. I had another letter from my tormentors this morning and it seems he's in league with them."

If his blackmailers knew to send the letter to the country that meant Benedick's movements were being carefully watched. "What are they threatening now?"

"It's more than just revealing the things I wrote to Falco all those years ago. He's here himself. In England. And, wittingly or not, he has aligned himself with my enemies."

Nora laid her head between Benedick's shoulder blades and tightened her grip around his slender waist. She felt the sense of betrayal emanating from his body in scalding waves. "I'm so sorry."

"So am I. He was such a lovely young man. Peasant stock, you understand, but he had a quick mind. We parted badly. I wanted more than he could give at the time, but when I left him behind in Genoa, I also left sufficient funds for him to secure a trade for himself."

It was like Benedick to provide liberally for his past lovers. He'd do the same for Nora once their supposed association ended. It was part of the gentlemanliness for which he was known.

"What trade did he pursue?"

"Falco became a doctor. He spends a good deal of time in his letter emphasizing that I will not be endangering the Prince Regent's bodily health by using the *Fides Pulvis* to influence him."

"You'll only endanger his mind."

"Exactly. Who knows how long the powder works? A malleable prince is a tempting thought. Think what I could accomplish with Prinny in my pocket. But what if this substance reduces him to imbecility? It's bad enough to have a mad king."

"And the prince's brothers are no prizes, either," Nora said, parroting back something Benedick had said once about the gaggle of royal dukes. Then she served up her own thoughts about the monarchy. "With a ruling family like the Hanoverians, perhaps we should consider following the Americans' example and try democracy."

"Careful, my dear," Benedick chided. "That's treason."

"So is using the *Fides Pulvis* on your future king."

Benedick's usually ramrod-straight posture slumped. "But I may not have a choice."

"So your letters to Falco are still being used against you. I must say, it is bad form of him to repay your generosity like this."

"He does promise to give my letters back after the Prince Regent changes his mind on the subject of the withdrawal of our troops from France." Benedick shrugged. "Not only will he return the letters. He's offered to come back to me as well."

"I'll bet Rivers loved that."

"He doesn't know and, please God, he never will. Dear Rivers is jealous enough of you, and he knows nothing ever passes between us but friendship. Heaven help me if he ever caught wind that there was a possibility that Falco might return to my life." He sighed wistfully. "That lovely Italian was the only man I've been with who was my intellectual equal. Rivers is a pretty valet, but he'll never be anything more."

Nora straightened her spine. She was grateful to Benedick for the way he provided for her and Emilia, but she, too, would never be anything to him but a pretty ornament to his arm. Was this all life held before her? To be a useful tool to her patron for a limited time and after that, to be set aside like a dull letter opener?

"So will you take Falco back?"

Benedick shook his head. "He's no longer the young man I left in Genoa, and I'm not the same, either. Too much time has passed and time wounds all heels, you know. It would be the height of hubris to think we might have a second chance."

Life didn't generally give second chances to women like her, either. But Nora couldn't help but feel there was a spark of hope in Pierce's declaration of love.

This night, the Duke of Camden's party descended upon Albion Abbey, and Benedick has prevailed upon His Grace to spend several days with us. He can be so very charming when he wants something and he definitely wants something from His Grace.

Tomorrow, we embark for the fair at Patterlane Green. If that gypsy wagon is there again, I shall not seek the old wise woman out. Last year, she predicted I would lead someone I love to destroy himself. Who pays a penny for that sort of fortune? Yet if she'd foretold a future of nosegays and bliss for me, I'd have known she was selling a bag of moonshine.

Which is why I fear she told me the truth.

~from the secret journal of Lady Nora
Claremont

Chapter Fifteen

The last place Pierce wanted to be was at the Patterlane Green fair. The sleepy little village probably would have been fine on a normal day. All the minds would have been focused on workaday things, uncomplicated things—how much meal to buy for supper, whether the cow needed to be freshened to sweeten her milk, or if the goat had broken down the garden fence and was into the leeks and potato plants again.

Pierce could let those kinds of thoughts wash over him like rainwater off an eave and into a barrel.

Today the problems were thornier. The villagers were worried about spending their hard-earned coin on shoes for the child who was growing so fast his feet were already bigger than his older brother's or trying to decide if partnering with a neighbor to invest in an iron plowshare would be worth the added expense.

Incomes for the entire year might be decided by a few deals made on this green. Everything felt more important, more critical, despite the outwardly gay atmosphere of a fair.

Pierce kept his mental shield up, but a bit of desperation, emanating from Nora, slipped around its edges. While she laughed and talked and hung on his arm as they moved from one booth to the next, her gaze darted furtively through the crowd.

"Who are you looking for?" he finally asked.

She cocked her head at him accusingly.

"No, I'm not listening to your thoughts," he assured her, though he was sorely tempted. It would be the best way to get a straight answer from her. She'd been evasive and distant since the Duke of Camden's party had settled into Albion Abbey. He hadn't had a moment's private speech with her after they had parted at that stream. When she condescended to allow him to squire her around the fair this morning, he expected to be able to pick up at least the conversational threads from their interrupted tryst. However, she seemed determined to keep the banter between them light and suitable for anyone's ears.

"What makes you think I'm looking for someone?" Her gaze flitted past him toward the puppeteer's booth and then jerked guiltily back to meet his eyes.

"It's Emilia, isn't it?" he guessed.

Her mouth drew into a tight line. "You promised."

"And I kept my word." He raised his hands in mock surrender. "It doesn't take a mind reader to know you're seeking a child when you scrutinize every sweetmeat seller and can't take your eyes off the Punchinello show."

She sighed. "All right. If you must know, Emilia is fostered by a couple who live near this village. Mr. and Mrs. Hobarth."

"And you've seen her here at the fair before?"

She made no pretense of trying to hide her search now, craning her neck to peer around him. "Last year and the one before that."

"You don't visit her between times?"

Her eyes flew wide. "No. How could I? What would I say? As far as Emilia knows, she is the natural daughter of the Hobarths." When a dark-haired girl the right age skittered past them, Nora started after her, but she stopped herself in mid-step. "That's not her."

"How can you be sure? Children change a good deal from year to year."

"Emilia has a strawberry mark above her right eyebrow. But truthfully, I usually recognize Mrs. Hobarth first. She's a slender little woman with a nose like a stork. But she has kind eyes."

"Do the Hobarths know you on sight?"

"No, they have no idea who I am. Everything was arranged by Mr. Trotter, my man of business. They receive their quarterly stipend through him."

He took her hand and tucked it possessively in the crook of his elbow. Her fingers trembled with nervousness. "How did you choose the Hobarths?"

"Before Emilia was born, Mr. Trotter arranged interviews with a number of potential guardians."

"And you trusted him to make this decision?"

She shook her head. "I listened to every conversation with prospective couples from behind a screen. I'm the one who chose Mr. and Mrs. Hobarth. She is barren, you see, and they desperately wanted a child. They have a tidy little farmstead. They're hardworking and honest, and they've been frugal with the moneys paid to them. Mr. Trotter says everything is used for my daughter's benefit. I've never regretted my decision."

Pierce knew that was a lie. Regret was etched in tiny lines around her eyes and in the firm set of her lips, but he let Nora's fib go unchallenged.

"More than that, they adore her," she went on. "If Emilia knows what it is to be loved, I'm satisfied."

"She just doesn't know *your* love."

"But *I* know it. She doesn't have to be aware of my love for it to be. Oh, there are the Hobarths now." A frown creased her brow.

Pierce followed the direction of her gaze and discovered a frantic-looking couple. He dropped his shield and over the hurdy-gurdy noise of the fair-goers' thoughts, he heard the Hobarths' minds churning furiously.

"They've lost her in the crowd," he said. "They don't know where she is."

Nora's hand went reflexively to her chest, and he was inundated by her panic.

"Steady on. This seems like a good little town. Emilia likely knows most of the people here. She's probably slipped away from her parents' side to play with her friends."

"They are not her parents. They are her guardians," Nora said fiercely. "I'm her parent. Her mother. Oh God. Where could she be?"

Pierce didn't know, but he knew someone who would. "We have to find Miss Anthony. She'll locate your girl."

Pierce strode across the green looking for Meg. One woman

looked very like another to him, except for Honora, of course.

There were a pair of ladies paused before the Punchinello show. One was a well-dressed matron in a pale blue pelisse and gown with a matching parasol to protect her fair complexion. The other lady was younger, judging from the slenderness of her waist. Her ensemble was just as fashionable, but her posture was slightly stooped, not nearly as confident as her older companion. A shovel-shaped bonnet obscured her features. Pierce wished he'd thought to mark the color of the ladies' ensembles before they'd parted ways earlier, but he was fairly sure they were Lady Easton and Meg. Then before he could reach them, a forceful thought broke through his shield.

I'll be damned. If it isn't Meg Jackson and in the flesh.

Pierce stopped near the puppet booth and heard frantic whispers from behind the curtain of the slapstick show.

"Did you see her?"

"See who?"

"Your cousin Meg, that's who. Look there through the slit in the curtain."

"Are you sure it's her?"

"Sure as there's a boil on my buttocks."

"It *is* her!"

"Too bloody right it is. Looks like she landed on her feet and no mistake."

"Do you suppose she's a companion or some such like for that other lady?"

"Could be. We need to find out who her ladyship is."

It sounded like the family Meg had run away from had finally caught up with her. If her uncle and cousin discovered Lady Easton's identity, they'd have a good idea where Meg was hiding from them. But Pierce couldn't worry about that now. Not with Lady Nora's Emilia missing.

He ran the rest of the way.

. . .

"Oh, dear, I don't think this is at all wise," Lady Easton said. "The duke specifically forbade you to use your gift until we discover a way for you to exercise it more safely."

"I know, but surely His Grace wouldn't mind if I just popped up and had a quick look round for a lost little girl," Meg said. "I'll *Find* her in a blink and be back before you can breathe twice."

"I doubt it'll be that fast," Pierce said. "You've never *Found* anything or anyone that easily."

You asked me to do it, ninny. You're supposed to be on my side.

Meg rolled her eyes at him as her thoughts rolled over him. So long as Emilia was missing, Pierce had lowered his shield completely in case he might overhear something of her whereabouts. So far, the voices of the fair clamored over one another, each more shrill than the last. Only those with whom he made eye contact tossed thoughts his way that could be discerned from the general commotion swirling around him.

He'd convinced Nora to remain at the glassblower's booth while he and the other two women had slipped into the makeshift lane behind the row of tradesmen. He'd explained to Nora that Miss Anthony could find Emilia, but he couldn't share Meg's method of doing so. Revealing the special ability of another Extraordinaire would violate the first rule in the Order of the M.U.S.E. and probably earn him expulsion from the duke's circle.

Convincing Meg to disregard a direct edict from Camden would likely lead to the same result, but he had to help Honora. Even though he wasn't with her, her panic washed over him in ever higher waves. Nora would be swamped in short order, reduced to piteous blubbering and not even able to tell anyone why.

"This is all highly irregular," Lady Easton said with a frustrated shake of her head. "Miss Anthony is usually seated comfortably when she enters her trance. Do you intend that she should slump on the grass?"

"No. I'll hold her." He suited his actions to his words, wrapping his arms around Meg and cradling her head against his chest so it wouldn't fall back once her spirit left her body.

"That'll do," Meg said. "If anyone happens by, they'll think we were having a lovers' tryst and have been caught at it by my chaperone. Emilia Hobarth, you say." He nodded confirmation of the missing child's name. Legally, the girl's name should have been Emilia Claremont, but Meg's *Finding* was tied to the name her subject was *known by*, which might not be their real name. Then before Lady Easton could raise any further objections, Meg said, "Wish me luck."

Her body went limp and boneless as a cat. A fairly heavy cat. Pierce was unprepared for the sudden dead weight in his arms. He held his own breath, counting off the seconds while Meg's essence flew free. Then as his lungs began to burn, she gasped and straightened back on her own two feet.

"She's playing by the river," Meg said.

"Is anyone with her?"

Meg shook her head. "Last I saw, she was peeling off her

shoes and stockings. Hurry."

• • •

As soon as Pierce told her where her daughter was, Nora lifted her hem, the better to run from the level green of the fair to the slope where the river wound around the village's edge. Rivers were dicey things. One moment they were placid and friendly, the next they'd tug unsuspecting waders down and carry them away. Emilia was only five and petite for her age, at that. She'd be nothing for the water to swallow in one gulp.

Pierce ran on ahead of her, leaving her to flail after him. He didn't stop for the thick woods and crashed through the tangled underbrush, barreling toward the water.

During the rare times when Nora allowed herself to think about Emilia, she always pictured her happy and sheltered. A perfect child in a perfect setting. The Emilia in her mind wore a perpetual angelic smile. She never dirtied the hem of her pristine gowns and always took her tea with her little pinky properly out. Nothing threatened her placid life in an idyllic home. Now Nora realized how false, how deceptive, that image was.

Emilia was a flesh-and-blood child. Fragile. Breakable.

Nora had lost her when she gave her care over to the Hobarths, but having the phantom Emilia had helped to deaden the pain. She could take her perfect imagined daughter and visualize the march of happy years ahead for her. Perhaps in the future, when she was grown, Nora might find a way to make her acquaintance and get to know her, in truth.

But Nora had nothing of her now. And *now* was all anyone ever had. If they didn't reach her in time, Emilia might not have much more *now*.

Nora would lose her afresh. A sob tore from her throat.

She couldn't see Pierce any longer, but she could hear him fighting his way through the heavy growth. The snapping and crackling of timber stopped and the air was rent by a high, thin wail. Then the scream ceased abruptly, like a thread snipped off by a pair of shears.

Women seem to be born into this world with a well-developed sense of what they want. Whatever their age, a man thwarts their designs at his peril.

~From the secret journal of Pierce Langdon,
Viscount Westfall

Chapter Sixteen

"Hold still," Pierce ordered the squirming child in his dripping arms. If she didn't settle, he was likely to drop her back into the brown water. Granted, she was already doused from head to toe, so it wasn't as if he could save her muslin gown. But the river was so thick with sediment, if she slipped under the surface again, he might not find her a second time.

"I want to see ducks!" Emilia protested.

"You can see ducks from the bank," he said as he slogged toward the shore. After his cruel treatments while he was in Bedlam, Pierce had a healthy respect for water and its power. But he hadn't paused at the river's edge when he first saw the little girl tumble into it. He had followed her into the spate without question. His footing shifted on the slippery rocks beneath him. The current tugged at his thighs, and he tensed with each step.

Emilia balled her fist and pounded his chest. "You are a mean, mean man."

"If it's mean not to allow you to drown, then I whole-heartedly concur. I am the meanest man alive."

The little girl started blubbering, which was much worse than having her call him names and pummel him. Tears streamed down her ruddy cheeks, and she shook in his arms.

How does one deal with children?

He opened his mind to hers and discovered that despite her bluster, she was not angry. Emilia was terrified. Pierce held her more tightly.

"You're all right. I've got you. We'll find your parents, and everything will be fine."

"No, it won't," she said with a sniff and a fresh round of tears. "Mamma will be mad because I soiled my new frock."

"She may well be," he said agreeably, which earned him a fresh pounding. "Women put a great deal of store in fripperies and such, but she'd be much more upset if you'd been swept away. A frock can be replaced. You cannot."

Emilia stopped knocking on his chest and swiped her eyes with the back of her little hand. "You think so?"

"I know so," Pierce assured her. Honora burst through the undergrowth and stood wringing her hands as they advanced toward the shore. Her relief crashed over him in palpable waves. "Your mamma loves you very much."

"Papa, too?"

"How could he not?"

Nora's face was etched with longing as she stumbled down to the muddy edge of the river, her arms outstretched to receive the child from him.

But before he could reach Nora, another couple came scuffling through the woods, breaking off saplings in their haste and calling Emilia's name. The man and woman burst through the thick greenery.

"Mamma!" the child sang out. "Papa, I'm here."

The woman scrambled down the embankment and pushed in front of Nora to snatch Emilia from Pierce's arms. Nora stepped back several paces, her expression stricken. Mrs. Hobarth hugged the little girl as if she'd never let her go.

Pierce watched Nora, amazed that the Hobarths didn't seem to notice her intensity. Her longing to hold her daughter was so sharp, it was a wonder she didn't prick herself on it and bleed all over the shoreline.

"Oh, Emilia, you wicked child, we were that worried, weren't we, Mr. H.?" But Mrs. Hobarth's tone belied her stern words. The woman fought back tears as she gave the girl a slight shake. "You mustn't wander off. Promise you'll never do that to your father and me again."

Mr. Hobarth pumped Pierce's hand, spouting his thanks in a flurry of grateful, sometimes incoherent, appreciation. When the couple took their leave, Emilia was between them, her hands firmly held by both adults.

"Well, they've had quite a scare," Pierce said as he sat on a driftwood log and tugged off his wet boots. "I doubt she'll slip away from them so easily again."

Mutely, Nora sank down beside him, her gaze glued to the opposite bank of the river. She knotted her fingers together so tightly, her knuckles went white. Once Pierce emptied the water from his boots and set them aside, he took her hands. They were icy, despite the warmth of the day.

A single tear glided down her cheek.

"I didn't get to hold her. You were coming toward me with her and I thought I'd...just once...only for a little while…" She turned her face away from him, as if that could hide her pain. "It wasn't too much to ask, was it?"

He shook his head. "No, it wasn't."

"I didn't hold her when she was born, you know. The midwife said it would be best not to. She was probably right. I couldn't have let her go otherwise." Nora covered her face with her hands and sobbed. "But who would it hurt if I held her now?"

"You," he said softly. "Because you'd still have to let her go."

He put his arm around her waist, and she turned back to him to lean her head on his shoulder. She shook with grief, but she made no sound. All her sorrow was bottled inside.

More than anything he wanted to fix this for her. That was what it meant to be a man, wasn't it? He was supposed to solve problems and make the world a good place, a safe place for those he loved. His questionable sanity hadn't made him someone anyone could depend upon for that sort of protection. Until now.

He ached for Nora to trust him with this.

The words blurted out of his mouth before he thought them through. "You should marry me."

"I should what?"

"Marry me," he said firmly. "I'll hire the right solicitor, and he'll arrange to void whatever agreement your man of business made with the Hobarths. I have a country estate. Emilia could come to live with us. Fresh air, sunshine, everything a growing child needs. She could even have a pony."

She sat up straight and met his gaze, a bit of wonderment in her expression as if she were seeing him clearly for the first time. Then a tremulous smile lifted her lips, and she palmed his cheeks. "You dear man, if only it were that simple."

"Why isn't it?"

"Because while it would be wonderful for me to have her, it wouldn't be the best thing for my daughter. My reputation would taint her. Besides, after seeing Emilia with the Hobarths, I couldn't take her from them. She loves them and they love her. Being torn from the only home she's ever known would be devastating. I may be many things, but I hope I'm not that selfish."

Nora knew what it was to be exiled from home, and it was something to consider before totally upending a child's world. But it pricked his feelings that she focused exclusively on how his proposal would affect Emilia. Didn't it mean anything to her that he wanted to marry her?

Perhaps if he solved this problem, she'd come round to the idea of marrying him. He could hire the Hobarths to work on his country estate in some capacity. If they all came to live there, Nora could watch her daughter grow to adulthood and become part of her world without disrupting her attachment to the Hobarths. He was about to suggest this alternate proposal, when Nora rose to her feet.

"Besides, I can't marry you, Pierce. What would happen to Benedick if I did?"

A heavy weight lodged in his chest. She cared more about her patron than she did him. "Albemarle would simply find a new mistress to hide behind."

"That's just it. He'd be taking a terrible risk by sharing his secret with yet another person." She began to pace along the riverbank. "He frequently has to deal with rumors over this issue, but gossip and sworn testimony are two different things. Participating in unnatural acts is a capital offense, you know. If the rumors were proved true, they'd hang him, for sure."

Pierce frowned at that. It didn't seem fair. Why were some loves sanctioned and others labeled unnatural? Wasn't love the same emotion no matter who was involved? And wasn't it rare enough for two souls to find each other that it ought to be celebrated each time it happened?

As if they'd conjured him by speaking his name, Lord Albemarle appeared farther down the river. His Grace walked by his side.

"Ah, I see Benedick is touting his plans to the duke." Nora stopped pacing.

"What plans?"

"This river changes too much with the seasons to be navigable year around. Benedick means to see a canal dug through this area and needs His Grace to support the effort in the House of Lords."

"That sounds like a good scheme," Pierce said woodenly. It irked him to say anything positive about Albemarle since the baron's needs seemed to be instrumental in keeping Nora from agreeing to marry him. "A canal would certainly benefit the village."

"True, though it will benefit Albemarle and his friends more. They've already formed a consortium and bought up the land along the proposed route."

How like a politician. Doing good on one hand while making good with the other. Pierce decided to take another tack and at least accomplish something positive for the Order.

"You fear he'll hang if his secret passions are unmasked, but just as surely, Lord Albemarle is risking hanging if he uses the *Fides Pulvis* on the Prince Regent. If you care about

Albemarle as much as you claim, you'd steal that powder and replace it with something less virulent."

"I could never betray Albemarle's trust like that." She sank down beside him again. "You don't understand how much he's done for me."

"Yes, yes, he makes it possible for you to provide for your daughter. I know."

"That's only part of it," she said. "He also saved me from having to sell myself again and again. Before him, I couldn't seem to keep a patron for longer than six months."

"Because your heart wasn't in it," Pierce said.

"Well, that's part of the whole arrangement, isn't it? Heaven help the courtesan who falls in love," she said defensively. "At any rate, when I hit a rough patch between patrons, my mentor in the business decided an auction would be the best way to relaunch me in demimonde society."

"Plenty of men would pay handsomely to use the daughter of an earl."

She looked at him sharply. "I wasn't going to put it that bluntly, but you're right. And plenty did bid high. If Benedick hadn't outbid them all, who knows how many lovers I'd have had by now?" She covered one of his hands with hers. "I may have the reputation of being a high flyer, but my protectors have actually been few and, until I met you, I've taken no man to my bed without a signed contract since my husband died."

So, she hadn't known so many men, after all. Pierce had decided that he could lay her livelihood aside, that it didn't matter to him, but the knowledge that she'd given herself willingly to him, and only him, pleased him out of all knowing. "I suppose I must be grateful to Lord Albemarle too, then."

"Yes, you must. Besides, it's not as if he *wants* to use the *Fides Pulvis* on the Prince Regent. He hasn't much choice as long as his enemies are in possession of some incriminating letters he wrote to an old lover."

So Albemarle was being blackmailed. "Have you any idea who has the letters?"

She nodded. "His Italian lover. And to make matters worse, the man is actually on English soil. His name is Falco."

A waterlogged memory nudged Pierce's brain. "*Dr. Falco?*"

"Yes," she said, eyeing him quizzically. "When they parted, Benedick left him with enough money to learn a trade, and he became a doctor. You see why I can't turn my back on him? Benedick is unfailingly generous. I don't know what I'd do without his patronage."

Marry me, Pierce thought desperately. He could be generous, too. If she wouldn't accept his love, why wouldn't she at least accept his help?

Maybe she could, he decided. If she didn't know he was giving it.

Pierce asked me to marry him today. No, that's not strictly correct. He said I should *marry him, as if a man's bald order is likely to move a woman to accept his proposal. But that's not why I turned him down. When Lewis proposed, I took no thought for the problems that might rear up to meet us. With Pierce, they are all I can see.*

Yet the real objection is not one I voiced to him. You see, with my first love, my heart was boundless. I gave freely out of a well which I thought would never run dry.

Now I'm a desert. It's not that I don't have feelings for Pierce. I assuredly do. But my heart is so shriveled, so desiccated, I can't offer it to him.

He deserves so much more.

~from the secret journal of Lady Nora
Claremont

Chapter Seventeen

Albion Abbey started as a refuge for a group of Franciscan monks who had invaded England with the gospel and a vow of poverty in the thirteenth century. Known as the Greyfriars, they had settled in London and then quickly spread out into the countryside. In keeping with the Order's commitment to austerity, the abbey had been designed simply, a square around a central cloister with the little jewel of a Gothic chapel in the middle of its northern arm.

When Lord Albemarle had acquired the abbey, he had removed all suggestion of poverty. The cells which had served as guest rooms were decorated with rich fabrics and elegant furnishings, with no expense spared to make them into oases of comfort for his lordship's guests.

However, Pierce could not get comfortable in his.

His problem was not one that would be solved by a thick feather tick. His difficulty was caused by architecture.

His room was too far from where he needed to be.

All the men's guest rooms were on the west side of the structure, while the ladies were housed on the eastern arm. They were separated by the large formal dining room and opulent parlors on the south and the imposing chapel on the north. Pierce knotted his banyan at his waist, decided to abandon the interior of the abbey, and slipped into the cloister so he could move along the covered porticos that ringed the open-to-the-sky courtyard in the center of the square structure.

His Grace and Lord Albemarle were still sipping sherry in one of the lighted rooms to the south, so Pierce opted for a northerly route, past the nail-studded door of the chapel. When he reached the door that should have let him enter the women's section of the abbey, he found it locked.

He was philosophical about the setback. Whether he entered by the door that led to the corridor outside the women's cells or by a window that opened to the courtyard, the lady would have to admit him in any case.

He wished it was Honora's room he sought. He ached to hold her. Ached to love her so well, she wouldn't keep saying no to his proposal. But if he couldn't prove his worth to her outside of her bed, he doubted he'd win a permanent place in it.

So he was looking for Meg Anthony.

Pierce lowered his shield and let the minds in the abbey flood into his. In the distant kitchen, the cook and the scullery maid were at odds with each other. Their argument about who let the white soup burn was over, but their thoughts were still hot enough to singe off each other's eyebrows. In the opulent parlor, His Grace was weighing Lord Albemarle's proposals and finding them a witch's brew of benefit to others and self-serving schemes. He could hear nothing of Lady Easton and surmised that she must be asleep.

From Nora, he felt barely contained frustration.

He tried to push her thoughts away. She wouldn't want him listening to them in any case, and if he sensed she needed him it would be that much harder not to go straight to her. Besides, she seemed to be at a greater distance from him than he expected.

Meg Anthony's mind was much nearer. Just on the other side of the nearest window, in fact. And she was desperately worried.

He rapped on the pane softly. When she came to peer out, he stepped into the light of her candle. Meg quickly set it down and opened the sash.

"Lord Westfall, what are you doing here?"

"Coming to see you, Miss Anthony. With your permission, of course."

Her gaze darted down the long row of windows that opened onto the cloister. "If I let you into my chamber, Lady Easton will have my head."

"Whether or not you admit me, most likely the outcome will be the same. I'm told even the appearance of impropriety is as injurious as actual—"

"Oh, for pity's sake, come in," Meg whispered furiously as she motioned for him to enter. "If I'm going to get into trouble in any case, I may as well deserve it."

He climbed through the low window and thanked her as she closed it and drew the damask drapes behind him.

"Now what do you want?" she demanded, arms crossed over her chest.

"First, I'm most grateful to you for finding the child today. It took courage to go against the duke's orders."

She waved away his thanks. "I'd do it again in a heartbeat." Then an impish smile turned her plain face almost pretty, and she indicated he should sit in one of the two frilly Sheridan chairs. "Besides, what the duke don't know won't hurt me."

"But you're worried about something that will," Pierce said as he took the seat she offered after she settled into the other one. "Perhaps someone, to be more precise."

She cast a slant-eyed gaze at him. "Have you been invading my mind?"

"Only long enough to locate you. However, I couldn't help but sense your dismay. How may I be of help?"

"I don't know that you can. You see, I saw someone today from my past and I didn't relish the sight. It was the uncle and cousin I ran away from."

Pierce narrowly resisted smacking his forehead. In the panic of trying to find Emilia, he'd forgotten to tell Meg about the conversation he'd overheard by the Punchinello show. "Did you tell His Grace?"

"No. I'm hoping Uncle Rowney didn't see me. Or if he did, that he didn't recognize me."

"I'm sorry to say that he must have," Pierce said. "I overheard the puppeteers discussing you. They not only knew you, they marked the fact that you were in Lady Easton's company."

"Then they'll be able to find me without much trouble."

"Even so, you are safer than houses in His Grace's care."

"That's true. How did Uncle Rowney and Oswald ever recognize me?" She glanced toward the long mirror over her vanity. "Honestly, sometimes, I don't know myself in the fancy things His Grace expects me to wear."

"The gown you wore today was very becoming," he said, because he'd been told that women liked to hear that sort of thing. He was rewarded with another of Meg Anthony's rare smiles.

"You didn't risk my reputation to come tell me that," she said. "I know you fancy Lady Nora."

"How do you know that?"

"I may not be able to hear your thoughts, but I have eyes. And yours never leave her if she's anywhere near. Now, why are you here, your lordship?"

Now that they came to it, he hesitated. Meg took a horrible risk each time she exercised her gift. It seemed the height of selfishness for him to ask it of her—especially since not much time had elapsed since the last time he needed her help.

"I need you to *Find* something for me," he admitted.

To his relief, Meg didn't seem distressed. If anything, excitement prickled from her. He'd heard some folk enjoyed dancing close to the edge of a precipice. Miss Anthony must be one of those who needed the spice of danger to feel truly alive.

"Is it something for the Order of the M.U.S.E.?" she asked.

"Yes."

"Does the duke know you're asking me to *Find* it?"

"No."

"That's a bit of stickiness then. I feel as if I dodged a bullet this afternoon with His Grace. Even though it was to find a lost child, I fear what he'd say if he knew I'd disobeyed him," she said. "Do you think he'd agree to me doing a search for you if we lay the matter before him?"

"No. He values you too much to risk you."

She shot him a wry grin. "And you don't."

"That's not true. I think very highly of you. I wouldn't ask this of you if I could find the information any other way." Then he explained what he sought and where she was likely to find it. After she pinpointed its location, the rest would be up to him. If he told His Grace his plans, the duke wouldn't approve them either. It was a risk only Pierce could take.

And he was determined to take it.

• • •

Meg Anthony had learned something about using her gift when she searched for Emilia that afternoon, she told Pierce. Instead of sitting apart from others while she slipped into her trance, having him hold her helped anchor her soul more firmly to her house of flesh.

"It seemed to strengthen the spiritual tether I use to find my way home and made it easier than usual for me to zip back to my body," she explained. "His Grace should be pleased about that."

Still, because the item Pierce asked her to locate was at a greater distance than the lost girl had been, he wasn't comforted by her assurance, at first.

"You don't understand," she explained. "Distance is not something that matters so much once I'm flying free. Everything happens quick as a thought in the realm of pure spirit. That's how I can cover so much ground. And it may seem as if I'm gone for a long time to you, but to me, it's like a blink."

"Therein lies your danger. You can't sense how your spirit's absence is affecting your body. I wish there were a way I could warn you when you've been gone too long.

"I don't know how you could," she said. "But let's not fret about it now. The sooner I go, the sooner I'll be back with your answers."

Pierce held his breath as she slumped in his arms, cursing himself for asking this of her. The place he'd asked her to search was so big, with so many nooks and crannies and hidey-holes. How would she ever find it quickly enough to stay safe?

He let the air escape from his lungs slowly. Still, she didn't return. He fought against the urge to inhale.

Come back, Meg.

He imagined himself in the water chair again, trying not to breathe lest his lungs fill with liquid. Panic crept along his spine on little spidery legs.

If anything happened to Miss Anthony, the duke would never forgive him. He'd never forgive himself.

Then, just as despair threatened to swamp him, she jerked to full awareness. Meg stared at him wide-eyed for about the space of ten heartbeats. Then her little face crumpled, and she wept uncontrollably for a good five minutes.

"I'm so sorry, your lordship. I had no idea." She blew her nose like a trumpet into a neatly embroidered handkerchief and swiped her eyes on the sleeve of her wrapper. "That place you had me search, it was… Well, I always figured there was a Hell. I just didn't think it was here on earth."

Pierce nodded grimly. He should have warned her, but she wouldn't have believed the horrors she'd encounter if she hadn't seen them for herself. "Did you find it?"

To his great relief, she nodded and launched into a detailed description of where the item was. He'd be able to retrieve it, if the rest of his plan bore fruit. He thanked her and headed for the window.

"Are you thinking about going in there to get it?" she asked as he climbed out.

He nodded. "More than thinking. I plan to do it. Don't tell His Grace."

"I must." She grasped his forearm to stop him.

"Then I shall be forced to tell him that you ignored his explicit orders not to use your gift, not once, but twice."

Meg glared at him. "You wouldn't."

"Don't try me, Miss Anthony. I never learned to bluff."

"Then I'm sorry I helped you, Westfall."

As the window banged down behind him, he was a little sorry, too. Not only had he angered one of the few people he might consider a friend, now he was honor-bound to act on the knowledge she'd given him.

He walked slowly around the perimeter of the cloister toward his chamber. The moon had risen, painting the statue of St. Francis in the center of the open space in shades of gray. He wandered out to study the art, wondering at the placid, sightless eyes of the saint staring unconcernedly into the distance. Was the real Francis's soul truly that peaceful?

Saints weren't supposed to love their lives so much they were afraid to hazard them. Pierce was no saint, though he wasn't afraid to die. But in this case, more than his life would be at risk.

He feared for his mind.

They say that Lucifer is armed with temptations aplenty, but I think there's only one thing that tempts him—human happiness. If we are happy or think we will be, the devil turns his minions loose to wreak havoc in our lives with redoubled efforts.

Perhaps that's why I've always been warned against wanting something too much.

~from the secret journal of Pierce Langdon,
Viscount Westfall

Chapter Eighteen

As soon as he opened the door to his cell, he was nearly knocked over by an intruder.

"Where have you been?" Nora said as she wrapped her arms around him and hugged him close. "I've been waiting for you."

She didn't wait for him to answer. Instead she pulled his head down for a long kiss. She didn't really want to talk. She wanted him.

He was more than happy to give himself to her. When he opened his mind to hers, only thoughts of him rushed in to greet him. Her mind was full of him, pressed down and overflowing. He was determined to fill the rest of her, too.

The first time they took each other that night, it was hard and fast. She didn't seem to want nuanced lovemaking from him. She was looking for something primal. Her touch was tinged with the same urgency he'd sensed from her while they had searched for Emilia. An emptiness demanding to be filled. She was welcome to all that he was, and he gave himself without reservation, pumping away with abandon for the sheer animal joy of rutting.

Spent and gasping, they clung to each other. Then, he took her slowly, savoring every inch of her. He drew out her climb till she ground her teeth in frustration. When he finally let her come, he covered her mouth with his hand to stifle her cry of release.

He knew without being told that as much as she wanted him, she wanted just as fervently not to be discovered in his bed.

Then they lay together, simply being still without speaking, for hours, snuggled close, touching lightly with hands and lips, reassuring each other of their bond. They had no need for words. Their bodies had said what was needful.

You are mine. I am yours. There is no space in between that we cannot fill with the glorious us.

Honora drifted to sleep in his arms.

Pierce didn't let himself follow her into oblivion. He didn't want to miss a moment of being with her. Even though he couldn't pry into her dreams, he sensed she was content, perhaps for the first time in years. Her happiness wrapped itself around his mind, caressing, soothing, calming him.

Just watching her sleep rested him. He wished he could look forward to a lifetime of lying beside her. Wished he could put his ring on her finger. Whether he would be allowed to or not was an open question, so he let it go as one of many things beyond his control.

Instead, he tried to commit every bit of this night to memory. He might need the comfort of such remembrance in the days to come.

As the moon set and the eastern sky began to lighten to pearl gray, he kissed her brow, and she stirred.

"Hello, you," she said, her tone sultry as she rolled toward him.

Pierce began to peel back the sheet to expose her luscious skin to the last of the moonlight streaming in his window. "Hello, you. Look what I discovered—an angel in my bed." He ran his thumb along the edge of the sheet, skimming under her breasts, then along her ribs and the curve of her waist.

"I'm no angel." She ran a hand down his flat belly and cupped his genitals.

"You are to me."

She leaned over and nipped his earlobe. "Allow me to convince you otherwise."

Her kiss swallowed up his laugh.

When will the man get on with it? Her thoughts were tight, as though she were thinking them with clenched teeth.

Not yet. Pierce nuzzled between her legs, drunk on her scent. He was desperate to draw this loving out, but equally desperate to sink into her sweet flesh and find release.

He knew it was the last time they'd be together for a long while. He wouldn't let himself think forever. He had to make it go on a little longer.

Nora arched herself into his mouth. He devoured her and didn't stop until he thought he detected the slightest pulse of a contraction in the soft lips of her sex.

When he pulled back, she moaned low in the back of her throat. His balls tightened in response to her need.

He moved up her body, poised to slide into her wet heat. His cock screamed at him to hurry.

It was past time.

He rushed in with one long stroke, and she molded around him in a warm, slick embrace. His balls drew up into a tense mound, coiled for release as pressure built in his shaft. He held himself motionless, willing the urgency to subside so he could revel in the joy of Nora a little longer. Only a little. His heartbeat pounded in his cock.

Her mouth gaped softly. Her brows tented in distress. He couldn't keep her suspended within finger-widths of her release. He couldn't withhold pleasure from her any longer. He loved her too much to keep any good thing from her. He had to let her go.

He covered her mouth with his and flicked his tongue in, loving her with his tongue and his cock in tandem. She moved beneath him, urging him in deeper with little noises of desperation that shredded his control.

He pounded into her as deeply as he could. Then he felt it start, a frenzy of pulsing.

Now, Nora, now.

Pierce arched his back, driving in as his life shot into her in a steady rhythm. Her walls contracted around him. It was like being born, only backward, trying to come in instead of fighting his way out.

She was his center. The source of all that was good and right and whole.

Her body convulsed under him. When it was over, he slumped down on her, breathing her air, inhaling her musky sweetness to his toes. Her chest rose and fell under his. Then he lifted his weight onto his elbows.

"Nora, I…"

She snored softly. She'd slipped off to asleep again. He'd unraveled her every kink and she'd sunk back into blissful slumber, too fully relaxed to maintain consciousness.

He'd meant to tell her he loved her again. Well, he supposed she knew. And if she didn't believe him now, she would hereafter.

He stood and began dressing in the dark. He was dimly aware that the euphoria of loving Nora had dissipated. He shut down, experiencing no feelings at all, save for the numbing despair that stole over him. If his plan didn't work, he'd lose everything, starting with Nora and his chance to be useful to the Order.

And ending with himself.

Pierce managed to saddle a horse and slip out of Lord Albemarle's stable without attracting any attention from the groomsmen. It bothered him that he was technically stealing his mount but, when weighed in the balance against the greater good, a little larceny was a small matter.

With any luck, Nora would think he'd risen early to ride before she tiptoed back to her own chamber. When he didn't appear at breakfast, it would cause no undo comment. He often took a tray alone, waiting until the evening to brave the company of other minds. He'd have most of the day to put as much distance between himself and Albion Abbey as he could.

Once they realized he was missing, he was counting on them believing he'd returned to Camden House in London and sending someone to search for him there. He could depend on Meg Anthony's silence. The last thing she wanted was to incur the duke's wrath by admitting she'd disobeyed him. And Meg was the only one who knew his ultimate destination.

But even Meg didn't know the route he intended to take to reach it. No one would expect him to return to Westphalia and his uncle's untender welcome.

His family's countryseat was two days distance from Albion Abbey, but he didn't stop at an inn when night fell. Instead, he turned aside from the deserted road, hobbled his mount, and slept in an open field. For his purposes, if he arrived in a less than well-turned-out state, so much the better.

At the end of his second day of travel, when he crested the final rise and saw the manor house in the distance, he expected to feel something about his return. After all, he'd grown up there. Been hidden away there, in truth, since his parents had kept him at home long past the age when other boys were off to school. They had protected him, he realized, and had been anxious to keep his unusual condition from becoming public knowledge. From the chalk hills in the east to the silver strip of river that defined the western boundary of the lands attached to the viscountcy, Westphalia had been his whole world.

But it didn't seem all that familiar. Instead, it was as if he'd never seen the ash grove, never played in the hollows and hills, never learned to ride in the paddock or do his sums in the third floor schoolroom of the staid, Tudor-style manor house. Even the fateful oak, the one he'd fallen from that had started the voices clamoring in his head, seemed like any other hundred-year-old leafy giant.

Westphalia was just a place. And even though the estate was technically his, he felt no pride in it, no surge of warmth for the land stretching out around the brick and mortar manor.

Perhaps when he saw a familiar face.

But there were none to be found. He was ushered into his own home by a stiff-lipped butler he'd never seen before, who looked down his long nose at him when Pierce announced himself as Lord Westfall. Of course, the general scruffiness of his person didn't lend credibility to his claim. However, he was asked to wait in the parlor while the butler fetched someone who could meet with him.

The someone turned out to be his Aunt Beatrice instead of his Uncle Horace.

"Oh, my!" the little bird of a woman said when she saw him. However, she recovered quickly and skittered across the room to him like a sandpiper running along the shore. She extended a frail hand, palm down. The veins stood out on it like a meandering map of her life. Pierce bowed over it correctly.

"Hello, Auntie. It's lovely to see you again."

"Er, likewise, I'm sure," she said, sounding not at all certain. She indicated that he should sit in one of the wing chairs and perched on the settee herself. It had been his mother's favorite piece, but Aunt Beatrice had re-covered it in an abominable floral pattern whose loud colors made Pierce's stomach queasy. She rang for tea and made innocuous comments about the weather while they waited for the snooty butler to bring a tray. When it arrived, Pierce fell on the finger sandwiches and petit fours as if he hadn't eaten in two days, which he hadn't.

His aunt sputtered her amazement at his gauche behavior, but didn't take him to task. Instead, she took refuge in the homely ritual of pouring out tea for both of them.

"Milk and sugar, if you please," Pierce said. "Four lumps."

Her eyes flared at the excess, but he supposed the more imbalanced he seemed, the quicker matters would progress.

"We understood you were in London with His Grace, the Duke of Camden," she said cautiously. "Of course, we have been concerned that your...medical treatment had been suspended, but the duke sent us every assurance that you'd be well cared for." She narrowed her eyes at his lapel where a foxtail was firmly embedded in the fabric. Clearly, she didn't feel the duke had lived up to his part of the bargain. "Your uncle will be so...surprised to see you."

"I expect he will. I'll be surprised to see him, too." Pierce licked the excess icing from one of the sweets off his fingers and then wiped his hands on his shirtfront. "Never thought we'd meet again in this life after he sent me off to Bedlam."

Appalled at his lack of manners, his aunt stared as if he'd sprouted a second head.

"About that..." She took a fortifying sip of her tea. "You must understand. Your uncle thought it best at the time."

"Best for him, you mean."

"No, dear boy. Best for you. How else will you ever get well?"

Her thoughts were like squirrels chasing each other around a tree trunk. Pierce struggled to catch one by the tail.

"Don't worry. Just because I'm back home, it doesn't mean I'll put you and my cousins out, Auntie," he assured her. "I'm not the vindictive sort."

But his uncle was. Horace Langdon ruled over the viscountcy in Pierce's absence like some decadent pasha, master of all he surveyed. He treated his family with the same heavy-handed domination.

"You needn't fret about that other thing, either, Aunt Beatrice."

"What other thing?"

"I can't see the bruises he left on your arm through your sleeve and neither can anyone else."

Her right hand covered her left forearm reflexively. "How did you—"

"You were thinking about how hot a day it is and what a shame it was that you'd have to wear long sleeves at supper this evening."

Her brows shot up. "Then you still think you can hear the thoughts of others."

"I don't think it. I know it. And so do you. I'm not mad," he said firmly. "I'm just different."

Her gaze swept the floor. "No, I won't believe it."

Pierce slurped up the last of his tea. "Well, you will when I move back in and take my rightful place."

Her spine straightened at that. She'd been kindly disposed toward him when she thought him helpless. Now he threatened not only her husband, but her children. There might not be any love lost between her and Pierce's uncle, but she was like a sow bear when it came to her offspring. With Pierce out of the way, her son would someday be Viscount Westfall.

"We'll see what your uncle has to say about that."

"So we shall." Pierce stood and stretched. "Dinner at eight, I assume. In the meantime, I'd like a place to rest."

"Not to put too fine a point on it, nephew, but your travels have not been kind to you or your wardrobe. Clean clothes and a bath would not come amiss, either." She bared her teeth at him. He did not mistake the expression for a smile. Then she rang for the butler again. "Mr. Dickens will sort you out. Ah, there he is. Show Lord Westfall to the Blue Room, if you please."

"No need. I'll just claim my old chamber, if it's all the same to you," Pierce said as he stood, sketched a quick bow, and strode out.

He ought to have felt a hole being bored into his retreating back. If looks could indeed kill, his aunt's glare should have reduced him to a quivering puddle. He heard the virulent, whispered conversation behind him as he walked away.

"Shall I tell Cook to set another place for dinner?" the butler asked.

"No need," she said. "I doubt my nephew will be staying that long."

It is said that no matter how close, no matter how intimate one's relationships, we never really know another because we are not privy to their secret thoughts.

But Pierce knew mine.

And knowing how I feel about him, how could he have vanished into thin air without a word?

~from the secret journal of Lady Nora Claremont

Chapter Nineteen

"I'm that sorry, yer lordship, but we can't find Lord Westfall anywheres." The head groom ran the brim of his thoroughly disreputable hat through his thick, work-roughened fingers, clearly distraught at having to bring Albemarle this unwelcome news. "We had the lads out beating the bushes all night. If he'd run into mischief here at Albion, we'd have found him. I'll lay my best shirt, he's not on the estate no longer."

Albemarle eyed his employee critically. Losing this man's best shirt would not be much of a loss but, poor grammar and personal habits aside, Harkins was an honest sort. If he said Westfall had quit Albion Abbey, he surely had. Nora hoped Benedick wouldn't be harsh with the groom. It wasn't his fault Pierce was missing.

The man shifted his weight from one foot to the other.

"I take it there is something you have not yet told me. Spit it out, man," Albemarle demanded.

"Your piebald Thoroughbred is gone, as well." Harkins

winced as he spoke the words. "I don't know how it happened, my lord. No one never heard Lord Westfall in the stable so I can't say when he made off with the gelding."

"So you're suggesting one of my guests stole a horse?"

"No, no, o' course not. Well, not exactly. I'd never accuse his lordship's guest of such a thing. But it seems both Lord Westfall and the gelding have gone missing at the same time, so it's hard not to jump to conclusions, if you see what I mean," Harkins said, clearly distressed. "When we noticed the horse gone yesterday morning, we assumed you'd given Lord Westfall permission to ride whenever he chose."

"Rightly assumed. And since the viscount is no horse thief, we must also assume Lord Westfall has met with foul play. Extend your search, Mr. Harkins, to include His Grace's property. Perhaps Westfall decided to ride back to Camden End. Off you go." He waved his groom away and sank into the chair behind his desk.

"I shall send Mr. LeGrand to London," the duke said from the wing chair before the cold fireplace. The continuous drumming of his fingers on the arm of the chair belied the air of calm His Grace tried to project. "We must consider that Lord Westfall might have returned to Camden House. He is most at home in the conservatory there."

"I thought he was enjoying the country," Lady Easton said from the opposite end of the chintz settee from Nora. Miss Anthony, who was seated between them, contributed nothing to the discussion. "Didn't you think so, Lady Nora?"

Nora nodded mutely. Pierce had seemed happy. Fewer voices, he'd said. And since His Grace's party had moved to Albion Abbey, she and Pierce were close enough to be able to steal away together. He'd loved her to exhaustion last night and then had let her sleep in his arms. She'd never felt so safe.

Now she'd never felt so betrayed. Her left knee jittered under her gown, and she was unable to stop its constant motion without concerted effort. Where could the man be?

She had thought it strange that he left her sleeping in his bed, but Pierce was unlike any man she'd ever known. He must have had his reasons. She assumed an early morning constitutional was at the heart of his disappearance from her side.

Nora wasn't surprised when he didn't appear for breakfast, but after luncheon, she began to make discreet inquiries of the servants. None of them had seen him since he retired the night before. When he couldn't be found for dinner, she made Albemarle launch a search, but by then Pierce had been missing for more than twelve hours.

And she couldn't shake the feeling that if only she'd told him what was in her heart, if she'd admitted that she loved him, he'd have told her his plans.

Or if she'd have accepted his awkward suggestion that she marry him, perhaps he wouldn't have disappeared at all.

• • •

His cheek scraped against rough wood. When he lifted his head, the stickiness and the coppery tang of blood in the stuffy compartment made him realize he'd been in that position a long time. His cheek had been rubbed against the wood hard enough to abrade the skin and start it bleeding.

Pierce struggled back to full awareness, but nothing made any sense. A strange jostling motion rattled his teeth and made every joint in his body ache. He couldn't move any of his limbs.

He forced his eyes open, but the small space in which he was confined was so dark, he was no better informed than if he'd kept them shut. He seemed to be in some sort of enclosed conveyance because he could feel every bump in the road they traveled. However, there were no tufted squabs to sit upon, no curtained windows to gaze through. The cart was obviously not designed to transport human beings.

His last coherent memory was of settling into a steaming hip bath to let the road dirt soak off. Mr. Dickens had left a tumbler with two fingers of whiskey on a small table for him to enjoy as he bathed, a gesture he had found particularly civilized. He thought it less civilized now. The drink had obviously been laced with some sort of opiate.

He supposed he should have been grateful that his uncle and aunt hadn't simply drowned him in the tub. Then he remembered where they were likely sending him. Even though he'd counted on this reaction from them when he came up with the plan, dreaming up a risky scheme and actually going through with it were two different things. He decided it was sensible not to be too grateful to his aunt and uncle.

Lying on his side, he realized that he'd been restrained as well as drugged. The straightjacket cut into his armpits and the tether binding his ankles forced him to bend his knees and curl his legs back. With his arms strapped across his chest, it was damnably uncomfortable.

As his tormentors had intended.

He sighed. He was either being shipped back to Bedlam

like a returned parcel or his aunt and uncle were going to have him drowned in the first river deep enough to do the job, far away from Westphalia, so as to remove any connection to them.

Still, his aunt's dire prediction about brevity of his visit aside, he'd thought he'd at least have one night in his own bed while they made up their minds as to what course to take.

Since he had no way of knowing how long he'd been insensate, he didn't know how long a journey to expect. Over the clack of wheels, he began to hear other noises. The cry of a fishmonger. Church bells. The shouts of carters and the low hum of a city waking to another day.

The distinctive tarry-fishy stench of the Thames began to creep through the chinks in his prison.

Southwark. He was headed back to Bethlem Hospital for the Insane, then.

He ought to be pleased. This was his plan, after all. He couldn't very well present himself at the hospital gate and demand to be allowed back in. He had to arrange for someone to commit him, and his aunt and uncle had already shown a readiness for the job. And becoming an inmate of Bedlam was the only way he'd be able to search Dr. Falco's office for those incriminating letters from Lord Albemarle.

But when his conveyance stopped and he heard the screech of the iron gates of Bedlam opening before him, fear made his balls try to retreat back up into his body. Then the cart rolled forward, and the gates closed behind him.

His soul froze.

The compartment in which he was bound was pried open, and light flooded the small space. Pierce blinked at the brightness as rough hands hauled him out and dropped him, without ceremony, onto the stone pavers before the hospital's entrance.

"Ah! We meet again, Mr. Langdon." The doctor who'd treated him previously was there to greet him. Pierce searched his memory for the quack's name, but where it ought to have been stored, there was only a watery miasma, a snot-running, bile-rising, ball-freezing glop of things best left forgotten. However, Pierce did remember the trim, dark-haired fellow at his side. It was Lord Albemarle's Dr. Falco.

Pierce's doctor summoned a great lummox of an orderly with an imperious wave. "We don't want his lordship to leave us again before his cure is complete." He leaned down and made a great show of examining Pierce's eyes, which were no doubt wild after the opiates he had ingested at his relatives' hands. "Mr. Langdon, what was your mother's maiden name?"

He tried to speak, but his throat was so dry little more than a croak came out. He swallowed hard. "Mycroft," he managed to whisper.

"Very well." The doctor made a note on the sheaf of papers and then handed them off to the orderly. "From now on, you'll be known as Mr. Mycroft. This way, if that infernal busybody, the Duke of Camden, suspects you're here and tries to have you released again, I can tell him with absolute integrity that we have no Mr. Langdon in residence."

Pierce's heart sank to his toes. The doctor had erased him. He'd gone from being a peer of the realm to Mr. Langdon to a nonentity in only a few blinks.

"Since he was here before, he may be recognized by some of the staff," Dr. Falco said. "I suggest he wear a mask or a hood for a while, in case there are inquiries from outside. We cannot allow his treatment to be interrupted again."

Before Pierce could dodge it, the doctors slipped a canvas hood over his head. It had holes for his eyes and mouth and fastened at his neck with a padlock.

His plan had seemed sound. Since the Finder had revealed where Lord Albemarle's letters were secreted away, he only needed the right moment to steal them back. Once Nora's patron was no longer being blackmailed, he would surely give up the *Fides Pulvis* and the Prince Regent would continue to support a plan that would ensure peace on the Continent. Nora would be beyond grateful to him for extricating her friend from his intolerable situation. Perhaps grateful enough to realize she could trust Pierce to handle other things for her. And for Emilia.

He hadn't told His Grace his plans ahead of time, on the theory that it was easier to ask forgiveness than permission. To escape from Bedlam with the letters tucked in his waistcoat, he had been counting on His Grace to figure out where he was and to use his influence to have him released.

His Grace would eventually come to Bedlam to ask if Mr. Langdon had been readmitted, but no one would look for someone named Mycroft. Since he was hooded, not even Meg would be able to *Find* him without knowing the name they had assigned him.

"Our patient has had a tiring journey. Perhaps he should have a day to rest before we resume treatments," Pierce's doctor said. "What do you think, Dr. Falco?"

"Has your research not shown the treatments, they are most effective when the brain is in a suggestible state?" the Italian said. "Extreme fatigue from his journey should put

Signor Mycroft into a receptive frame of mind."

"I concur. The damage done while he has been gone from us must be countermanded immediately. Dodsworth," he said to the lumbering orderly, "Prepare the patient for the water chair."

Pierce felt as though he'd been gut-punched. He had never dreamed he'd be sent to the chair first thing. He had planned to be a model patient. He'd agree to everything his doctor said and be as docile as a lamb. He figured only a few days of that subterfuge would earn him free rein of the facility as one of the trusted "inmate wardens." With the ability to come and go within Bedlam's walls, he'd be able to sneak into Falco's office and steal the letters.

Now, even though he was still bound hand and foot, Pierce struggled against Dodsworth and his minions. He might have had a chance without the straightjacket. He was a good fighter in a tight spot. But not only did the restraint keep him from doing anything but thrashing about and screaming obscenities he hadn't known were in him, it provided admirable handles for the orderlies to use as they carted him off to the scene of his recurring nightmare.

And he couldn't do a damned thing about it.

The first time I was committed, part of the hell of Bedlam was that I was never alone, not even in my solitary cell. All those diseased minds poked at me constantly. Day and night, coherent or gibberish, their disjointed thoughts pounded away at my brain.

This time, thanks to the Duke of Camden's mental exercises, my shield will keep them out. However, nothing will keep their piteous bleating and miserable cries from assaulting my unprotected ears.

~from the secret journal of Pierce Langdon,
Viscount Westfall

Chapter Twenty

Vesta LaMotte found the duke in the Albion Abbey chapel, wandering from one stained glass window to the next. His shoulders slumped. Even from across the space, she felt his despondency and wished with all her heart she could ease it. She slipped down the aisle to join him as he stood before a depiction of the miracle at Cana.

"Turning water into wine. Now there's a truly useful miracle for you," she said, trying to lighten his mood.

"All miracles are useful. Why would they happen unless they were needed?" Camden sighed. "We could certainly do with one. I can't sense Westfall at all."

"Well, that could simply mean that he's using the skills you taught him and is shielding his mind. Which also shields his gift from you."

Camden massaged his temple, obviously trying to stave off one of his horrendous headaches. They always accompanied times when he overtaxed himself, trying to locate the source of psychic energy emanating from another Extraordinaire. Or in this case, trying to sense a missing viscount.

"Or Westfall is no longer among the living," he said wearily. "I've yet to be able to sense the presence of the dead."

Vesta bit back the retort that danced on the tip of her tongue. She sympathized with Edward's loss of his wife and child, but the longer he continued to seek a medium to force a way to communicate with Mercedes, the longer he put off dealing with the fact that she was gone.

"Edward, you don't have to do everything yourself. You have other assets, you know." She linked her arm with his and started to walk back up the aisle. Even though Vesta was a courtesan, she wasn't the least uncomfortable in churches or chapels. After all, some of Christ's best friends had been the worst sinners. She fit into that category with ease, but Edward wasn't as at home in sacred spaces. He still blamed the Almighty too much for his losses.

"Miss Anthony could search for Pierce," she suggested. "You sense your Extraordinaires based on their psychic abilities. But Meg can *Find* people and objects regardless of whether they have any supernatural attributes."

He shook his head. "Since we know how dangerous using her gift is, I can't order her to search for him."

"Perhaps not. An order would be heavy-handed in this instance, even for you, but you might *ask* her if she'd be willing to try. She and Pierce are friends, you know."

His raised brows said he didn't. "I wasn't aware that Westfall had made any such attachments. Is there…a romantic element to their friendship?"

"Heavens, you truly are oblivious, aren't you?" Vesta rolled her eyes. "Our dear Pierce is hopelessly smitten with

Lady Nora."

"Ah, and his fondness is returned," Camden nodded as if a candle of understanding had just been kindled in his mind. "No wonder the lady was so upset when he absented himself from Albion Abbey suddenly and inexplicably. Does Lord Albemarle suspect his mistress's affections are elsewhere engaged?" Camden's brows lowered in a frown. "Do you suppose the baron might have done something underhanded to Westfall?"

"No, I'm sure he hasn't. Benedick isn't the jealous type."

"Benedick? I had no idea you were on such intimate terms with the man."

"Now who's sounding jealous?" Vesta chuckled. "But you have no need to be. Intimate is not a word I'd use to describe my friendship with Albemarle. We share a love of poets and other starveling artists, nothing more."

If Edward hadn't heard the rumors about Benedick's sexual preferences, Vesta saw no need to enlighten him. What two adults did in private was their own business. It should have no bearing on the public aspects of their lives. Of course, she knew her opinion was in the minority and not likely to become more generally endorsed by the *ton* any time soon, but one of the lovely things about being a courtesan was that she was expected to have a few outrageous opinions.

"But back to Miss Anthony," Vesta said as they neared the nail-studded door that led out to the open cloister. "You need to give her a chance to help you. She wants to be useful. Lud, I've never seen such a puppy of a person as she. She lives to please you, Your Grace."

And so would I. If only you'd let me.

. . .

A gentle rain fell on the cloister, painting the statue of the saint dark gray and leaving all the shrubbery in the enclosed space a slick, vibrant green. Camden turned away from the window in one of Lord Albemarle's parlors to survey his remaining Extraordinaires. Since Benedick and his household retainers were still knee-deep in the search for Westfall, Camden and his associates were able to assemble in privacy.

"LeGrand, you've been posing as Westfall's valet," he said. "Did he give any indication that something odd was afoot?"

"Monsieur le Viscount, he did not confide in me, Your Grace. In truth, he rarely allowed me to even pretend to serve him," the water mage said. "I do not think he enjoys the company of others. Perhaps he has merely gone away to seek solitude for selfish reasons."

Lady Easton shook her head. "Lord Westfall is one of the least selfish individuals I've ever known. If he were leaving the Order for personal reasons, he would have told someone. He is far too mannerly not to extend us that courtesy."

"Which means he thinks he is advancing the Order's cause by his absence somehow," Camden said. "What are your thoughts on the matter, Miss Anthony?"

Meg startled a bit at the sound of her name, and Camden might have suspected the Finder had been wool-gathering if not for the look of concern on her face.

"If we knew where he was, we'd be closer to knowing

why he left. Let me *Find* him for you," Meg said. "I know you're concerned for me, Your Grace, and I'm ever so grateful for it, but I can do this without too much risk. I feel certain of it."

Now that he knew Meg courted death each time her spirit flew free of her body, Camden was torn. If anything happened to her, he'd never forgive himself. But if he didn't let her *Find* Westfall and something harmed the viscount, he'd be burdened with just as heavy a load of guilt.

"How can we minimize the danger to you?" he asked.

"If you all come around and put your hands on me. Somehow, the physical contact creates a stronger anchor for me," she explained. "It will help me return more quickly, once I *Find* his lordship."

Camden arched a brow at her. "I believe I should not ask how you discovered this."

"That's good, Your Grace, because I believe I shouldn't want to answer." She moved to the center of the tufted settee and waited while Vesta and Lady Easton settled themselves on either side of her and took her hands in theirs. Camden and LeGrand stood behind the settee and placed their palms on Miss Anthony's shoulders.

"Pierce Langdon, Viscount Westfall," she said, repeating his name. When she sought an object, a description of the item was more helpful to her, but when she launched her soul skyward in search of a person, it was the name by which they were known that pulled her essence to them. She stiffened suddenly. Then her eyes rolled back in her head and her body slumped.

Camden wished he could follow her spirit's progress. Wished he could take the risk she ran on himself, but

Vesta was right. He couldn't do it all. He needed to let the members of the Order exercise their gifts. Just as a cord of many strands was stronger than a single one, the Order was stronger together than any of them were apart.

The seconds ticked by. They turned into minutes and still Miss Anthony didn't return. Her lips had gone bloodless, and there was a blue tinge around her sightless eyes.

"Enough, Miss Anthony," Camden whispered. "Come back at once."

"She can't hear you, Edward," Vesta said, but he noticed she gripped Meg's hand tighter.

"It is almost two minutes, Your Grace," LeGrand said. He flicked his hand at Meg and droplets of water shot from his fingertips to land on her unresponsive face. The water mage shook his head ruefully. "That is usually enough to revive a lady in a swoon."

"This is no swoon," Camden said, resisting the urge to give her a shake. This was death. Without her spirit, Meg's body was dying by inches. Why had he ever allowed her to conduct this search?

Then, without warning, Meg shuddered. She gasped, dragging in a lungful of air, as her eyelids fluttered uncontrollably. Vesta hugged her tightly. Lady Easton was up at once, fetching a glass of sherry for the Finder from the liquor cabinet in the corner.

"Here you are, dear, safe and sound," Lady Easton said as she pressed the glass of fortified wine into Meg's hand.

"Where is—" Camden began.

"Not yet," Vesta interrupted. "Give her a moment to collect herself."

Meg continued to breathe heavily between sips of sherry. Her hands shook. "I don't need a moment. I have nothing to report. I couldn't *Find* him, and I thought I knew exactly where to look," she said disbelievingly, "but I couldn't *Find* him anywhere."

• • •

Plink. Plink. Plink.

Pierce curled tighter into the fetal position and covered his ears with his palms.

He could still hear the incessant drips. They landed near, but not on him. He seemed to feel them in any case. It was as if the drops were boring into his forehead, wearing a hole in his skull. It wasn't so daft a fancy. Water would eat away at even granite given enough time, and his head surely wasn't as hard as that.

Water sloshed over his whole world. He was never dry. Either he was in the chair where the deluge rained down without mercy or in his dank cell in the basement of the hospital where moisture condensed on the ceiling and pattered to the stone floor with soul-deadening constancy. Then there was the watery soup that comprised his daily meals and the slop bucket in the corner that served as his latrine.

Water everywhere.

But none to bathe with and precious little to drink.

He tried to sleep as much as possible because keeping up his mental shield taxed his strength at every turn. In a moment of weakness, he lost the fight and the voices from nearby cells rushed into him.

Pick a posy, pick a pocket, pick a peck of pickled pumpernickel, peddler's pockmarks, pimples and piss...

Wicked boy. Nasty boy. You'll get yours. Then the voice turned sugary. *Where's that mother's angel?*

Did you see that knife? God, the blood, so much blood. The blade still drips with it.

He sat up and put all his effort into rebuilding his shield. The voices became muted, but he could still hear them, buzzing at the edge of his consciousness like a hornet's nest. "As long as I can tell which thoughts are mine, I am not mad," he muttered.

"Oh, I greatly fear you are not competent to make that assessment, Signor Mycroft," came a voice from the slot in his door. He'd not realized he was being watched until he saw the pair of dark eyes that stared through the opening.

Dr. Falco.

"If you are thinking thoughts they are, of course, yours, *capisci? Scusi,* I mean, you understand?"

He understood. The Italian doctor expected him to agree. He expected him to admit that he couldn't hear the thoughts of others. In fact, Falco was thinking it so loudly now, it drowned out the other voices and became the only one he could hear.

Pierce thought he could deceive his doctors easily enough. All he had to do was say what they wanted to hear.

How hard could it be?

Very hard, as it happened.

"The truth is all I have." Westfall repeated the phrase under his breath like some yogi's mantra. He *could* hear the thoughts of others. He couldn't surrender his truth. If he denied this fact about himself, something inside him would break, and he didn't think he'd ever be able to put it back together again.

"Ah! *Veritas*," Falco said. "The search for that elusive quality, it is the search of the ages, no? But if it is the truth you seek, I have something that might help—a new treatment."

Pierce couldn't stifle his groan. *Dear God, not a new one.* The water chair was torture enough.

"Do not fear, my troubled friend. It is not so…strenuous as the water chair. It involves the simple ingestion of a mushroom."

Pierce had heard of such things. Before his friend Stanstead had joined the Order of the M.U.S.E. he had regularly medicated himself with opiates to try to rid himself of the nightmares he dreamed that inevitably came true. Could a cure for him be as simple as taking some mind-altering substance?

"You think it will work?" he said, ashamed of the naked hope in his voice. If there was a chance to be normal, he'd jump at it.

"After the curative properties in the mushroom have worked its way into your system, your senses will be enhanced," Dr. Falco said. "Patients report being able to smell colors and taste words."

"That's ridiculous." And of no benefit whatsoever. Hearing thoughts was bad enough. He didn't need to smell colors or taste words, too.

"Of course it is. Utterly ridiculous. And it is a good sign that you recognize it. *Bene.* This level of self-awareness makes you the perfect candidate for the treatment."

"What if I refuse?"

"During the time you have bided here, have you successfully refused any other treatment? Ah, I thought not." Falco cast him the thin-lipped smile of a cat before a mousehole. "Once you have had a few sessions with this miraculous substance, perhaps you will also see that it is equally ridiculous for you to believe you hear the thoughts of others. According to my colleagues in France, they are seeing great changes in their patients."

Colleagues in France. The *Fides Pulvis*. For a few moments, the real reason he'd allowed himself to be taken into Bedlam again had flitted from his mind. He'd allowed himself to hope, however briefly, that there was a way for him to lay aside what the duke called his "gift." Now his true purpose slammed back into him. He had to find those incriminating letters in Falco's office and escape with them. Then he would trade them for Lord Albemarle's Trust Powder, free Honora from her patently false relationship with the baron, and hire the Hobarths at his country estate so Honora could see her daughter anytime she wished.

Then, maybe, she would marry him.

And it wouldn't matter if he heard other people's thoughts or not, so long as he could hear hers every day.

"Dodsworth," Dr. Falco said to the orderly who hung on his every word. "Prepare Mr. Mycroft for a dose of Myconia Fantasma."

He might have a troubled brainpan, but he was not going to let this Italian quack take who he was from him. "I'm not Mycroft."

"You will be," Falco assured him. "After floating with the mushroom for a while, you will be anyone or anything I tell you to be."

It is the perversity of human nature to want what we don't have. Worse, we never seem to appreciate what we do have until it is taken from us.

~from the secret journal of Lady Nora Claremont

Chapter Twenty-One

Meg Anthony looked up from her book and blinked in surprise. "Lady Nora is here? To see me?"

"Yes, miss," Mr. Bernard, the hard-working steward of Camden House, said. "I've directed the lady to the parlor. She awaits you there. I have also ordered tea. I hope that is in accordance with your wishes."

"Oh yes, and quite the correct thing to do, I'm sure. I'll come at once." Meg rose from the overstuffed chair in His Grace's library and replaced the simple hornbook on the shelf. Once Lady Easton had learned that Meg could neither read nor write, it had become yet another task for the Finder to accomplish in her quest to pass as a wellborn young lady. She worked at it every day, and while she could now decipher most words, she struggled with being able to read them quickly enough to make sense of entire sentences.

Meg climbed the grand staircase to the first floor parlor, her heart racing. She'd practiced taking tea with Lady Easton.

This would be her first time with someone who didn't know she would be more at home washing up the used cups in the scullery than pouring out the brew in a ritual of gentility in the duke's fancy parlor.

She paused at the parlor doorway and found Lady Nora pacing before the heavily curtained windows like a caged lynx. Meg dropped a shallow curtsy. "Good afternoon, my lady."

Lady Nora's pacing stopped, and her gaze cut to Meg sharply. She returned Meg's curtsy. "Thank you for receiving me, Miss Anthony. Many respectable women wouldn't, you know."

Meg's mouth twitched. She was an accomplished pickpocket and drawlatch. Masquerading as a lady made her an utter fraud. It was amusing to be considered a respectable woman. But she couldn't remain amused while her guest was in such obvious discomfort.

"Won't you please be seated?"

"No, I shan't be staying long," Lady Nora said. She hadn't removed her bonnet, the signal for an extended visit according to Lady Easton. "I realize how improper it is of me to intrude on you like this, but you were so helpful in finding that little girl at the fair. I feel as if I know you better than our short acquaintance warrants, and I had to speak to somebody."

The courtesan's ensemble was as elegant as ever. Her artfully made up face was beyond striking. But there was a glint of something Meg recognized as terror in her wide eyes.

"Please tell me you have heard from him," Nora said.

Meg didn't pretend to misunderstand her. "We have received no word of Lord Westfall."

"What about his family? Might he have gone home?"

Meg shook her head. After her efforts to locate Westfall had failed, the duke's party had returned to London, and His Grace had turned to mundane methods of finding the missing lord. He had employed half a dozen Bow Street runners to chase down clues. At first, the viscount's countryseat had looked promising, but Westfall's aunt and uncle swore their nephew was not there. In fact, Horace Langdon was incensed that the duke had lost track of Lord Westfall after faithfully promising to be responsible for his well-being since he'd been released from Bedlam to Camden's care. Over a week had passed, and they were no closer to finding Westfall than they had been on the day he'd gone missing without a trace.

Lady Nora began to pace again.

This was no way to conduct a proper visit. Meg had to get a handle on the situation. "Please, won't you be seated?"

"I can't. Every time I sit, my knee begins to bounce so, and I can't keep it still. I can't eat. I can't sleep. I shall go completely dotty if I don't hear from the man soon."

A hostess's first task is to make her guests feel comfortable. Lady Easton had drummed that cardinal rule of etiquette into Meg's head. How could she set Lady Nora at ease? If Lady Easton came in and discovered Meg couldn't preside over her first official call, she'd be so disappointed. Meg was determined not to let that happen.

"Lord Westfall wouldn't want you to take on so, my lady. He—" She stopped herself when one of the footmen entered the room. Lady Easton had also drummed it into her head that conversation was not to be continued in the presence of servants, especially when the conversation was as fraught with emotion as this one. The footman bore a tray of finger sandwiches and petit fours along with the tea service, which he placed on the low table before the settee. When he retired, Meg went on. "Allow me to offer you refreshment. You'll feel ever so much better after a nice hot cup."

Lady Nora met her gaze squarely and sighed. "You're right. I'm sorry for being so difficult. I can't seem to think straight these days."

"That's understandable. You are fond of his lordship. We all are."

"Fond," Lady Nora repeated as she sank into one of the Sheridan chairs. "Such a bland word, fond. As if the man were an éclair I couldn't resist. Fond is woefully inadequate, I fear."

Oh, dear. Meg had insulted her by using the wrong word. She'd never get the hang of this being-a-lady business. "I beg pardon. I didn't mean to—"

"No, I'm the one who should apologize." Nora waved away Meg's attempt to smooth things over with her lace-gloved hand. "It's terribly gauche of me to offer confidences where none have been encouraged."

"I'm all for encouraging confidence, my lady."

Lady Nora's lips tightened in a suppressed smile, and Meg suspected her words had come out wrong somehow. Then the lady leaned toward her.

"The truth is, I love Lord Westfall. Most desperately. I know I shouldn't. He deserves the love of a fine lady. Someone worthy of the name. But I can't seem to help myself." Her lovely face crumpled, and tears trembled on her long lashes. How could Lady Nora be so distraught and so attractive at the same time? Meg wasn't a pretty crier. Her nose turned red and her eyes became puffy instead of glistening and interesting. "If he cannot be found, I don't know what I shall do."

Meg laced Lady Nora's cup with milk and two sugars without asking how she preferred it. Someone suffering that badly from a fit of the blue devils deserved milk and sugar, whether she wanted it or not.

"His Grace is searching for his lordship," she assured the courtesan as she handed her guest a full cup and saucer without sloshing a bit. "Trust to that."

"But I can't sit by and do nothing." Lady Nora raised the cup to her lips and went through the motions of sipping. Meg doubted she tasted more than a drop. "Do you think it possible that Westfall's family had him committed again without His Grace's knowledge?"

"No, I'm certain he's not in Bedlam." That was the one thing Meg was sure of. She'd looked high and low and no one called Pierce Langdon was trapped behind those barred gates.

Meg was beyond surprised not to have *Found* him, because he'd told her his intention to go there. She feared he'd met with foul play somewhere between Albion Abbey and the hospital for the insane. For a few months, her Uncle Rowney and Cousin Oswald had hired out as part of a press gang to waylay solitary travelers. After a solid clout to the head, the unfortunate victim was deposited on a departing ship and forced to work as part of the crew. If that's what had happened to Westfall, he might be halfway to the Horn of Africa by now.

"Even if His Grace made inquiries, which I'm assuming he has, the keepers at Bedlam could be convinced to lie," Lady Nora said as she drummed her fingers on her knee.

"Cross someone's palm with enough money and you can generally get them to agree to most anything."

Is that why she became a courtesan? For the money? Or was it the fine clothes and the jewels winking at her throat?

Nora rose and began pacing again. "I should go and see for myself."

"You? Go to Bedlam?"

"Yes, of course."

"How?"

"With the right size 'donation,' anyone can enter the hospital and view the unhappy souls held there. Some claim altruistic motives, Societies for the Improvement-of-Whatever-They-Can-Think-to-Criticize-This-Week sorts. I'm sure you recognize the type. Others treat it like visiting a freak show." Lady Nora lifted a hand toward her. "I can see I've shocked you. Since you've been gently reared, Miss Anthony, I'm sure you've never heard such a repugnant notion."

All Meg heard was that Lady Nora thought she'd been gently reared. Uncle Rowney would have a laugh over that, but Lady Easton would be so proud.

"Of course, I've never done it, but I've listened to stories from those who have." Nora's voice sank to a whisper. "Pitiable. Horrendous. I almost hope I don't find him."

"If you're determined to go, I'll go with you," Meg offered. She'd seen Bedlam while in spirit form and found it disturbing enough. It made her flesh crawl to think about walking those filthy halls in person. But Lady Nora would need her support when she didn't discover Lord Westfall in that hellacious place.

"No, I don't think that would be wise." She sat again and returned her cup and saucer to the tray. She'd hardly touched the tea. "Since His Grace has already inquired about Lord Westfall, and you're known to be part of the duke's household, if Pierce is there, they'd make sure we didn't see him."

She uses his Christian name. Dear me. This is serious!

"But you dare not go alone, surely," Meg said. She'd taken off by herself when she ran away from Uncle Rowney and had to disappear into London. *Not* being gently reared, she figured she could hold her own in the chanciest of neighborhoods. But even Meg would hesitate to enter Bedlam without someone at her side.

"I can't take Mr. Whittles," Lady Nora said.

"Who is that?"

"He's my butler and, while he's handy with a chafing dish, he'd be of no use whatsoever in a tight spot. Besides, he'd feel the need to tell Lord Albemarle about this little expedition, and that would never do."

"No, I suppose not." How did Lady Nora manage to juggle a patron and a lover at the same time? She obviously knew how to handle men. But even a clever woman like Lady Nora might need a man's protection in a place like Bedlam. "Oh! What about Mr. LeGrand?"

"Who is he?"

"Westfall's valet, but he hasn't been with him long enough for anyone to put the two of them together. I'd feel ever so much better about this if you'd take him with you."

Nora cocked her head to one side, considering. "That might answer, but I should still have a female companion as well, I suppose. Benedick would want me to if this little excursion comes to his attention. I wonder if Miss LaMotte would—"

"I'm sure she will," Meg cut in and then clapped her hand over her mouth because she'd made the mistake of interrupting her guest. How did the Quality ever manage to get anything accomplished when there were so many rules to be mindful of? "Of course, she and the duke are known to be friends, but Miss LaMotte has lots of friends."

"Lots of friends," Nora repeated. "You dear girl, what a sweet way you have of putting things."

The words sounded like a compliment on their face, but something about the way Nora said them suggested that Meg was a bit feebleminded. That was rot. Meg knew perfectly well what Vesta did for a living and, while she couldn't imagine the confidence it took for a woman to become a top tier "bird-of-paradise," she wouldn't fault Vesta for her choices. Just as Vesta hadn't ostracized her when she learned that Meg was a master of the cutpurse's art. Meg straightened her spine.

"Miss LaMotte is my friend, as well. I do hope your comment wasn't meant to malign her." *Or me.* Just because Meg was out of her depth in social situations didn't mean she couldn't or wouldn't defend herself.

"Heavens, no. I meant no disrespect. I only meant…oh, dear, I'm hopelessly out of practice in a proper parlor. I've spent far too much time in snide conversations about the *ton* with Albemarle's salon guests." Lady Nora threw her graceful hands in the air. "You see, Miss Anthony, it is rare for a respectable woman like you to receive a woman like me. Or Miss LaMotte, for that matter."

Since she had joined the Order of the M.U.S.E., Meg had regularly associated with all manner of "respectable" people, starting with His Grace. She counted Lord and Lady

Stanstead her friends, and she'd have been lost without Lady Easton. She and Westfall almost behaved like brother and sister. But getting to know Vesta had been a treat, albeit quite a spicy one, at times. Meg had more friends now than she'd ever had in her whole life. Even though Lady Nora was often seen out and about on the town and presided as hostess over Lord Albemarle's numerous fetes, she actually seemed to lead a very lonely life.

"I admit I'm not terribly sophisticated," Meg said, pleased that she'd remembered the two-guinea word Lady Easton had taught her. "But in my case, innocence and ignorance do not clasp hands. You have not offended me. Please think no more on such things, my lady." Here was her golden opportunity to put Lady Easton's training to good use and make her guest feel completely at home. "I'd be honored to count you my friend. And if you'll allow it, I'll make arrangements with Mr. LeGrand and Miss LaMotte to accompany you to Bedlam on the morrow."

"If you would, I'd be so grateful." Lady Nora's tight shoulders relaxed and, to Meg's surprise, she removed her bonnet.

She intended to stay for a longer visit!

Meg could report to Lady Easton that her handling of her first social caller had been an unqualified success.

Subject: Mr. Mycroft

*When first admitted, the unfortunate gentleman presented
with auditory hallucinations. Since that time, his condition
has deteriorated, and he is experiencing what can only be
described as general sensory displacement. He smells what
he should experience as tactile stimulation. He claims to
see sounds. The stench of his slop bucket grates on his ears.
The poor fellow is nothing if not inventive. Manic laughter
is a frequent occurrence, and his pupils are fully dilated for
hours at a time. During lucid periods (and one uses that
term loosely), he seems too weak for continued treatment
with the water chair, though he is still adamant about being
able to hear the thoughts of others.*

*Dr. Falco has attempted an alternative treatment, something
of a pharmacological nature. My colleague is welcome to try,
though one is more inclined to trust the efficacy of behavior
modification by mechanical means. Judicious and frequent
sessions in the water chair are Mr. Mycroft's best hope.*

*If there is no improvement soon, however, one may be
forced to concede that no cure can be affected. Mr. Mycroft
will be released to the general population of the hospital to*

live out his remaining days roaming the halls in bewildered confusion, a lost soul trapped in a diseased mind.

Once he expires, and in his wretched condition one may be forgiven for hoping his release comes swiftly, an autopsy of his cranium in particular should offer advances in treatment for future sufferers.

~from the chart of Mr. Mycroft, patient, Bethlem Hospital

Chapter Twenty-Two

Nora skittered after the doctor, testing the limits of her narrow column dress with each stride. Even so, she wished the tour would move along faster. She held a scented handkerchief to her nose in an attempt to mask the foul odor, but the perfumed cloth was woefully inadequate to the task.

"I shall have to burn this dress," Vesta muttered under her breath.

Nora was of similar mind, but she couldn't be bothered about her wardrobe at the moment, not when every turn in the corridor brought a new horror to her eyes. Mr. LeGrand, disguised as a footman in elegant livery that could not be identified with any particular noble house, followed the women at a respectful couple of steps behind. He wasn't a large man, but his misshapen nose pointed to a bout of fisticuffs or two in his past. Though he was the quiet sort, Nora felt better for his presence as her rear guard.

They encountered a number of inmates wandering the

halls who shrieked at first sight of them or blasted them with obscenities. When they crossed an open door, a chamber pot came rolling toward them, spilling its contents over the already dirty-looking floor.

"Why aren't the patients in their rooms?" Nora asked the doctor who'd taken her handful of sovereigns quickly enough when she and Vesta had arrived asking to see over the place.

"Those who are deemed not to be a danger to themselves or others—careful there, my lady, mind your skirts—are allowed free run of the place, up to the barred gate, of course. Since we have determined that further treatment will not be of use in their cases, we strive merely to make them comfortable."

"If comfortable means allowing them to wallow in their own filth, the policy is a staggering success," Vesta whispered.

The doctor seemed not to hear her, for he continued to lead them up a flight of stairs. A beefy-armed orderly stood guard at the top step. "On this level, you'll find the patients who are confined to their rooms by night. During the day, they may take their exercise in the corridors, but must remain on this floor. We can't allow them to mingle with the general population."

"Why not?" Nora asked.

"Because they've shown a propensity for unexpected violence. Don't get too close to Violet there." He hurried them past a seemingly feeble scarecrow of a woman with cottony tufts of hair sprouting on her head. "She's here because she has a nasty habit of shoving hatpins between people's ribs."

"Why on earth do you allow her access to pins?" Vesta demanded.

"Oh, she doesn't use pins now, but she has been known to sharpen spoons and anything else she can get her hands on," the doctor said as another orderly approached.

"The machine is ready for Mrs. Mounsey," the hulking servant said. Nora wondered if they employed anyone who didn't look as if they'd be more at home in a pugilists' ring.

"Very good." The doctor turned to the women. "You know, I usually don't include ongoing treatments as part of the tour, but this sad woman's malady should be of particular interest to you ladies."

"And why is that?" Vesta asked

"You'll see. This way, if you please." He led them down several flights of stairs to the sub-basement level. The air was ripe with toadstools and unwholesome earth and mold. Nora decided if misery had a smell, they had discovered it. They stopped before a metal door which the doctor opened using a heavy key.

"Your footman will have to wait here," he said.

"Why?" Nora was loath to give up LeGrand's comforting presence.

"It will become self-evident."

Nora tossed a look at the footman. He stepped to the side of the door and assumed the bland mask of a servant waiting at table. The doctor ushered them into a large chamber that was dominated by a single wooden chair in the center of the space. A nude woman was strapped to it. When she lifted her head to eye the doctor, Nora thought she'd never seen such naked hate on a human face.

"As you can see, we are ever mindful of the dignity of our patients." The doctor seemed oblivious to the woman's expression as he strode forward to check the tightness of her bonds. "Since Mrs. Mounsey's treatment must be administered without benefit of clothing, it wouldn't have been seemly for your footman to view the proceedings."

"I'm not certain it's seemly for us to view it, either," Nora said as an aside to Vesta.

"This water chair is a device of my own design," the doctor began, preening his mustache with the back of his hand. "You see, the goal of the treatment is—"

"What is Mrs. Mounsey's ailment, if I may ask?" Vesta said.

"Oh, that. She refuses her husband's bed."

Nora was sure she'd misheard him. "She what?"

"I know. It's a sad case." The doctor shook his head. "She completely shuns her wifely duty. Such unwomanly rebellion defies understanding, does it not?"

"You'd understand it right enough if you was the one Mr. Mounsey was poking," the woman in the chair said, her voice thick with loathing. "The man is a pig."

The doctor tut-tutted and pulled a small book from his pocket to make a note. "Patient believes husband is an animal. Obviously, more treatments are needed to clear up this delusion."

Nora had been shocked when her family disowned her, but her outrage over that indignity paled when compared to the plight of poor Mrs. Mounsey. She was about to launch into a blistering setdown that would have the doctor reeling. She'd unstrap the unhappy patient and spirit her away from this awful place, but just as she took a step forward, Vesta stopped her with a hand to her forearm.

"Remember where you are, my dear," she whispered urgently. "If you interfere, the good doctor may decide you're a bit touched yourself and need a treatment or two. And they might elect to keep LeGrand and me, as well, based solely on our decision to keep company with you."

That brought her up short. Nora hadn't thought her actions through. If she tried to intervene, she might well be endangering Vesta and her erstwhile "footman."

Then the door behind them opened with a sinister creak.

"Ah! Dr. Falco, I'm so gratified you could join us. Ladies, may I introduce my Italian colleague?"

Falco? Benedick's Falco? Nora turned to discover a darkly handsome man of medium height advancing toward her. He had the chiseled features Benedick favored in his lovers, a strong chin and aquiline nose. His hooded eyes swept over her and Vesta while the other doctor made the introductions.

So this was the man Benedick had befriended. He had supported him and made his career as a doctor possible. How could Falco turn on his old lover like that? Nora's outrage over Mrs. Mounsey's situation now transferred to the turncoat Dr. Falco, but she was in no better position to act at the moment.

"Lady Nora," Dr. Falco bowed over her gloved hand. "Who has not heard of your beauty? How pleased I am to finally meet you."

She thought she detected the hard edge of jealousy in his tone. If he knew of her, he undoubtedly knew she was Benedick's mistress. Did he see her as a rival? Was that why he was siding with Benedick's enemies?

Love spurned was a powerful motivator, but to hear Benedick tell it, Falco was the one who'd bowed out of their relationship years ago. She'd have to find a way to wheedle more information from Benedick about his old love.

But then the doctor pulled a lever, and all thoughts of her patron and his problems fled away. In the center of the room, the ceiling appeared to open and poor Mrs. Mounsey was caught in a downpour. She sputtered. She coughed. She made pitiful strangled noises, but the water kept falling.

My God, they did this to Pierce.

Mrs. Mounsey's head drooped to her chest, and she sagged against her bonds. She was clearly unconscious, but the water continued to fall.

"Stop," Nora chanted under her breath. "Oh, please stop."

"I would, since the patient is insensible, but the machine is calibrated to deliver so many gallons per minute for a certain duration," the doctor explained. "If we end treatment prematurely, we will not be able to assess how much water was used to create the desired result."

"And the desired result is for her to want to return to her husband's bed?" Vesta said dryly. "I can't imagine why this wouldn't send her screaming back to him."

"Indeed, but in the interest of future patients, we need accurate records," Dr. Falco said. "Science which cannot be quantified is not worthy of the name."

Mrs. Mounsey began to rouse, moaning and snuffling. She was going to drown in that chair before Nora's eyes, and there was no way to stop it. Her belly roiled. Watching without intervening made her part of this horror. The back of her throat spasmed. She feared she'd retch, so she turned and threw all her weight against the heavy metal door.

She pushed through the opening. Heedless of whether Vesta or LeGrand joined her, she lifted her skirts and fled to the staircase leading out of the watery hell. But as she ran by countless closed and locked doors, she heard something.

Her name.

When she'd first lost Lewis, she'd often wake with a start in the dark watches of the night, certain she'd heard him call her. His voice wasn't its usual full-timbred sound at those times. It was hollow. Bloodless. But somehow, she'd known it was her dead husband. Knew he'd spoken to her.

This voice was like that, a shadow of itself, not of this world. But it didn't belong to Lewis. This deathly summons came from someone else.

The only man who'd ever called her Honora.

A sob tore from her throat as she kept running.

• • •

A swirl of mint undulated over Mycroft's head. It was joined by an explosion of lavender leaves and splashed with the tart freshness of apple. The smells coalesced into a woman's face floating above him, translucent, shimmering, and far larger than life.

"Honora," he whispered.

Mycroft could make out the mold-stained walls through the apparition, but somehow this slightly see-through woman seemed more real to him than the cold stone. Her skin glowed. Her eyes glistened down on him with love.

If she wasn't real, he didn't want to return to reality.

"Honora," he called, louder this time.

The flurry of footfalls past his door seemed to tramp through his head, leaving prints in the brain pudding between his ears. They slowed for half a heartbeat, then tripped on.

The woman above him began to fade.

A tear streaked his cheek. She wasn't real, after all. Mycroft supposed he should have known that, since all he'd seen of her was her face, floating disembodied there. It took more than a face to make a person. Then he remembered that Dr. Falco and a couple of orderlies had forced more of the mushroom down him. The woman was only a bit of digesting fungus.

Mycroft wasn't losing his mind. It was being systematically taken from him. But maybe hallucinating Honora was his way of taking it back.

"She was Honora," he said to himself stubbornly. "And Honora is real."

But she hadn't really been hovering in his cell. He was glad of that. As he came more to himself, he was certain he didn't want her there with him.

But if she wasn't with him and yet she was real—dear God, she must be real or there was no reason to keep breathing— that meant there was a world beyond these gray walls. He had a life somewhere else. He had a purpose...

As the effects of the mushroom continued to fade, that life came back to him in flashes and starts. He was part of something larger than himself. He had meaningful work to do. And in the doing of it, he would be serving the woman he loved, as well.

He sat up straight. The next time Dr. Falco came with his *Myconia Fantasma*, he'd take it without a qualm. He'd chew it up and pretend to swallow. Then as soon as the doctor left the cell, he'd spit out the poison and stick a finger down his throat to bring up anything he might have inadvertently let slide into his gullet.

"I am not Mr. Mycroft," he said to the walls. "I am

Viscount Westfall, a peer of the realm."

The words tasted a little grandiose, even to his own tongue, and he wondered if he were still under the fungus's influence. So he amended his proclamation and ticked off the things he knew for certain about himself on his fingers.

"My name is Pierce Langdon. I love Lady Honora Claremont. I can hear the thoughts of others as easily as if they'd been given voice. I can shield my mind if I need to, but if I choose, I can strip another person's secrets from them before the introductions are finished."

He decided the next time Dr. Falco came into his cell, his shield would definitely be down.

Having been considered mad for most of my childhood and all of my adult life, it is no great feat to pretend to be so. I find it as natural as breathing.

~from the secret journal of Pierce Langdon,
Viscount Westfall

Chapter Twenty-Three

"You don't understand, Vesta." Honora was expected to appear at Benedick's town house later that evening to serve as hostess at a small dinner party, so she had received her friend in her boudoir while she completed her toilette.

It wasn't such an unusual use of the space. Her canopied bed in the corner notwithstanding, the large room was set up for entertaining intimates with plenty of seating and even a table in one corner should a guest wish to play a hand of whist. Vesta, not being interested in cards, was comfortably ensconced on a velvet fainting couch, while Honora continued to brush her own hair before the vanity mirror.

The rough bristles against her scalp were a penance of sorts for the cowardice she had shown at Bedlam. She hadn't helped poor Mrs. Mounsey, and she hadn't stayed long enough to find Pierce. She scraped the brush over her head harder.

"I *heard* him," Nora said. "I'm certain of it."

"I'm willing to believe you *thought* you heard Pierce's voice," Vesta allowed, "but you didn't stop to try to discover where the sound came from."

"No, and I've regretted it every minute since." At the time, Nora could think of nothing but escaping the scene of poor Mrs. Mounsey's torment. And the voice she'd heard calling her name had many of the same qualities as her dead husband's imagined one. She had feared it was only in her mind. Or worse, that hearing him call to her like that meant Pierce was as dead as Lewis. "The voice I heard in Bedlam was so different from Pierce's normal one."

"Well, there you have it," Vesta said. "It couldn't have been him."

"But isn't it likely that he wouldn't sound like himself after being subjected to torture like Mrs. Mounsey?"

Vesta sat up straight and swung her legs to one side so that her neatly shod feet were planted firmly on the polished hardwood. "Nora, please believe that I want to find Pierce, almost as much as you obviously do. But he is not in Bedlam."

Nora met her friend's concerned gaze in the mirror. "We didn't begin to see all of it." Even as she said the words, her stomach quaked with that hollowed-out, shaky feeling again. The hospital had horrified her to her marrow. "There are any number of cells in that horrible place where he might be hidden away."

"He's not."

"How can you be so sure?"

"The Duke of Camden has made exhaustive inquiries at Bedlam, and His Grace is satisfied on that point." Vesta rose and sauntered to the window to look out over the fashionable St. James block. "Trust me, he has resources the likes of which you cannot imagine."

"I can imagine quite a lot."

"Not this, my dear. In a way, I'm relieved that we have eliminated the place," Vesta said. "We must be thankful that wherever Pierce is, it cannot be worse than Bedlam."

"But not knowing where he is, is likely to make me lunatic enough to land in hospital myself." He was all she could think of. She'd even tried to beg off when Benedick sent the request for her to come to him, which she'd never done before. He wrote back, saying unless she was physically ill, he expected her presence and full attention. She wondered how she'd manage to pretend interest in Lord Albemarle's troubles. There was simply no room for anyone else. Pierce filled her completely.

Had it really only been a little over a month since she met him at Albemarle's soiree? Their first kiss at the opera rushed back to her. It was unlike any kiss she'd ever experienced, more honest, more true. Pierce had marked her then, she realized. She'd never be free of him, though she really ought to make sure he was free of her. Once he was safe, she must steel herself to let him go so he could find someone more worthy than her to love.

Nora laid down the brush and shook her head. "I didn't accept his proposal, Vesta."

"Pierce asked you to marry him?" The shock in her voice would have been insulting if not for the fact that Nora agreed with her. There was no reason for a viscount to wed a courtesan when he might reasonably keep her for the right price and then bid her adieu when he tired of her and she was no longer useful. "I must say I'm surprised. Pierce Langdon is a very private man. To allow you into his life as his wife, well, this is a far more daunting commitment on his part than the wedding vows are to most men."

"Oh, so you know about his ability to hear the thoughts of others, too?"

Vesta blanched beneath her artful makeup. "He may have mentioned something about that particular fancy in passing. No doubt he was shining us on. I gave it no heed."

"I didn't either at first, but now I'm convinced it's true. The man *knows* me, Vesta. He knows me inside out. And even that didn't keep him from proposing." Nora buried her face in her hands. "Do you suppose that's why he left us at Albion Abbey? What have I done?"

Vesta hurried over and smoothed down Nora's curls with a surprisingly motherly hand.

"Oh, my dear," she said to Nora's reflection in the mirror. "There's no sense fretting over what you've done in the past. All any of us have power over is our present."

"And what we'll do in the future," Nora said pensively.

"Assuredly. Tomorrow will seem brighter. You'll see."

Nora took leave to doubt it.

Honora...

She closed her eyes as the memory of his voice shivered over her. This time she knew it wasn't real, but no matter what the Duke of Camden said, she'd swear on a stack of bibles that reached to the moon that she'd heard Pierce call her name at Bedlam.

She feathered the tip of her finger across her bottom lip. Pierce's kiss still lingered there.

That night at the opera when their lips had first met, the repertory company had been singing Beethoven's *Fidelio*. The story of the faithful wife who pretended to be a lad so she could search for her missing husband in prison scrolled across Nora's mind.

She could do that.

She could go back to Bedlam, not as Lady Nora, a well-heeled visitor willing to pay for the privilege of gawking at the unfortunates, but as someone who was looking for work of any kind. Once she was in, she'd be able to search for Pierce in a more thorough way. She had to know for certain. She'd go batty if she didn't. If only she could screw her courage to act.

Her plans spilled out her mouth before she thought better of them.

"Oh, Nora, don't. It's reckless in the extreme," Vesta said. "Please reconsider."

"No, my mind's made up." Speaking her plan aloud cemented it in her mind. Now she had to do something irreversible to put it into motion. She rang the bellpull for Mr. Whittles. When he appeared at her door, she asked him to bring the sharpest pair of scissors in the house.

"Honestly, dear, are you sure you want to pattern your behavior after something you saw at the opera?" Vesta said, twining her beringed fingers in consternation. "Everybody tends to die by the time the last curtain falls in those things, you know."

Her butler arrived with the shears she'd requested.

"Mr. Whittles, I haven't time to write a note. Please take a message to Lord Albemarle."

"Me, my lady?"

"Yes, I don't want you to send a footman. This is important enough for you to go yourself. Give Lord Albemarle my apologies, and tell his lordship that I am indisposed. I will not be joining him this evening…or any other evening for the next fortnight. Off you go."

Whittles didn't voice his disapproval. He was too well trained for that, but his tight-lipped expression spoke volumes. After a quick bow, the butler left.

"Oh, my dear, was that wise?" Vesta said. "We are business-women, you and I. You're likely to upset your patron with that faradiddle. One look at you and anyone can see that you're not ill."

"Yes, I am. I'm sick at heart. And I'll prove it." Nora lifted a long lock and cut it off close to her scalp before she lost her nerve. Her pinkish skin showed through the dark stubble. There was no going back now. "I'll cut my hair and pass as a young man, just like Leonore in *Fidelio*. Everyone dies at the opera, you say. I say, if I don't find Pierce, I may as well be dead already."

• • •

The clack of footsteps outside his cell warned Pierce that someone was coming. He hurriedly replaced the flagstone he'd dislodged from under his chamber pot and returned the stinking vessel to its place.

For the past couple of days, he'd been using the handle of his spoon to scrape out mortar around the stone to reveal a narrow void under the flooring. Once he found Lord Albemarle's letters to Dr. Falco, he'd need a place to hide them until he could make good his escape. He couldn't chance tucking them into his pocket. If he were taken to the water chair again, the orderlies who stripped him would find the missives for sure.

All that remained was to win free of his cell. Thanks to being able to eavesdrop on his doctors when they thought he was insensible, he'd been working toward that end. All he had to do was continue to show no "improvement," and the quack would give up treating him. His doctor seemed near to throwing in the towel.

Pierce scrambled back to the worm-eaten pallet that served as his bed and lay on his side in a fetal position.

"Good morning, Mr. Mycroft," the doctor said as he and the orderly Dodsworth entered. "How are we feeling today?"

Pierce made a few sounds, taking care that none of them should remotely resemble actual words.

The doctor shook his head and labored over his notebook for a moment. "Remove his hood. Take Mr. Mycroft to the ground floor and release him into the general population."

"You want I should move him to the west wing, Doc?"

"No, no. Too many changes at once might be unsettling. Return him to this chamber by night for a week. We'll see how he does. Perhaps he can be moved to a room above ground after that."

The doctor jotted another line or two while Dodsworth grunted with the effort of getting Pierce on his feet. Pierce saw no need to help him overmuch and went limp as a dishrag.

"Oh, and in case I don't see Dr. Falco before he makes rounds, please tell him I have ordered all treatment for Mr. Mycroft stopped. This includes the good doctor's experiments with Myconia Fantasma."

Dodsworth propped Pierce against the wall. He promptly slid down, settling with his knees under his chin.

Dodsworth scratched his head, which sent his resident lice scurrying, and turned back to the doctor. "Dr. Falco won't like that, nary a bit. He says on account of them mushrooms, Mycroft here was near to what you call a breakthrough."

"More like a breakdown. Look at him, Dodsworth. The man is a jellyfish with feet. Not that I fault my esteemed colleague. No indeed," the doctor was quick to add. "Dr. Falco has done his best. No, I blame that interfering Duke of Camden. If he hadn't demanded we release Lord Westfa— but that's neither here nor there. For better or worse, our Mr. *Mycroft* will be with us from now on."

"Till he leaves in a pine box," Dodsworth said with a laugh as he jerked Pierce to his feet and frog-marched him out of the cell and up the stairs. He deposited him in the main hall and left Pierce to his own devices among the pitiful flotsam of other inmates who wandered to and fro.

Though he was beyond relieved to be free of the hood and his cell, Pierce kept his eyes downcast for a good ten minutes. For one thing, he was unused to the brightness of the aboveground world. For another, he hoped to effectively disappear from anyone's notice before he started to move.

Meg Anthony had told him Lord Albemarle's incriminating letters were in Dr. Falco's desk in his office on the third floor. She'd even drawn out a crude map of the place so he knew exactly where to go. He retraced the route in his mind. The trick would be to arrive there unnoticed, slip in and snag the letters, then make it out and back down to his basement cell without being stopped or searched. If the doctor kept to his plan not to relocate Pierce to another wing right away, he'd have only a week to find a way over the wall.

All while keeping up the appearance of making no

improvement in his mental state.

He was careful to keep his mental shield raised. If he lowered it now, the diseased minds parading past him would engulf him entirely. It was bad enough that he could hear and — merciful God! — smell them.

His time spent floating with Dr. Falco's mushroom seemed to have left him with heightened senses. He wished the effect had dulled him instead. A whisper was like a shout. The most muted color seemed brilliant. And the other patients. They made him ponder what a wonder the human body was, how fitly joined, how godlike in its strength and beauty. And how foul it became when it was left untended.

Finally, he deemed it safe to rise and join the shuffling throng of other lunatics in aimless wandering for a bit. It helped him unkink his legs to walk farther. For the whole time he'd been at Bedlam his only exercise had been pacing his small cell or being dragged down the dank corridor to the water chair. When he started up a staircase, he was surprised to find he was winded by the time he reached the first landing.

Above him, he heard a pair of angry voices. One put him in the mind of a bull standing at stud, while the other was shriller but no less full of fury.

"Empty all the pots on this level before you skip to the next, boy. Then, mind you, mop the floors. And make sure they're clean or I'll make you eat off them." Dodsworth was the one bellowing orders. Pierce couldn't make out the other person's words, but the boy was clearly sassing the big orderly. Then there was a clatter of buckets and mop handles and a loud thump.

Pierce used the distraction to slip around the landing

that looked down that corridor but he managed a peek as he did. Dodsworth had laid the lad out. He was prone in a puddle of wash water, scrabbling to rise. Dodsworth laughed and headed back toward the staircase.

"Stay down," Pierce advised the lad in a whisper as he moved stealthily upward.

And promised himself that he'd find a way to make Dodsworth pay before he left Bedlam. Not for what the orderly had done to him, but for the way he terrorized everyone under him, patients and workers alike, in this horrible place.

Then, as he continued to climb, he found he needed something to bolster his flagging energy, so he said her name, the sweetest word ever to cross his tongue.

"Honora."

It gave him strength.

What constitutes being of sound mind? Is it as simple as doing what is expected? Following the rules and fitting in? Or when faced with a difficult choice, is it being guided by one's heart, devil take the hindermost?

~From the secret journal of Lady Nora Claremont

Chapter Twenty-Four

"There it is again," Nora muttered as she dragged herself to her knees. After she had cropped off her hair, bound her breasts, and disguised herself as a lad in a cheap set of secondhand work clothes, she'd presented herself at the Bedlam gate an hour before dawn. Evidently, it was hard for them to keep employees, for she was hired on the spot by the man named Dodsworth. She had been working like a drudge since then. No matter how hard she scrubbed the vile corridors, they'd never come clean. Now she'd thought she'd heard Pierce's voice call her name. Perhaps Vesta was right. She was going dotty.

"There what is again?"

Nora looked up into the hard-featured face of Mrs. Mounsey. The patient was leaning against a doorjamb, arms crossed over her bony chest. Evidently, even time spent in the water chair wasn't sufficient inducement to lure her back to the bed of her pig of a husband, Mr. Mounsey.

"I thought I heard someone call...a woman's name."

Nora rose to her feet, thankful she'd bound her breasts tight with strips of linen. Her boy's things were hopelessly wet, and a corset would have shown through.

"Ah, it'd be someone what's sharp of ear to hear anything over Dodsworth's bellowing," Mrs. Mounsey said confidingly, "but just between you and me and the doorknob, I heard a voice, too."

"You did? What did your voice say?"

"Same as yours, I'll warrant. I'm not really balmy, you understand. Not like these other poor bastards. No, I heard someone call for Anna Ora or somesuch like."

"Honora?"

"Mighta been. What's it to you?"

"Nothing," she said and started mopping furiously. "Nothing at all."

"Now you're pitching the gammon and no mistake," Mrs. Mounsey said. "I was willing to overlook the fact that you're not what you're trying to seem, but I'll not stand for a bald-faced lie."

"What do you mean?"

"I mean, young master whoever-you-are, you're no more a lad than I am. Don't mistake me. I understand. Times is tough and a lass can't make as much in most situations as a young man can." Mrs. Mounsey shrugged eloquently. "Leastwise not if she's opposed to lying on her back and kicking up her heels. Likely you've got a bairn or two to support, so I won't peach on you. But you'd better tell me why you're looking for this Honora person, or I'll go straight to Dodsworth."

"I'm not looking for Honora. I *am* Honora," she whispered. "I'm looking for Viscount Westfall."

Mrs. Mounsey shook her head. "Ain't nobody here

by that name. I hear about all of them as they come in. Dodsworth talks in his sleep, you collect."

So the skinny little woman wasn't opposed to letting any man into her bed, just her husband. But it made Honora wonder how bad Mr. Mounsey truly must be if the odious Dodsworth was an acceptable bedfellow.

"Of course, that don't mean your viscount ain't here under another name." Mrs. Mounsey poked at the center of Nora's chest. "Sometimes they do that. Especially if someone comes looking for a patient and the family don't want him found particularly."

That made sense. If Pierce's uncle had returned him to hospital and didn't want His Grace to have him released again, they might ask that he be committed under another name.

"Thank you, Mrs. Mounsey. You've given me hope. I'll try to do you a good turn if I can."

"Get me out of here without Mr. Mounsey hearing about it, and we'll call it square." The woman smiled wryly. "What is it you think you'll be doing then?"

"The voice I heard seemed to come from up that stairwell." Honora pointed in that direction. "I intend to follow it. Have you any idea what's up there?"

"Think the doctors keep rooms on the upper story. Won't do for you to be caught wandering where you shouldn't ought, though. No telling what they'll do if they catch you snooping about."

Nora planted the mophead in the bucket and made for the stairs. "That can't be helped."

"Suit yourself, Anna Ora, but after you have a look-see, best you nip back double quick and finish up the floors. Dodsworth don't make no idle threats."

. . .

Pierce continued to climb. He passed by the second story where seriously disturbed patients spent their days chained to their bed rails. The windows were all barred, so he assumed the doctors were afraid of someone taking a running leap if they slipped their chains. He knew the truly difficult cases, like his, were kept in cells in the basement. On the first floor, the violent sorts were housed. He decided it was simpler for staff if some of the inmates were confined on the second level. Perhaps they were rotated with the ones from the ground floor where wandering was encouraged. He hoped so.

On the third level, several windows stood open, so perhaps the second story patients were chained to keep them from sneaking up to this level and then slipping out to teeter on the parapets. But one benefit of the open windows was fresh air. Pierce stuck his head out into the sunshine and inhaled clear to his toes.

Then he started down the deserted hallway. None of the rooms were marked, so he peered through the keyholes to see if they were occupied. He jerked back when he looked into one of the offices and saw his doctor behind a desk. The man's balding pate was bent over a stack of paperwork. Pierce moved on.

The next room was similarly furnished, but it was empty, so he opened the door and slipped in.

"Thank God for those blasted mushrooms," he muttered. He caught a whiff of civet, lemon oil, and garlic, smells he associated with Dr. Falco. This was the right office. Now Pierce only had to search the desk. Meg Anthony had assured him the letters were there, tied up with a length of pink ribbon.

He'd only gone through half the drawers when the doorknob jiggled and started to turn. Pierce grabbed the paperweight from the desk, hurried across the room, and stood behind the door as it opened. If he had to, he'd bean the intruder over the head.

But it wasn't Dodsworth or one of the other orderlies, and it wasn't Dr. Falco. It was a thin slip of a lad. Then when the boy turned around, he saw that it wasn't a boy at all.

"Honora." The paperweight fell from his nerveless fingers, thudding harmlessly to the floor. "Are you real?"

She came to him, arms outstretched, and suddenly he was holding her tight. If she wasn't real, she was the best hallucination he'd ever had. She'd applied no fresh fragrance, but the smell of mint, lavender, and apples was part of her skin. It was so faint, no one who hadn't spent time with Falco's infernal mushroom could have smelled it, but Pierce thought he might drown in the scent and not care one whit. As he kissed her, all the worry, all the longing of the past days, sloughed off him in the wonder of her mouth. He clasped her head to his chest, and her sloppy boy's hat slid off.

"What happened to your hair?" He ran his hand over her cropped do.

"I did it myself so I could get in here to find you." She palmed his cheeks, and he saw a rising bruise on hers. In fact, her left eye was beginning to swell shut.

"You didn't do this to yourself."

"No, that was Dodsworth."

Pierce had never been a violent man, but if the orderly were within reach, he'd have strangled him.

"Come," she said. "We have to get out of here. I think I

know a way—"

"Not until we have what I came for—Albemarle's letters. I'm certain they're here in this desk."

"You mean you willingly allowed yourself to be committed just so you could help Benedick?"

"No, I did it for you. If Albemarle has his letters, maybe you'll feel you can leave him and marry me." He grasped her hands and kissed her reddened knuckles. "I can't live without you, Honora. I don't want to try."

"Oh, Pierce." She hugged him close, but he noticed she didn't say she'd become his wife. "Let's find those letters."

They began anew, rifling through all the drawers, but they came up empty each time.

"Are you sure the letters are here?" Nora asked.

"They were as of the last night I was at Albion Abbey."

"How can you know that?" Nora asked, then waved the question away. "Never mind. I've given up trying to understand all your secrets. It doesn't matter how you know it. I believe you. Do you think Falco might have moved the letters?"

"No, I think we haven't searched thoroughly enough. Some desks have secret compartments." Pierce lay down on his back under the desk and felt the dark wood for seams. There seemed to be a place where the wood gave a bit in the far corner. He pushed up on it and a secret space sprang open. "Here."

The letters fell out, about twenty of them, judging from the heft of the packet, all tied up, as Meg had said, with a bow.

"You take them," he said, shoving them down the front of her ill-fitting trousers. "I have a place to hide them in my cell, but I still haven't figured out how to leave this place. You can simply quit your position and walk out the front gates with the letters. No one will be the wiser."

"No, Pierce, we go together or not at all."

But before they could come to an agreement, the sound of voices in the hallway tabled all discussion.

"Here is how it will go," Pierce said. "If you love me, say you found me wandering here. Then get out of hospital as soon as you can." He picked up a sheaf of papers stacked on the desk and flung it skyward. As the door opened, reams of foolscap fluttered to the hardwood floor.

When Falco entered with Dodsworth on his heels, it certainly looked as if a madman had ransacked the place.

• • •

"What is going on here?" Falco demanded as he glared at Nora. "Who are you?"

"Oh, that's just Clarence," Dodsworth said. "Hired him this morning, but if he don't follow orders no better than this, he won't be around for long. Why aren't you cleaning like I told you?"

"I was, Mr. Dodsworth." Nora bobbed her head and slapped her cap back on her shorn locks. The skin on her cheek felt tight, and she was grateful for the shiner because it altered her appearance enough so that Falco didn't seem to recognize her as the well-dressed courtesan who'd visited the day before. "I was working, just like you told me, when I spied this gentleman—"

"No gentlemen are committed here," Falco corrected.

"Oh, right. In any case, I saw him slipping up the stairs and thought to myself you might not want him wandering up here." At her words, Pierce smiled, a big dopey smile that would convince anyone he was shy of sense. "I'm sorry I didn't catch him before he made a mess."

She took Pierce's hand and started to lead him out.

"Where do you think you're going?" Falco demanded.

"The patient seems harmless enough. I'm going to take him back down to the ground floor."

"No, this office you are going to straighten," Falco said. "Dodsworth, he will take Mr. Mycroft to his treatment."

"But his doc said no more treatments for this fellow," the orderly complained.

"If the patient is exhibiting new symptoms, and wanton destruction of property seems to me to qualify, then new treatment is in order," Dr. Falco said with a frown. "If you question my judgment again, Dodsworth, you may spend the rest of the day looking for a new position."

Sullenly, Dodsworth grabbed Pierce by the collar. "Come on, you."

Pierce met Nora's gaze for a heartbeat and she read a silent message in them. *Get out now.* Then his eyes seemed to glaze over, and he went with Dodsworth as meekly as a sheep to its shearer.

Anything to lead them away from her, she realized. She didn't deserve his devotion. She brought disaster to everyone she loved. Her family had had to face disgrace because of her. Lewis had died trying to be a hero to impress her father because of her. Even Emilia was forced to live a lie because of her. She was damaged and she might not mean to, but she hurt everyone she touched, eventually. Once he was free, she needed to help him understand it, too. For his sake.

"Where am I taking him?" Dodsworth asked as they neared the door.

"Mr. Mycroft needs something to wake him up," Dr. Falco said. "The water chair should do nicely."

Honora loves me. She might not have said it straight out, but she showed that she does when she told Falco she'd caught me wandering like I asked her to. She loves me, I know it. I can face anything after that.

~from the secret journal of Pierce Langdon, Viscount Westfall

Chapter Twenty-Five

As soon as the door swung shut behind Pierce and his captors, Nora sank to her knees. She clutched her chest, lest her heart pound its way out. The letters Pierce had risked so much to find were still tucked into her trousers. Clearly, he wanted her to take them and run. Those letters would free Albemarle from his blackmailers and protect the Prince Regent from having that infernal Trust Powder used on him. And if Benedick was free, she could be free, too.

But her freedom was worthless without Pierce.

She couldn't leave him to the chair. She wouldn't.

Since she and Vesta had visited the subterranean parts of Bedlam yesterday, the route to that underworld was still fresh in her mind. She took the stairs on tiptoe lest Dodsworth or Dr. Falco hear her above them. Once she reached the basement, she waited for their footfalls to die away before stealing after them.

The water chamber door closed behind them like a

coffin lid.

She hurried to the door, put a hand to the knob, then drew back. How could she face down both Dodsworth and Dr. Falco at once? She had only one card to play. She had to make it count.

Her thoughts bounced around like rubber balls. She was never quick enough to catch one. Then as she reached for the knob again, it began to turn on its own. She quickly hid behind the door as it opened.

Dodsworth came out and plodded down the hall.

"Hey Dods, how come you're not with the doc in the water room?" one of the inmates yelled through the small grate in his door. "They always have two watchers. Always."

"Dr. Falco sent me away. Think he means to drown this one and don't want no witnesses. Even did the strappin' down his own self. All right by me," the orderly said as he strode on down the hall. "If there's trouble over it, I won't be the one who'll swing for killing the bastard."

Nora didn't wait for more. She pulled open the door to the chamber she'd fled from yesterday, squared her shoulders, and went in.

Pierce was already in the chair. Dr. Falco hadn't bothered to have him stripped in his hurry to administer the "treatment." Water poured over him in torrents, obscuring his form beneath its pounding.

"What do you think you're doing here, boy?" Dr. Falco demanded from his position beside the lever that worked the mechanism.

"Let him out," Nora said. "Now."

Garbled noises came from the chair. Pierce had heard her and was probably trying to tell her to leave him.

Oh, don't try to talk, love. It will only mean more water pouring into you.

She'd intended to barter with Falco for Pierce, to offer to return the letters in exchange for his freedom. She'd betray Benedick. She'd let the royal take his chances with the Trust Powder. Pierce was all that mattered. She had to stop his torture. She dashed forward into the falling water with him.

It pummeled her head and shoulders, but she managed to tuck her chin and breathe through her mouth. Her fingers found the strap binding one of his arms, and she worked furiously at the buckles. Then a hand grabbed the back of her collar and yanked her out of the indoor waterfall.

"I will not tolerate this interruption of—wait a moment. You're not Clarence. You're not even a boy." Falco eyed her like a robin might a worm. "You're Lady Nora Claremont. Benedick's bitch."

She opened her mouth to answer, but his hand closed over her throat. Clawing at him, she fought to free herself, but Falco was too strong. Pinpricks of stars burst behind her eyes. Her vision tunneled.

Nora sank to her knees. She almost winked out entirely, but then Falco released her, and his feet left the flagstones as if he were capable of levitation. He screamed and then went crashing to the floor. As oxygen streamed into her, her vision came into sharp focus. She must have been successful at freeing one of Pierce's hands because he'd unfastened the rest of his bonds. He was loose now and bearing a frown worthy of an avenging angel.

The doctor rolled and crabbed backward trying to get away, but Pierce yanked him to his feet. Falco took a wild swing at him. Pierce dodged the blow and answered it with one of his own. When Pierce's jab connected with the doctor's jaw, he collapsed in a heap.

Then Pierce hurried to Nora and lifted her to her feet. "We have to get you out of here," he said, his voice hoarse from the water.

"Only if you come with me."

"Say the word and I'll never leave your side again."

The door creaked open and Pierce positioned himself in front of her, fists raised. Then his shoulders relaxed, and he dropped his arms.

"Come in, Stanstead. I can hear you thinking out there," he said. "Besides, the hard part is done."

Lord Stanstead peered around the door and then entered with Mr. LeGrand dogging his steps. He cast an approving look at the fallen Dr. Falco. "The letters, do you have them?"

Pierce nodded. "Lady Nora does."

"Well done, both of you."

"How did you know where we were?" Pierce asked.

"Miss Anthony is outside the gate," Stanstead explained. "She couldn't *Find* you before, and it fretted her terribly. Finally, she decided the doctors had changed your name and obscured your appearance somehow."

"I was called Mr. Mycroft and made to wear a hood until today."

"Ah, that explains it. Good thing the hood is gone. Even without the correct name, Miss Anthony was able to *Find* you based on recognizing your ugly face. She confirmed your location just now, and here we are to help. LeGrand, what are you doing?"

Nora had no idea what to make of that cryptic conversation, but she didn't have time to ask for explanations.

The wiry Frenchman had Dr. Falco draped over his shoulder and was bearing him to the chair in the center of the room. "I have heard of such devices as this. We shall see if the good doctor finds it as beneficial for himself as he seems to think it is for his patients."

LeGrand began strapping Falco into the chair.

"Right. Come now, Westfall," Stanstead said. "We're here to break you and Lady Nora out of here."

"How will you do that?" she asked.

"Why, we'll walk right out the front door, of course," Stanstead said with a grin. "I'll be *Sending* to cover our escape every step of the way."

"I need to do something first." Nora didn't think much of Lord Stanstead's plan, and had no idea what he meant by "sending," but she didn't have a better suggestion to make at the moment. "There is a patient on the first floor named Mrs. Mounsey. She's no more insane than Lord Westfall is, but she's stubborn enough to die here if we don't bring her with us."

"I'll get her," Pierce said. "Stanstead, see Lady Honora to safety."

"Consider it done," Lord Stanstead said with a bow to Nora. "My lady."

"Pierce, I don't think we should split up—"

He pulled her to him for a quick kiss. "Just keep thinking that. I'll join you as soon as I can with Mrs. Mounsey in tow, and then we'll never be parted again. Agreed?"

She nodded, not trusting her voice. She let Lord Stanstead lead her away.

• • •

As Nora left with Lord Stanstead, LeGrand started the water falling without touching the lever. Dr. Falco roused and began making a pathetic bleating sound, amid intermittent sputtering and coughing.

"Don't kill him," Pierce said, feeling the doctor's terror as if it were his own before he raised his mental shield against Falco's thoughts.

"He would have killed you," LeGrand said.

"Dr. Falco feels dead inside most of the time already. He hates himself," Pierce said. "It makes him hate other people, too. Have a little mercy, LeGrand."

"Only a little," LeGrand said. "I'll leave him here long enough to make sure he doesn't use this thing on anyone else ever again."

When Pierce left the chamber, the water was still falling.

Still dripping from his stint in the water chair, he squelched along the corridor and up the stairs to the first floor. "Mrs. Mounsey," he called as loudly as he dared.

There was no answer.

He peered into a number of rooms, but no one responded with a sensible answer when he asked where Mrs. Mounsey might be.

A woman with white tufts of hair ambled toward him with a beatific smile. She babbled in sweet tones and even managed to singsong "I love you" intelligibly once or twice.

If the only thing her mental disease left her with was "I love you," Pierce decided she must have been a wonderful person at one time. But as she neared him, her hand dipped into her pocket, and something metallic flashed.

"Violet!" came a voice from behind him. "You put that shank back in your pocket now, or I'll tell Dodsworth on you."

Violet's shoulders hunched, and her smile turned into a gargoyle's frown. The old woman scuttled back the way she came.

Pierce lowered his mental shield and realized the person who'd intervened was Mrs. Mounsey. He turned to face her. "Lady Honora Claremont has sent me to find you and take you away from here."

"*Lady* Honora?" The woman chuckled. "You mean to say that skinny little Clarence is not only a woman, but a lady to boot? Lud, that do beat all. Well, don't be standing there like a ninny. If you're here to save me, get to saving."

Pierce wondered if the woman would have said anything differently if she'd known he was a viscount. He doubted it.

"This way," he said, indicating that she should precede him down the hall to the stairwell. They moved smoothly through the ranks of wandering patients until they reached the ground floor. Then Pierce decided this was no time to be gentlemanly. It would be better if he led the way, in case they encountered trouble.

He kept his shield up, knowing he'd be inundated with too many minds chattering at once to give him useful information. As he rounded the last corner before the vestibule at the front door, he nearly ran into Dodsworth.

Before he could strike a blow, the big orderly pulled out his wooden club and landed a solid clout to Westfall's temple. He staggered and collapsed to the floor. His last coherent thought was that the front door must be open, because he could see only light.

Lord, I have not asked You for much over the last few years. In fact, I doubt You'd listen if I did. But I'm not asking for myself this time. I ask, no, I beg, for the life and mind of Pierce Langdon. Bring him back to me and I will never ask You for more.

~from the secret journal of Lady Nora Claremont

Chapter Twenty-Six

"He's so pale," Nora said as she tucked the fine cotton sheets under Pierce's chin. She reached out to stroke his cheek. The muscles under his skin didn't so much as twitch.

"As I understand it," Lady Easton said, "Westfall was insensible for about a week when he was a child. He has only been out for a day this time."

Every hour felt like an eternity to Nora.

After Lord Stanstead had escorted her, as he'd promised, directly out the front door of Bedlam, he'd ducked back in. Within minutes, the earl had reappeared with Dodsworth, bearing an unconscious Pierce over his shoulder. Mrs. Mounsey dogged his steps, berating the big orderly all the way with language worthy of the saltiest sailor.

Nora had sent Mrs. Mounsey to present herself at her residence in St. James Park with instructions for Mr. Whittles to find a position for her within Nora's household.

She'd refused to be parted from Pierce, demanding to be

allowed to accompany him back to Camden House.

The Duke of Camden had made her welcome. She'd even been taken into the confidence of the Order of the M.U.S.E. The secret work of the Order explained so much about Pierce. Her heart constricted with love and pride for him.

And fear.

If he didn't wake…

"You've not had much rest," Lady Easton said. "I'll sit with him a while."

"I'm fine." Nora settled onto a straight-backed chair at Pierce's bedside. When they had first arrived at Camden House, the duke's sister had tended to Pierce, and His Grace's servants had prepared a bath for Nora. Only time would help her hopeless hair, but at least she was clean and wearing a borrowed gown. Fortunately, Lady Easton wouldn't allow a quack to be brought in for Pierce. He'd suffered far too much at the hands of medical professionals already. "I can't leave him."

"Of course. Speak to him. Perhaps he'll follow the sound of your voice back to us," Lady Easton said as she withdrew from the chamber. "Ring if you need me."

Nora leaned forward and placed a trembling hand on Pierce's chest. She was comforted by the regular rise and fall, but her belly still writhed like a bucketful of eels. Even if he wakened, she would lose him, because she'd decided to set him free. She didn't deserve to keep him.

"Why did you risk so much for me?" she whispered.

Because I love you.

She could almost hear his voice. Did that mean she was going mad, too? If she was, it might be a blessing. She couldn't face the world stone-cold sane without him.

"I haven't told you before now," she began softly. "I don't know how to say it except to come straight out with it. I love you most desperately."

His chest continued to rise and fall.

"I shouldn't, you know. You deserve to be loved by someone so much better than me. Someone worthy of your love."

His eyelid twitched a bit, and she gasped.

"If I were the unselfish sort, I'd leave right now so you could be free to find that someone. You were trapped back in Bedlam because of me. Who knows what calamity will befall you next on my account? I ruin everyone I touch, and I can't bear to ruin you," she continued as his eyes opened slowly.

"What if being ruined by you is the best thing that could ever happen to me?"

"You can't mean that." A sob tore at her throat. She didn't deserve such love, such unqualified acceptance.

"I do."

A tear teetered on her eyelid and then streaked her cheek. She couldn't resist his relentless love. He wore her down with his constancy and made her believe she could trust him with all of her. "Then I will be selfish. I won't leave you."

His hand reached up and covered hers.

"You'd better not," he said.

"Oh, Pierce." Nora meant to only buss his cheek and settle sedately back into the chair, but before she knew it, she was climbing into bed with him, snuggling close, and peppering his dear face with kisses. When she finally settled beside him, he sighed.

"What happened while I was…gone?" he asked.

"So much I don't know where to begin."

"Start with how I got here."

"After Lord Stanstead saw me out of hospital, he went back into Bedlam and *Sent* a thought to Dodsworth that he should carry you out to the waiting coach." Nora giggled. "And while he was at it, Stanstead suggested to the orderly that if he ever laid a hand in anger on a patient again, he'd be promptly sick all over his own shoes."

"*Sent*, you said. So you know about Stanstead's ability to project his thoughts into the minds of others."

"I know about all the Extraordinaires. The duke has told me about your work with the Order of the M.U.S.E."

He frowned quizzically at her. "What about the letters?"

"I gave them to His Grace. He has already been to see Benedick. They have reached a gentleman's agreement. Benedick is in possession of those incriminating letters, and the duke has custody of the Trust Powder. The prince regent is safe."

Pierce closed his eyes. "So much done while I lay here helpless as a naked chick."

"You are not helpless." She raised herself on her elbow so she could grin down on him. "But you are naked."

He smiled back at her and started to pull her closer. "So I am."

She straight-armed him. "Not so fast, my love. You need to recover your strength first. You've had quite a blow. And besides, you shouldn't think this wasn't your doing. None of the good that has come to pass would have happened without you. You're the one who risked everything to find the letters."

"And you risked everything to find me." He pulled her

close, and this time she let him. His kiss was a benediction. This man knew her—all the flaws and odd angles of her soul—and he loved her in spite of them. She melted on the inside, all warm and sweet as pie filling.

"Seems to me we found each other," she said.

"Does that mean you'll marry me?"

"Yes, Pierce, with all my heart."

He sat up straight. "Then I'll send for the Hobarths right away so you can have Emilia with—"

She stopped him by pressing two fingers to his lips. "That's a lovely thought, and I love you all the more for it. I hope you'll do it and everything will work together so that I can see my daughter grow up. But I don't ever want you to think I'm marrying you for anything other than yourself. You, all by yourself, are more than enough for me."

He gazed at her intently. "I can't tell if you mean it."

"Lower your shield. I have no secrets from you." He was welcome to all of her—unreservedly. "I love you, Pierce, now and for always."

"That's just it." He rubbed the lump at his temple. "My shield has been down since my eyes opened and I haven't heard a single one of your thoughts."

Epilogue

My initial confusion about hearing the thoughts of others was nothing compared to the day when the voices stopped.

~from the secret journal of Pierce Langdon,
Viscount Westfall

The sun dropped below a blanket of clouds and shot a parting shaft of mellow light across Westphalia on its way to its westerly bed. Pierce leaned on the parapet of his family's country manor and surveyed his viscountcy with a satisfied heart.

He missed hearing the voices of other minds in his head, missed the way they washed over him, bathing him in a jumbled up sea of emotions and cogitations. He never would have guessed that he'd become attached to the droning tide that had formed the background for his own thoughts, but somehow he had.

"It's the perversity of human nature to want what we don't have," he said to himself with a shake of his head.

In the stable yard below, a hostler was putting a new trotter through its paces, growling out commands to the horse. Pierce hadn't erected his mental shields since he escaped from Bedlam a second time, but he still couldn't hear what the working man was thinking.

One of the housemaids came out to lean on the fence. The hostler stopped work to speak with her in low tones. Then the maid gave him a resounding slap, turned on her heel, and flounced back inside. Shoulders slumping, the hostler hung his head. Pierce stared at him fixedly.

Trollop. Just when I was about ready to plight my trough, too.

Pierce jerked in surprise. He'd heard the man's thought as clearly as if he'd spoken the words in his ear. What had changed to make it possible?

After a bit, he reasoned that his gift wasn't completely gone. It had simply undergone a change. It was no longer passive. Instead of having thoughts roll over him, Pierce had to go get this one by concentrating on the fellow.

Elation flooded his chest. If he was right, his gift was finally going to be both manageable and of great use. He'd be able to pick and choose which mind he invaded, like his friend Stanstead did. He'd be of use to the Order once more. He'd—

"I thought I'd find you up here," Honora said as she came up behind him and slipped her arms around his waist.

"I never grow tired of looking at it." He never thought he'd be back in his rightful place, either. But once he'd convinced the magistrate who'd ruled him unfit that he no longer believed he heard the thoughts of others, he was able to take the reins of the estate and send his uncle and aunt packing. While he and Honora had honeymooned in Scotland, his man of business had moved the Hobarths into the caretaker's cottage with Mr. Hobarth as the new steward of the estate. Hobarth quickly replaced all the staff loyal to Pierce's uncle and set the place humming. Mrs. Hobarth came on as head housekeeper, and Emilia was given full run of the manor house.

The child was an affectionate sort with all the adults on the estate, giving out hugs whenever she felt they were needed. The day Honora finally got to hold her daughter in her arms was one of the happiest days of Pierce's life.

"No, I never tire of looking at the place." Pierce turned and tucked his wife's head under his chin. Her glorious hair was still a cropped bob, but it curled enticingly around her ears and nape. "And I never tire of looking at you, either."

"Are you sorry not to be an Extraordinaire any longer?"

He shrugged. He needed more time to experiment with this new aspect of his gift to make sure he was right, that the business with the hostler wasn't a singular occurrence. The ability to actively decide to hear someone's thoughts was radically different from being inundated with them willy-nilly. But Honora didn't need to know about his suspicions until he was sure. "The duke knows he can call on me if I can render the Order any service."

Likewise, the powerful Lord Albemarle would be hard pressed to deny him or Honora a favor should they ever need his assistance. Benedick was quick to give his former mistress his blessing when she left him and had decided not to fill her position with another young courtesan.

"I'm reaching the age," Benedick had told them, "when no one will think it odd that I'm satisfied with my own company. As far as the world knows, the snow gathering on the roof has effectively guttered the fire in the chimney."

Pierce doubted Benedick was going to remain that solitary, but he was equally sure the baron would never be foolish enough to betray any other company he kept by leaving a written record. At least, not until the world changed quite a bit.

"Do you miss not being able to hear what I'm thinking?" Honora interrupted his thoughts.

"Sometimes." Even though he'd not been married long, he knew better than to experiment on his wife with this new manifestation of his psychic gift. Honora would be the first to demand the privacy of her own mind. Besides, she deserved it. "It was both painful and useful to know what's buzzing in the brains of others. But in this case, I'll make an educated guess at your thoughts."

He cupped his hand around his mouth and whispered something deliciously filthy into her ear, something he thought his lovely wife would like done to her, slowly, repeatedly, and with feeling.

"Pierce!" She slapped his chest playfully. "What a wicked idea!"

"Am I wrong?"

She smiled impishly. "We've an hour till the dressing gong sounds for supper."

"Only an hour, *hmm*? I may have to rush things, but I believe we can make a credible start." He scooped her up and carried her to the stairway that led from the roof back down into the manor house. "To bed, wife."

"To bed, my lord. But, just to be on the safe side, let's hide the dressing gong first."

"Even if I can't hear the thought before it comes out of your mouth," Pierce said with a grin, "I do love the way you think."

OTHER BOOKS BY MIA MARLOWE

The Curse of Lord Stanstead

Author's Notes

Thank you, dear reader, for spending time with me and the M.U.S.E.s. I hope you enjoyed your visit to my imaginary psychic Regency and will want to return to us often.

Even though many of my characters possess psychic abilities, their gifts don't always help them solve the mysteries of the heart. *The Madness of Lord Westfall* is about forgiveness and receiving second chances we don't deserve. Honora and Pierce both needed to forgive their families for the wrongs done them. And they needed to forgive themselves for the roads they wish they hadn't taken. But since, in the end, their paths intersected, I don't think they'd change a thing.

As always, I try to make the history in my books as accurate as possible. I'm sad to report that my description of Bedlam was probably not horrific enough. It was not unusual for people to pay admission to make sport of the unfortunates housed there. The water chair used by Pierce's doctor was considered a real treatment for madness at that time and was thought to be an improvement over the head-first dunking tank that preceded it. At least the number of drownings went down. And there is a report of a woman, like poor Mrs. Mounsey, who was judged to be mad and was committed to hospital simply because she refused to allow her husband in her bed. In her case, the water chair put her in a more biddable frame of mind, and she was released to her spouse's dubious care.

About Lord Albemarle's homosexuality...a number of well-known Regency personages were probably gay, but since the act itself was considered criminal, there was no coming-out. Lord Byron, for one, reportedly had male lovers. The laws against "buggery" were considered "The Blackmailer's Charter" because gay men were willing to pay an extortioner's price rather than be exposed. And no wonder. In 1806, more men were hanged for sodomy than for murder. The last two men to be hanged in Britain for "unnatural acts" were executed in 1835, but the law punishing homosexuality by death was on the books until the 1860's.

What a terrible time to be different. Or a woman. Makes me thankful for now.

I love to hear from readers! For more about me and my books, please visit www.miamarlowe.com. And let me extend a special invitation for you to join my newsletter. That way, you'll be notified when the next M.U.S.E. book comes out!

Happy Reading,

Mia

Acknowledgments

No book is the work of only one person. *The Madness of Lord Westfall* wouldn't have happened without help from lots of people. I'd like to thank a few here:

Erin Molta, my editor. She pored over the manuscript and poked and prodded until the story was the best it could be. I'm thankful for her grasp of storytelling hot buttons, "spot-on" good taste and—above all—her stamina! It's an honor to work with her.

Louisa Maggio, my cover artist. Kudos for capturing the flavor of the M.U.S.E. series. And thank you to Nancy Cantor, my copy editor. Any errors that slipped through her grammar gauntlet are definitely my fault.

Natasha Kern, my tireless agent. I don't know what I'd do without her!

Ashlyn Chase and Marcy Weinbeck, my critique partner and my beta reader. The feedback from these two never fails to motivate and encourage me.

My husband, the love of my life. After all these years, he still knows how to show a girl a good time! Definitely hero material!

And last, but assuredly not least, YOU, dear reader. Thank you for investing a few hours of your life in my book. I'm thrilled to share the story with you. Thanks for bringing your imagination along for the ride. It means the world to me. Truly.

About the Author

Mia Marlowe didn't intend on making things up for a living, but she says it's the best job she ever had. Her work was featured in the Best of 2010 issue of PEOPLE magazine. One of her books is on display at the Museum of London Docklands next to Johnny Depp memorabilia. The RITA nominated author has over 20 books in print with more on the way! Mia loves art, music, history, and travel. Good thing about the travel because she's lived in 9 different states, 4 different time zones. For more, visit www.miamarlowe.com.

CPSIA information can be obtained at www.ICGtesting.com
Printed in the USA
LVOW08s2118010516

486216LV00001B/7/P